BLOOD KNOT

S.W. HUBBARD

Chapter 1

Irene Delafield was dead and Frank Bennett was glad.

It wasn't the first time he'd been happy to hear of someone's passing. When Ronald Beemis, serial child molester, had been shanked in the exercise yard of the Missouri state prison, Frank couldn't help but feel that the world was a better place. And when Osvaldo Merguez and Tyrone "Teeko" Mills had taken each other down in a blaze of semiautomatic gunfire over contested drug turf in Kansas City, Frank had joined his fellow cops in a genial celebration at their local bar.

Irene Delafield didn't have a rap sheet–she was the organist at the Presbyterian Church in Trout Run, New York—but what she did to the fine old melodies in the Presbyterian Hymnbook was positively criminal. Under Irene's inept fingers, "Jesus Christ Is Risen Today" became a dirge. She was so flummoxed by the syncopations of "A Mighty Fortress Is Our God" that she lost the entire congregation before the first verse ended and left each person valiantly singing whatever he thought best. As the widower of a very fine church musician, Frank couldn't bear to listen to Irene play. When he occasionally got in a churchgoing mood, he headed down to the Congregational Church in Keene Valley, where the organist put on a creditable show. Frank's flagrant disloyalty did not go unremarked in his adopted hometown. He was, after all, the police chief of Trout Run and should set an example.

So he had chosen the first Sunday in November, All Saints' Day, to rejoin the fold now that a heart attack had taken Irene off the organ bench for good. And it hadn't been bad. The service had ended with a rousing rendition of "When the Saints Go Marching In" that made sitting through Pastor Bob Rush's meandering sermon worthwhile.

He was still humming under his breath when Reid Burlingame and Ardyth Munger cornered him during fellowship hour.

"Good to see you here, Frank," Reid said. As chairman of the town council, Reid was his boss, so Frank was glad his attendance had been duly noted. "What did you think of today's music?"

Frank swallowed the last morsel of his crumb cake. "Terrific. Stepping outside the hymnal with that last number, no?"

"Matthew wanted to play it, and Bob said it was okay," Ardyth explained.

"Matthew?"

"Matthew Portman. That was him playing the piano during the service."

"Ah, *that* Matthew." Matthew Portman was only fourteen years old when he had filled in on piano last year while Irene visited her sister in Toledo, and church attendance had risen dramatically. After that, Pastor Bob had thoughtfully encouraged Irene to take more vacations, but she had clung to her organ bench with barnacle-like tenacity, and Matthew hadn't gotten another shot.

"Did you see this?" Ardyth tapped the back page of her bulletin, which proclaimed in boldface print: Hymn Sing and Pie Social, Saturday, November 14. "It's a fund-raiser so we can send Matthew for organ lessons."

Reid beamed. "We've had a real stroke of luck. Oliver Greffe, the music teacher at the North Country Academy, is quite an accomplished organist. He's agreed to instruct Matthew. It's another example of the good things that school is doing for our town now that it's under new management."

Frank braced himself for another one of Reid's rah-rah speeches. He'd hardly had a conversation with the man lately that didn't revolve around what a boon to the local economy the new North Country Academy was proving to be. The academy used to be a third-rate boarding school catering to kids who couldn't get into—or had been kicked out of—better institutions. But its remote location and indifferent academic reputation had finally driven it out of existence at the end of the last school year. Trout Run greeted the news with a big yawn—although technically within the town limits, the school had never seemed like part of the community. Only one person from Trout Run taught there, and all the local kids went to Trout Run Elementary, then on to High Peaks High School.

Then, at the end of the summer, a man named MacArthur Payne had bought the North Country Academy and the place had been reborn as what Reid liked to call a "therapeutic school." Frank, who hadn't mastered political correctness, referred to it as "that high-priced private reform school."

"So Matthew's going to the North Country Academy for organ lessons, huh," he said. "What'll they do if he doesn't practice—lock him up?"

Reid glared at him. "Frank, that's a very unfair remark. You—"

"Joking, I was joking!" Geez, Reid had really lost his sense of humor over this place.

"The lessons will be here in the church, where the organ is," Reid explained. "Plus, Matthew will be able to walk here."

"His father won't help out at all," Ardyth interjected. "He wasn't going to let Matthew take the lessons until Pastor Bob went and spoke to him. Those poor kids are really struggling without their mom."

Ardyth had a tendency to dwell on misfortune, while Reid was a determined optimist. "That's why the organ lessons are such a godsend. And, have you heard about the latest two people to get good jobs at the academy? Lorrie Betz and Ray Stulke."

Frank's hand hung suspended over the Danish tray. Lorrie had crammed more heartache into thirty years of living than most people manage in a lifetime. And Ray was Trout Run's foremost blockhead. "What in the world are those two qualified to do at a school? Cleaning?"

"Oh, no. They're going to be Pathfinders."

"The only path Ray can find is from his barstool to the john. What kind of position is a *Pathfinder?*"

"Fine for you to be so cavalier, Frank," Reid said. "You have a good, secure job. Most people in this town aren't so lucky. We're losing our young people because there are no opportunities for them here. And with Clyde being so sick, we can't count on Stevenson's Lumberyard to continue as our prime employer."

Reid straightened the lapels of his tweed sports coat. "This town needs to diversify. If MacArthur Payne makes a success of this school, it will be a source of good steady work with benefits for years to come. Steady work keeps people out of trouble. *You* should appreciate that."

Ardyth studied her shoes as if she'd never seen patent leather before. The thump of the big coffee urn being hauled away broke the uncomfortable silence, and Frank grabbed the opportunity to leave as Ardyth began helping with the cleanup.

He trudged across the green toward his truck, trying to shake off the sting of Reid's words. Last night's jack-o'-lanterns mocked him, their cheerful gap-toothed grins now transformed into grotesque snarls by the gnawing of hungry squirrels.

Unspoken in Reid's tirade was the fact that Frank was an outsider who'd taken the position of police chief away from a local. True, the job didn't pay well enough for a man to support a family. For twenty years his predecessor had combined the police chief's job with furniture refinishing to make ends meet.

Herv's retirement had touched off a great debate: increase the pay of the chief's position and induce a local man to train for the job at the police academy, or abolish it altogether and turn Trout Run's law enforcement over to the state police. In the middle of the fray, Frank had washed up on the town's doorstep: a man with twenty years' experience marred by one big mistake that had forced his resignation, willing to work cheap because he had a decent pension from the Kansas City force. His hiring had been an uneasy compromise, and Frank knew, even though Reid would never be so crass as to remind him, that he had cast the deciding vote in Frank's favor.

Now with a few unguarded wisecracks about the North Country Academy, he'd given Reid the impression that he didn't care about the fortunes of other people in town as long as his own bread was buttered.

Frank looked up at the towering peak of Mount Marcy in the distance, and the smaller mountains that tumbled toward the town, shutting out the problems of the wider world. If he knew what was good for him, he'd start showing some enthusiasm for the North Country Academy. But really, how excited could he get about a school that imported scores of juvenile delinquents into his jurisdiction?

Chapter 2

Frank jolted awake from a deep and dreamless sleep. The surge of adrenaline produced by the sound of a phone ringing in the middle of the night brought him to instant alertness.

"Bennett," he answered, and as he listened his eyes registered the time on his bedside clock: 4:55 a.m., only an hour before dawn on Friday.

"I'll be right there," he said, already on his feet and reaching for his uniform. A bear had attacked some campers on Corkscrew Mountain. The Trout Run volunteer ambulance squad was en route. The local environmental conservation officer had been notified and the state police were on their way, but Frank could be at the scene faster.

As he walked out to his truck, the frost-covered grass crunched under his feet. So far they'd had only a few light flurries of snow in the valleys, although the peaks of Whiteface and Marcy were already cloaked in white. The days had been pleasant, but the nights were damn cold. He couldn't see the joy of sleeping on the ground in a tent in this weather.

The campers who'd been attacked were from the North Country Academy. Frank wondered if anyone at the school knew the proper procedures for bear-proof storage of food on a campout. There were plenty of sightings of black bears in the Adirondacks by hikers and campers, but the bears were generally shy of people and went on their way if you backed away slowly and made some loud noise. The only thing that upset the relationship was food.

Last summer, some moron had been cuffed when he offered a bear a granola bar so he could take its picture. The man hadn't realized a bear that enjoys one granola bar is going to want another and might get a little testy when it's not forthcoming. Now it seemed North Country Academy students were learning what happened when food was left lying around a campsite. You couldn't blame bears for acting like bears. Usually they took the food and left, but Rollie Fister, who'd called Frank, said at least one camper had been seriously injured on Corkscrew.

He made it to the trailhead in less than twenty minutes. The ambulance was there, and so was a Department of Environmental Conservation Jeep, both empty. The horizon was beginning to lighten to gray, but Frank needed his flashlight to make his way up the dark and rocky trail. Within minutes he heard voices ahead of him.

"All right, there's a big step down here—keep him level." Roger Einhorn, head of the rescue squad, called out instructions to Orrin Snyder as they carried a stretcher down the steep path, while Rusty Magill, the conservation officer, walked ahead, illuminating the way. A pack of teenagers tramped along silently behind them.

"What do we have, Rusty?" Frank asked.

"Tent invasion. The bear attacked the teacher who was leading the camping trip. One of the kids came down for help, but it's been more than two hours. He's lost a lot of blood—it doesn't look good."

Roger, built like a lumberjack, plowed steadily down the trail, but Orrin seemed to be struggling to keep up.

"Let me give you a break, Orrin," Frank offered. As soon as he picked up the handles of the stretcher, he felt his legs tremble—not from the weight, but from the shock of seeing the man he carried. His face was a bloody mass; one ear seemed to be completely torn off. Blood continued to soak through the bandages Roger had wrapped around his neck.

"Jesus, I've never known a bear to attack like that!"

"Neither have I," said Rusty. "So far as I know, there's never been a serious mauling incident in the High Peaks. Most of our calls on bears are simply nuisance reports."

Orrin said, "His down sleeping bag protected his body some, but it trapped him, too. He couldn't get away."

"What finally stopped the attack?"

"The noise woke the kids. One of them threw a rock at the bear, and it ran off."

Frank glanced over his shoulder, "Are all the kids accounted for?"

"Yep, we did a head count before we started down. The only one not here is the one who called it in. He hiked out and over to Rollie Fister's house. Rollie called us—said the kid was just shook up, and he would take him back to school."

A branch snapped; some beechnuts rained down on the trail. One of the girls shrieked.

"The bear's back. He's following us!"

Rusty shone his flashlight into the forest to the left of the trail. An animal crashed through the underbrush, toward them or away from them, Frank couldn't tell.

Before Frank could set the stretcher down and reach for his service revolver, Rusty had his rifle up on his shoulder. The action threw the teenagers into turmoil. The girl who had first screamed leapt onto the taller boy's back, practically knocking him over. She clearly meant to keep him between herself and whatever creature was out in those woods.

"Jesus, Heather—get off me!" He shook himself free, and Heather landed on her backside. The two boys grabbed the other girl and bolted down the trail.

"Don't run!" Rusty warned, but the kids didn't stop. Rusty cocked his head, listening intently despite all the commotion around him. "That wasn't a bear," he announced. "Probably just a raccoon."

Frank helped the girl up. The baseball cap she'd been wearing had fallen onto the trail, and Frank saw that only a faint stubble of fair hair covered her head. Was the poor kid a cancer victim? What kind of parent would ship a sick teenager off to boarding school?

She snatched the cap up from the ground. "What're you looking at?"

Before he could respond, she trotted ahead to catch up with the other kids, who were running full tilt now that they realized how close they were to the end of the trail.

Frank, Orrin, and Roger were the last to step out into the trailhead parking area. The sun was up, the state police had arrived, and so had MacArthur Payne.

Frank saw the headmaster engaged in a finger-wagging, brow-furrowing dialogue with State Trooper Pauline Phelps. Payne had a buzz cut that revealed every bump on his bullet-shaped head, and a beaky nose, flattened at the tip, as if he'd crashed into a brick wall in his formative years. About as tall as Frank, he was a good thirty pounds of muscle heavier.

The rational part of Frank's mind told him to steer clear of the obviously angry Payne. Orrin and Roger had the victim loaded into the ambulance; the kids were accounted for. A bacon and eggs breakfast called to him from Malone's. But the part of him that always needed to be on top of things, always needed to be in control, drew him magnetically into the discussion.

"You absolutely cannot go up there, Mr. Payne," Pauline was telling the headmaster as Frank approached.

"Doctor," Payne corrected. "My students have left their personal belongings at the campsite. Two of my employees need to go and retrieve them."

"Trooper Phelps is correct. It's not safe. There's a rogue bear roaming this mountain." By this time, Rusty had joined the debate as well.

Frank watched Payne's lips purse in annoyance at Rusty's words. But he must have pegged Pauline as the more formidable obstacle, because he continued to direct his arguments to her. "With all the commotion made bringing Jake and the kids out, that bear has gone to ground," Payne said. "He won't bother my men."

"You can't be sure of that, Dr. Payne," Pauline answered with exaggerated deference.

"My men are experienced hunters—they'll take a rifle with them."

"No!" Rusty, normally so soft-spoken, practically jumped into the air. "The Department of Environmental Conservation will capture that bear. No one else is going near it. We have to determine what caused it to attack. It may be rabid."

Frank stepped into the fray. "Mr. Payne, there's no need to worry about the kids' camping gear. The conservation officers will collect it and bring it down. You'll have it by the end of the day."

"Not soon enough," Payne barked.

The quizzical look on Frank's face mirrored Rusty's and Pauline's. What possible urgent need could the students have for their camping gear? Those poor kids were never going to want to camp out again after what happened this morning.

"It's not the camping gear I'm concerned about," Payne explained. "Each student keeps a journal. Writing in it is a daily requirement. Most of them left their journals behind in their backpacks. They need them back immediately."

"Oh, a diary-writing emergency. Now I understand," Pauline said.

Frank fought a smile and took on the good-cop role. "Listen, Dr. Payne—we're all a little worked up over this incident. There hasn't been a life-threatening bear attack around here in years. Let Rusty and the DEC crew do their jobs, and I'll make it my business to get those journals back to you by midday. All right?"

Payne glowered at them all. "You don't seem to appreciate that you are keeping me from doing *my* job. These. Children. Must. Follow. A. Routine." He punctuated each word with a thump of one fist in the other palm. "It's essential to their recovery. Let them skip the routine once—just once—and everything you've worked for is lost."

Pauline spread her legs and folded her arms across her chest. "You are not—"

Frank interrupted, using his most reasonable tone. "Surely the kids can do today's writing on a separate sheet of paper and put it into the journal later. Wouldn't that work?"

Payne had the look of a chess master who'd been checked by a rank amateur. "Highly unsatisfactory." He pivoted, his shiny dress shoes grinding against the stony dirt of the parking area. "I will expect you to keep your commitment to deliver all my students' possessions by midday," he called back as he marched toward a van where the students sat waiting for him.

"Geez," Pauline said, shaking her head. "Just when you think you've seen it all, an entirely new kind of nut shows up."

"Thank you both for your help." Rusty turned his earnest, freckled face toward Frank. "We need to carefully examine the campsite to determine what provoked that attack. I'm really not sure if I can get those journals to you by noon."

Frank snorted. Rusty thought everyone was as sincere as he was. "Don't worry about it. When I deliver them to Payne, I'll blame the lateness on the DEC bureaucracy."

Rusty smiled, then shook his head. "Do you really think those journals could be so important to him that he'd put two more of his employees at risk to get them?"

Frank looked up at a hawk wheeling over the meadow across the road. "Makes you wonder what's in them, doesn't it?"

Chapter 3

Rusty paced anxiously waiting for his crew of DEC officers to arrive. Frank was about to reach out a hand to stop him when the young ranger announced, "I'm heading back up the trail—send them up when they get here, would you?"

"Don't go alone—it's not safe," Pauline said.

Rusty hesitated.

Frank understood how hard it was for him not to be at the scene of the attack. "I'm not sure how much help I'll be, but I'll go up with you, Rusty."

"Great!" Rusty sprang into action before Pauline could offer any further objections, and Frank followed him up the path.

After an hour of steady climbing, the trail switched back, then leveled out. Before them lay the campsite.

A small campfire had been built on a cleared patch of ground, and the damp, charred remains showed that it had been carefully extinguished. Three two-man tents surrounded the campfire like strangely shaped yellow and green mushrooms. A fourth tent was collapsed, its bright yellow fabric shredded and stained with streaks of deep red. Small white feathers floated around in the breeze. It took Frank a moment to realize they were escaping from the torn sleeping bag. Dark blots marked the bare earth: the blood of Jake Reiger.

Rusty said nothing as he set to work, his usually cheerful face a grim mask. Frank stayed out of his way, alert for any sound of the returning bear.

Occasionally Rusty spoke aloud the observations he was recording in his notebook. "Here are the remains of the campers' dinner wrapped up inside a bear-proof canister, like you're supposed to do. There's no other food visible anywhere here."

"Maybe the smell of cooking attracted him. Bears will go after the grease on camp grills, right?" Frank asked.

"Yes, but it looks like all they did was boil water to add to those freeze-dried trail food packs." Rusty held an unopened one up for Frank to see.

"These really don't smell like much when you mix them, and they've cleaned all their utensils."

Rusty continued to go through the standing tents, looking for food or strong-smelling lotions that could have attracted the bear.

"Nothing," he said as he emerged from the third tent. They stood looking at the collapsed tent. "Well, obviously Reiger had something in there," Frank said.

Rusty continued to look baffled. "Tent invasions are more common at busy public campgrounds filled with inexperienced campers. The bears come to associate tents with food, and will go in after it. Reiger seemed like such a responsible, knowledgeable guy when he came into my office last week to get advice on where to camp. I gave him the drill on bears. He used to live out west, where they have grizzlies—I could tell he was taking me seriously."

They heard the sound of the other DEC officers coming up the trail. "I'll wait for them to take this tent apart," Rusty said.

When three rangers and Pauline Phelps entered the clearing, Rusty asked, "Any word on—" The look on their faces made him break off.

"Jake Reiger died on the way to the hospital. He lost too much blood—there was nothing they could do," Pauline said.

They all stood awkwardly, looking at the scene of Jake Reiger's terrible death.

Rusty shivered. "Thirty-two years old," he said in a whisper.

"Did he have family around here?"

"I don't think so. He lived on campus. I only met him once, he seemed like a really nice guy. I can't believe his life is over."

Frank recognized the young person's unshakable belief that death only occurred to the old or to those who had done something to deserve it. He'd felt that way himself until three years ago.

Working as a cop should have convinced him of death's utter randomness, but for years it hadn't. He'd managed to convince himself that if you didn't run with a crowd of punks, didn't live with violent, crazy relatives, didn't have any bad habits, you could beat death and live until you were ready to die.

But Estelle's death had taught him that death can come to anyone at any time, without justice or reason or mercy. One day she had been his good, healthy, clean-living wife; the next she lay wired to machines in a hospital room, her brain flooded by her own blood, the victim of an aneurysm that couldn't be anticipated or cured. She hadn't deserved death, hadn't been ready for it, but it had come for her anyway, just as it had come for Jake Reiger.

"Have you had reports of aggressive bears on Corkscrew before?" Frank asked. Talking business was the only consolation he could offer Rusty.

"Never. Several hikers have reported seeing a young male around there, but he's always run off when he saw them. A mature male can be aggressive when he's protecting his turf, and of course you don't want to come between a mother and her cubs, but the adolescents are rarely threatening. The whole episode is just bizarre. Well, let's take apart this tent."

As Frank watched, the rangers carefully disassembled the tent. From the expressions on their faces, they were all as shocked as Rusty.

"I've never seen anything like it," one officer said. "It's like the bear was in a feeding frenzy. There has to be something in here that he was after."

They bagged the pieces of tent fabric and then the broken pieces of the frame. Finally, they got to the sleeping bag. The blood-soaked, tattered nylon and feathers were hardly recognizable as camping gear.

Rusty lifted a piece up, and the other officer looked away as he held a bag open to receive it. After he dropped it in, Rusty rubbed his fingers together. "There's something greasy on my fingers." He sniffed them, and looked up with wide eyes. "It's bacon grease!"

"Well, that explains it," Frank said. "Isn't bacon grease what you guys use as the bait when you trap bears?"

"There's nothing they like better. When we set a culvert trap, we collect a big container of bacon grease from the diner and smear it on a board. The bear can smell it from half a mile away. He goes right into the trap and starts licking and gnawing on the board, knocks it down, and the trap door closes behind him. It's foolproof."

Rusty looked around. "But they didn't cook any bacon here. All they did was boil water for those freeze- dried meals."

"It must have been left on the bag from a previous trip. Man, what awful luck!"

Rusty's pale brows were drawn down in concentration. "There had to be a hell of a lot of grease on that bag to provoke this kind of reaction. That bear was eating, not just sniffing around. Reiger surely would have noticed it when he climbed into the bag."

"Maybe he did, but it's so cold out, what choice did he have but to use it?" Pauline said.

Rusty exchanged glances with the other conservation officers, who were all shaking their heads. "He could have improvised something—he would have known better than to use a bag soaked in bacon grease." Rusty stared at his slippery fingers. "Could someone have sabotaged Reiger's sleeping bag?"

"Whoa, whoa, Rusty. That's a big leap you're making," Frank said.

"I think Reiger was a very sound sleeper," Rusty continued. "He made some comment to me about how he could sleep anywhere, no matter how cold it was. So they must've smeared it on after he fell asleep."

"Who? You think the kids did this as a prank, not realizing how danger-ous it could be?" Pauline asked.

"Maybe they didn't realize; maybe they did."

"Do you realize what you're saying?" Frank asked. "That would be pre-meditated murder. And for that, my friend, you need a motive."

"Look, these kids have all been in trouble before, right? They must hate being at the academy, hate their teachers—"

Frank interrupted. "I hated Miss Hecht for rapping me with a ruler when I wrote my *B* s backwards in first grade. I still hate that bitch, but I never once considered murdering her."

Pauline nodded. "Frank's right, Rusty. You're upset because you knew this guy." She turned to the other DEC officers. "What do you think?"

The older of the two spoke first. "Rusty's got a point. I've never seen a bear attack like that. A trace amount of grease on the bag might have attract-ed him, but he probably would've sniffed around and left when he realized there was nothing to eat. This bear was in a feeding frenzy—there had to be a lot of bacon grease. And I don't see how a lot of grease could've gotten on that bag unless someone put it there intentionally."

"How hard could it be for one of the kids to slip into the kitchen and get bacon grease?" Rusty said. "Or maybe it's that fellow Vreeland—he's not a student, he's one of those Pathfinders."

"Why would he want to harm Reiger?" Frank objected.

"I don't know!"

Frank had never seen the young officer so agitated. "I'm telling you, this is not normal. An experienced camper does not crawl into a sleeping bag soaked in bacon grease in bear country." His eyes blinked rapidly. "What a horrible way to die."

Frank glanced away. He'd been trying to keep the image of Jake Reiger waking up with a bear gnawing on him buried in a dark corner of his consciousness. Man was supposed to be at the top of the food chain; being eaten shouldn't be a worry.

"Bad enough to die that way in a terrible accident. But what if he really was set up—literally fed to a wild animal?" Rusty said, turning toward Pauline. "Surely there's something the state police can do?"

Pauline's broad, pragmatic face didn't show a ripple of emotion. "I'll mention it to Lieutenant Meyerson. If he agrees, we'll go over and speak to Dr. Payne."

Frank felt a stab of alarm. Pauline had already gotten off to a bad start with Payne, and Lew Meyerson, her boss, conformed to every hard-nosed state trooper stereotype in the book. He could only imagine the outraged response from Reid Burlingame if the state police and the DEC started making wild accusations against the students of the North Country Academy. But if Rusty was right, then the attack had to be investigated.

"You guys are awfully busy. Why don't you let me handle it?" Frank offered.

Pauline looked relieved. "That's a good idea. The school *is* in your jurisdiction."

"Let's keep this information about the bacon grease quiet until we get the test results back from the lab and we're absolutely sure of what we're talking about, all right?" Frank said.

Rusty turned on him. "You're going to hush this up, aren't you?"

"No, but I can't go marching over to the academy and start accusing Payne's students of murdering one of his teachers with no proof. We're talking about people's livelihoods here. Accusations of murder could undermine the school right as it's getting started. And if we're wrong, what do we say? 'Oh, never mind?' " Frank jammed his hands in his pockets. "We have no hard evidence of murder."

Rusty hoisted a loaded pack onto his back. "That's what I'm asking you to look for, Frank."

Chapter 4

"What's going on at the old flower shop?" Frank stood at his office window, looking at the line of pickup trucks parked in front of the long-deserted store. A steady stream of men carried two-by-fours, wallboard, and other construction supplies into the building.

The sound of the phrase "what's going on" brought Doris, the town secretary, in on the trot.

"Haven't you heard? Clyde Stevenson is turning the old flower shop into a library for the town."

"You're kidding! That's a really great idea. But he's owned that building for years. Why's he suddenly doing it now?"

"You know," Doris said darkly. "With the end being near, and all—"

"It's going to be the Clyde P. Stevenson Memorial Library." Earl, Frank's civilian assistant, joined the conversation. "Ever since Clyde found out he's got liver cancer, he's been doing all kinds of charity stuff. I guess he thinks it'll help him out." Earl glanced heavenward.

Frank snorted. "A last-minute rush to get a few hatch marks in the plus side of the column, eh?"

"Frank!"

Frank was immune to Doris's scolding. People often reproached him for saying aloud what they had been thinking. He did feel a little guilty though. Clyde had always been a thorn in his side, but in a matter of months, the poor guy had gone from feisty and energetic to frail and cadaverous. He was dying, and the doctors had told him there was nothing they could do.

"I think a memorial library is a wonderful legacy to leave to the town," Frank said. He felt Earl scrutinizing him for traces of sarcasm. "What? You know I love to read. I'll be that library's first customer. I just hope that they have some good books." Clyde's legendary thriftiness didn't bode well for an extensive collection.

"You don't have to worry about that," Earl assured him. "Guess who's helping him organize all the books, and stuff? Penny Stevenson."

Frank completely missed the cup with the coffee he was pouring. "No way!"

Earl and Doris nodded in unison. "She's up here right now," Doris said. "I saw her with Clyde at Malone's. They had the plans spread out and she was showing him how the shelves should be arranged."

"Penny's over at Malone's right now?" Frank's face lit up and he grabbed his jacket. "I'm going to go say hello."

Doris and Earl exchanged a glance.

"What's that look for?" Frank asked. "The last time I saw the kid, she was all banged up in the hospital. I'd like to know how she's doing, all right?"

He strode across the green, his hands shoved in his jacket pockets. Earl drove him nuts with this Cupid routine. No matter how often he insisted he wasn't heartbroken over Beth Abercrombie leaving town, Earl refused to believe it. Whenever a woman somewhere between the age of consent and assisted living crossed his radar screen, Earl started eyebrow raising, winking, and elbowing to draw Frank's attention to her. Naturally Penny, as pretty as she was, would set Earl's alarms off. But Penny was young enough to be his daughter. Almost.

Clyde Stevenson and his wife, Elinor, were slowly making their way to the door of Malone's Diner as Frank entered. He held the door open for them as Clyde, his face ashen with pain, shuffled forward clinging to his wife's arm.

"Thank you, Frank," Elinor said as she passed through the door. "I'm afraid Clyde's overdone it this morning. I've got to get him home." Frank watched to be sure they made it to their car before turning to scan the crowd at the diner. At first he thought he must have missed Penny, but then he spotted a dark head bent intently over some papers in the back booth.

She didn't hear him approaching until he spoke. "Hi, Penny—I didn't expect to see you here again."

She glanced up through her long bangs, then sprang out of her seat. "Frank! How great to see you!" She threw her arms around him and kissed him on the cheek.

He hadn't expected such an enthusiastic greeting, especially in the middle of Malone's. He sized Penny up: still the same long legs, the same chin-length dark hair, the trademark beads and jangly earrings. The only thing missing was the big diamond engagement ring and platinum band that she used to wear on her left hand.

"You're looking good. You're all healed up from the accident?"

"Yes. At first the doctors thought I might always walk with a limp, but I had a great physical therapist. I'm all better now." She smiled and Frank noticed another change. The former thousand-watt grin had dimmed a bit.

"So what's this I hear—you're helping your father-in-law plan the new library?"

"Ex-father-in-law," she corrected. "I was shocked when he called. But he wants to mend fences, and it's a fun project. Besides, believe it or not, I've missed this place."

"Now *that* surprises me. You must be having a great time working as a librarian in Manhattan."

"Oh, yeah . . . definitely." Penny fidgeted with her beads. "But it's nice to get out of the city occasionally. So, have you seen these plans? Look what we're going to do." She slid the library plans across the table to Frank and began to point out the children's room, the shelves for fiction and nonfiction, and the reference section. They sat with their heads bowed over the blueprints until the sound of a throat being cleared roused them.

Earl stood beside the table. "Frank, Rusty's here with those backpacks you're supposed to take back to the North Country Academy."

Frank glanced at his watch and jumped up. "Gee, I didn't realize it was so late. Well, Penny, nice talking to you. I guess we'll see you around."

"Sure. Bye, Frank."

As Frank and Earl walked back across the town green, Earl looked over his shoulder and waved.

"Who are you waving at?" Frank asked.

"Penny. She was looking out the window of Malone's."

RUSTY SAT IN THE DRIVER'S seat of his Jeep, head flung back, eyes shut. His wiry red hair, unruly under the best of circumstances, stood up in tufts. A filthy uniform, muddy boots, and scratched hands and face told the story of his day.

"Find the bear?" Frank asked.

"Eight guys walked every inch of that mountain with trained bear-tracking dogs. We could see which direction he headed, but we lost him. We're going out again tonight to set a trap. Until we get him, that trail is closed."

It only took a few minutes to load the gear into Frank's trunk and send Rusty on his way. Frank surveyed the jumble of backpacks and bedrolls. An unzipped pack on the top of the pile revealed the corner of a spiral-bound notebook. Frank knew he shouldn't, but temptation got the better of him. With the deserted office behind him and the open trunk shielding him from view from the street, he pulled out the notebook, opened it at random, and began to read:

October 28

I woke up feeling strong today. I am sure I can attain Level Two soon if I continue on this path. Today's goals are: replace negative thoughts with positive thoughts, complete all assignments in a timely manner, follow all directions given by Pathfinders.

So much for worrying that he was intruding on the most personal musings of a troubled teenager. Frank flipped to another page.

November 3

Today will be a better day than yesterday. Although I encountered some setbacks in my quest to attain a Level Two because of my inappropriate display of emotion with Christa, I understand and accept the disciplinary action imposed by Pathfinder Steve.

Very interesting. Frank wondered what the "inappropriate display of emotion" was. Had Christa and the writer been caught in the sack together, or had they merely called each other names? And what was "the disciplinary action imposed by Pathfinder Steve"? Frank read on, but each subsequent entry read like the first, with repeated mentions of the writer's desire to obtain the elusive Level Two. The whole tone of the thing reminded him of a news report during Chairman Mao's reign.

Frank replaced the notebook and searched for another to read. The cover of this one said it belonged to Heather LeBron, the girl with no hair. More of the same: the positive thinking, the goals, the reiteration of the commitment to following the Pathfinders. Frank closed it after scanning two pages. Hard to believe that all a kid's progress in school would unravel if she didn't write this drivel for a day.

Frank got into the town patrol car and drove north. The hamlet of Trout Run extended for only two blocks from the central green in any direction, but the town limits stretched in a roughly ten-mile radius. It took Frank about five minutes to arrive at the junction of Route 12 and High Meadow Lane, a sparsely traveled road that ran past the academy. He'd only gone a quarter of a mile down it when he noticed a sign: caution, don't pick up hitchhikers, students not permitted to leave grounds. He slowed to look at it more closely. Made of metal, it reminded him of the kind of sign used on interstates when they ran close to prisons. He drove on and encountered two more of the signs before he came to the North Country Academy, where he was stopped by locked gates.

This was new—he didn't recall the gates ever being locked under the previous administration. He rolled down his window to press the intercom button and waited to be admitted.

The drive led up to a grand old gray stone building in the Gothic tradition. Off to the side, the dorms—two clapboard buildings painted a muted green—nestled in a grove of trees. A one-lane paved road branched off the main drive, and Frank could see a few small cottages fronting on it before it twisted down a hill. Grassy playing fields stretched out behind the dorms, but no teams practiced there. In fact, he didn't see any kids outside at all, despite the sunny weather.

On the drive over, he had debated how to present Payne with the sabotage idea. He didn't see a way to inquire delicately about such an outrageous notion without setting MacArthur Payne off. And an angry headmaster would lead to an outraged town council, which would lead to an unemployed police chief. He knew what he should do, and he knew what he wanted to do—but he hadn't decided if guilt would trump desire.

Chapter 5

An athletically built young man emerged from the gatehouse and directed Frank to pull up alongside a parked van. "Dr. Payne has been expecting you," he said, as he transferred the camping equipment to the van. He didn't speak again and appeared to be counting under his breath. When he moved the last of the backpacks, bedrolls, and tents, he turned to Frank. "Two are missing."

"Mr. Reiger's tent and sleeping bag were destroyed by the bear," Frank explained.

"Nevertheless, we'd like them back."

"They're beyond repair," Frank assured him. "Torn, soaked with blood. The state police lab has them. An analysis may show what caused the bear to attack."

The young man stared at Frank for a long moment. "Dr. Payne will want to speak with you about this." He picked up a phone in the office and dialed four numbers. "This is Steve. Chief Bennett has returned the camping gear and backpacks, but Mr. Reiger's equipment isn't with the rest. He says the state police are examining it." Frank could hear Payne's voice booming through the line. It didn't sound encouraging.

"Follow me," the young man said after he hung up. Frank walked in silence with his escort toward Payne's office. The young man had announced himself as Steve when he made the call—he might be Steve Vreeland, the Pathfinder on the hike.

"So, Steve, were you the one who hiked out for help this morning after the attack?"

"That is correct." Steve kept his eyes focused straight ahead as he answered.

"Brave of you to come down that trail by yourself in the dark, knowing the bear was still out there."

"As the Pathfinder, I was second in command. It was my responsibility," Steve said. For a man who'd seen his colleague virtually eaten alive, he seemed remarkably free of emotion.

"Very unusual for a bear to attack like that. Any idea what could've set him off? Did Jake Reiger mention there was anything wrong with his sleeping bag?"

Steve clenched his teeth until the tendons in his neck stood out. "I already answered the questions of the state police and the DEC officer. We followed all appropriate guidelines for preparing and storing our food. The bear invaded his tent in the middle of the night without provocation."

They had arrived at Payne's office. Steve rapped on the solid oak door and after receiving a muffled "Enter" from within, he opened the door, turned on his heel, and left without a word.

MacArthur Payne marched across the room with his right hand extended. "It's well past the time you said you'd have the equipment back," he said, crushing Frank's hand in his grip. "I was just about to call. And while you're here, I have another police matter to discuss."

Frank freed himself from the painful handshake and took a step backwards. What kind of macho alpha dog behavior was this? If Payne expected an apology for the response time of the Trout Run police, he could pull up a chair to wait. No, no—wrong attitude. This was supposed to be a courtesy call. He let the remark pass and smiled at the headmaster. "Oh? What's that?"

Motioning Frank to sit down, Payne went behind his huge mahogany desk but remained standing. "Trespassers," he spat out with the distaste usually reserved for terms like "pedophiles," or "crackheads."

Frank said nothing, just watched the fellow.

"People from *your* town have been sneaking onto the grounds of the North Country Academy," Payne said. "Can't have it. Upsets the order of things. Order is paramount to what we do here."

Upset the order of things . . . what was that supposed to mean? "I'm sorry, Dr. Payne. Let me clarify this—are you concerned that hunters are poaching on school property?" The academy property spread for more than a hundred acres, much of it wooded, but it was all posted no hunting.

Payne's straight, black brows drew down. "No, this is what concerns me." With a snap, Payne spread a section of the *New York Times* across his vast, uncluttered desk. He leaned over, picked up a brown paper bag, and shook out the contents: a Snickers wrapper, a Doritos bag, and a crushed soda cup imprinted with the Stop'N'Buy market logo.

"Litter?" Frank asked. The guy wanted police intervention because he found some *litter* on the school grounds? "And what makes you think that's from people in town? Maybe your own students dropped it."

"Contraband," Payne spit out. "Academy students are not permitted to eat any food not served in the school dining hall."

Frank smiled. "Kids aren't easily separated from their junk food. It'd be easy enough to smuggle it in."

"I think not, Chief Bennett. The repercussions for such behavior are well known among the students."

"Really? What are the repercussions for eating chips on campus?"

Payne dismissed the question with a flip of his hand. "Not germane to our discussion. Let's walk out to the perimeter of the property and I'll show you what concerns me." He put on his overcoat and pulled a black beret over his nearly hairless head. A man with less self-confidence might have looked silly, but Payne carried it off.

"The North Country Academy is no longer an ordinary boarding school," Payne said as they set off across the broad lawn. "It's an institution dedicated to saving lives. We admit troubled teens here, kids who have failed in every school environment that they have been placed in, and we turn them into successes."

Payne was leading him toward the high wrought-iron fence separating the school grounds from the road. The campus was far too large to be entirely enclosed by fencing, but as Frank walked, he realized how difficult it would be for a student to run away. The school buildings, all with large spotlights on every corner, stood in the center of the campus, surrounded by several acres of open meadows and playing fields with no place to hide. On three sides, the fields ran up to state-owned forest preserve, a protected wilderness area with very few marked trails. Going over the fence to the road would be too risky, with those signs warning drivers not to pick up hitchhikers. And of course, Trout Run had no bus or train service.

Payne must have been watching Frank scan the scene. "It's a beautiful setting, but quite inaccessible. That's what made this property so attractive to me. We have two guards on duty twenty-four hours a day. One up there." He pointed to the turret on the Gothic main building. "And one at the gatehouse."

"But a kid could slip across those fields at night and make a break for the woods," Frank said.

"A skilled hiker could make his way down to Keene Valley if he knew the lay of the land and had a compass and some supplies," Payne agreed. "That's why we keep the hiking and camping gear under lock and key. After every outing, all the equipment—even the water bottles—is counted and logged in by two employees. And we don't allow any food to leave the dining room, so they'd be running on an empty stomach. There's really only one weak link in the setup, and that's what I want to show you."

Frank's ears perked up—these details about the camping gear he wanted to hear more of, but Payne seemed hell-bent on showing him something else.

They arrived at the far front corner of the campus, where a deep, fast-moving stream ran between the end of the fence and the beginning of the forest. Frank knew the road wasn't far away, but he couldn't see it through the trees.

Payne pointed across the stream to a large flat rock. "I find the remains of small fires on that rock, beer cans, snack food wrappers. Someone is parking and hiking in from the road. I've posted a sign that this is private property, but it hasn't done any good."

It was a pretty spot that might appeal to local kids looking for a place to hang out. Frank couldn't see why this was a big deal.

His lack of alarm was apparent to Payne. "These are kids with a history of running away, Bennett. They run away from home, run away from school, but really what they're trying to do is run away from themselves. At the North Country Academy, we make them understand that there's no place left to run. They have to stop and face their problems and overcome them." Payne held up one gloved finger. "We do that by first making them accept the literal impossibility of running away. Then we move on to the metaphorical level. Do you see what I'm getting at?"

As much as Frank had his doubts about Payne, he had to admit that he did. He'd seen men who came face-to-face with themselves for the first time in prison and realized they had to change. But he also knew it didn't work for most of them; they kept on doing more of what had brought them there in the first place. Of course, there wasn't much encouragement in prison. Presumably the academy did more to help the kids change.

"They receive some counseling, I guess, to help them solve their problems?"

"I'll be honest with you, Bennett, I'm not a big believer in therapy. Most of these kids have already been to every shrink in the book, and it hasn't done them one lick of good. What's the point of sitting around in big sob sessions, blaming all your problems on your parents and your teachers and your so-called learning disabilities? Change the behavior, that's what I endorse. Change the bad behavior, and the bad attitude will change right along with it."

Frank could see how parents at the end of their ropes would eat this up. Here was a man who didn't blame them for the way their kids had turned out and who promised to break their children's bad habits the way you'd train a dog to stay off the furniture.

"You make it sound easy."

"Not easy, Bennett. It's hard work, but not complex, if you catch my drift." He gestured to the horizon. "Climbing these mountains takes strength, stamina, perseverance—you can't think your way to the summit, you get there by putting one foot in front of the other. These kids have spent way too much time thinking about their problems. It's time for them to climb their way out."

Frank found himself smiling. You couldn't deny the man's power of persuasion. And maybe he was right. Maybe the kids got more value from six hours of hard winter hiking than they got from fifty minutes on the shrink's couch.

"So can you see why I feel it's important that these trespassers be kept away, Bennett? This location allows us to minimize inappropriate distractions. But if the students believe that their old lives lie within reach, just on the other side of that stream, they won't buy into the necessity of working their way to freedom."

Frank nodded. "I see your point. I tell you what— I'll park the patrol car out here a few nights. It's probably local kids, and a warning will send them on their way."

"An excellent plan. Thank you."

They turned and began to stroll back. The forced friendliness between them had gradually turned more genuine. Frank commented on the view, naming some of the High Peaks visible on the horizon.

"Thank you for returning our camping equipment," Payne said. "I understand there was some, er, delay with Jake's gear?"

"What's left of it—and there's not much—is at the state police lab."

Payne jingled the change in his pocket. "And why is that? I thought that Rusty Magill fellow believed the bear to be rabid. They have to test the bear's brain for that. The sleeping bag won't tell you a thing."

"That's true. But the DEC officer detected what smelled and felt like bacon grease on Jake Reiger's sleeping bag. Bacon grease is a very strong lure for bears. We know your group didn't cook or eat bacon on this trip."

A furrow of concentration creased Payne's high forehead. "We use freeze-dried meals on every camping trip."

"But you do serve bacon here at the dining hall?" They had reached the door to Payne's office and the headmaster held it open for Frank to enter. "Only occasionally. I prefer to offer the students a high-fiber, low-fat diet. A healthy diet helps restore healthy thinking." Payne glanced sideways at Frank. "What are you getting at?"

"Just trying to determine when and how that particular sleeping bag could have come in contact with a substantial amount of bacon grease."

Payne strode across the office to a dry-erase board in the corner. "Let's be logical about this." He picked up a red marker and pointed it at Frank as he spoke. "After every camping trip the gear is checked, counted, and returned to the locked storage room."

"By whom?" Frank asked.

"Jake Reiger himself. He was the director of our Wilderness Experience program. And Jake was the only person, apart from myself, who had a key to that room." Payne printed "Equipment secure" in bold red letters on the whiteboard.

"Now, as I mentioned earlier, the kitchen is off limits to the students, but not, of course, to the staff. They may request special meals, within reason. Let's call in Mrs. Pershing, the head cook." Payne picked up the phone and barked into it. While they waited, Payne beckoned to Frank to join him in front of a wall filled with framed photos.

"This is what makes my life worthwhile. These are my triumphs." He pointed at a photo. "That's Senator Bruce Carmore. I saved his son's life."

Frank squinted at the picture. Sure enough—it was that Republican from out west, the one always clamoring for an anti-flag-burning amendment.

"The boy came to me drunk, drug-addicted, and suicidal. Today, he's a sophomore at Penn State. Accounting major."

Frank scanned the wall. Every frame held a happy group photo—a clean-cut teenager surrounded by, often embraced by, his or her beaming parents. Payne was in most of the photos, as well. This selection of kids certainly didn't look homicidal.

"Any of your kids have criminal records?" Frank asked.

"Drug offenses, drunk and disorderly, vandalism— that sort of thing."

"No violent crimes?"

"I won't take them if they have a history of sex assaults or any violence with a weapon. Too risky."

Frank continued to study the pictures. "Was Jake Reiger popular with the students?"

Payne snorted. "None of our teachers is popular, Bennett. Popularity isn't what we're aiming for; respect is."

"Well, did they respect him?"

"He was earning their respect. He'd only been with this group for a few weeks. Jake always worked with the new arrivals."

"Always? You'd worked with him before?"

"Hmm?" Payne adjusted a crooked picture. "Yes, we were acquainted professionally for a few years. The therapeutic school community is a small one—we all know each other."

"You recruited him from another school?"

"He was ready for a change of scene." Payne inclined his head with a knowing look on his face. "Trouble with a woman."

"Some change! Will there be a memorial service?"

"His sister in Utah is taking care of that."

The door opened after a timid tap, and a middle-aged woman in a white uniform stepped into the room, looking like Dorothy in the presence of the great Oz.

"You wanted me, Dr. Payne?"

"Yes, Mrs. Pershing." Payne didn't bother to offer her a seat, but left her standing there, trembling. "I wanted to ask you about your procedures for disposing of bacon grease."

A blotchy red flush appeared on her neck and face. "I never throw it down the drain! Honest, I never do—I scrape it into the garbage so my sinks don't get clogged up."

"Excellent." Payne smiled at her, but the poor woman wasn't reassured. "And the trash is thrown in the Dumpster, which is enclosed by a fence with a locked gate."

"Who has the key to that?" Frank asked.

Mrs. Pershing pulled on a lanyard that hung around her neck with three keys on a ring. "These are the keys to the kitchen, the pantry, and the garbage enclosure. I wear them around my neck the whole time I'm on duty, and on my days off, Francine wears them. After the kitchen is locked for the night, I give the keys to Dr. Payne before I go home."

"And when is the last time you prepared bacon, Mrs. Pershing?" Payne asked.

She bit her lip and looked up and the ceiling. "Let's see—it must be about a week ago. Randy and Bill asked if I could make bacon for Sunday breakfast, so I did."

Frank wanted to ask her more about the keys, the menu, and access to the kitchen, but it was obvious that if Mrs. Pershing had ever deviated slightly from the established procedure, she'd never admit it in front of Payne. She looked vaguely familiar to him, but he didn't think she lived in Trout Run.

"You live here on campus, Mrs. Pershing?" he asked.

"No, I live over in Verona. I used to be a cook at the Sunnyside Cafe, but when that closed, I was out of work until I got the job here." She smiled at Payne. "This here is a real good job. I like it a lot."

Frank nodded. The Sunnyside Cafe had closed over a year ago, a long time to be unemployed. No wonder Mrs. Pershing was so jumpy.

"Thank you for your time, Mrs. Pershing," Payne said. "You may go."

She took a few steps backwards, as if leaving the presence of royalty, and then turned and slipped out the door. Meanwhile, Payne was writing another phrase on the board: Garbage Secure.

He tapped the board with the capped pen. "That only leaves one possibility. The grease got on the bag during the trip, but not from our campers. There aren't many areas on that mountain that offer a good place to camp. That spot's level, not too rocky, and protected from the wind. Jake's group wasn't the first to camp there and they won't be the last. A previous camping group must have disposed of bacon grease in that area. It soaked into the ground or was covered by leaves, but the bear could still smell it, even if Jake overlooked it."

Frank considered Payne's theory. It was a little improbable, but hell, no more so than Rusty's insistence on sabotage. But how did Payne know so much about the spot where the group had camped?

"You never went up the trail to the camp spot, Dr. Payne. How are you able to describe it so accurately?"

"I didn't go up this morning, but I had hiked there this summer with Jake. I've done all the wilderness outings in the program, so I can honestly tell the students that I don't expect them to do anything I haven't done myself."

Payne turned his back on Frank and gazed out the window. "I've always loved the mountains. I grew up in Montana—hiking, fishing, skiing. What better way is there to spend your time, in touch with the natural world, testing your mind and body against the challenges of the wilderness? Jake shared my passion. He understood the restorative effect that wilderness training can have for these troubled kids. A terrible loss ..." Payne stopped talking for a minute, then coughed and turned to face Frank. "I want to thank you for coming here today." He grabbed Frank's hand and pumped it vigorously, his sallow face flushed with emotion. "It was splendid of you to work with me to discover the cause of this tragic accident, and to look into our trespassing problem."

He put his hand on Frank's shoulder and locked eyes with him. "You're a man of influence in Trout Run. Act as an ambassador for the North Country Academy. Let it be known that I am still hiring people of good character for well-paying jobs with benefits. But also let it be known that this trespassing must stop."

Frank edged away. He was willing to handle the trespassers, but accepting the title of ambassador was pushing the envelope. "I'll bear it in mind."

Frank made it all the way to his patrol car before it registered that Payne had pressed his business card on him as he was leaving, and that he'd been mauling it as he walked.

He flattened it out and read:

North Country Academy MacArthur Payne, PhD Headmaster

"No Payne, no Gain"

Chapter 6

Frank tossed restlessly in his bed, his mind still in the office with MacArthur Payne. The man confounded him. There were plenty of things about Payne to dislike. The way he tried to intimidate people, the pompous boasting, the adherence to this crackpot system—all of it rubbed Frank the wrong way.

Yet there was something compelling about the guy. Not quite likeable, but admirable, somehow. You had to give him credit for turning these kids around when so many others had failed them. And he seemed to be sincere in his love of the outdoor life and genuinely saddened by Reiger's death.

Just when you expected him to blow smoke in your face, he'd surprise you with total honesty, like when he'd admitted that none of the teachers were well liked. That performance with the marker and the board was a little over the top, but in the final analysis, Payne's explanation for how the grease got on the bag had some merit, at least to him.

Frank rolled over and slept.

THE BARE BRANCHES OF the maples in the town green etched a jagged black pattern against the bright blue sky, as Frank walked to the office after grabbing a cup of coffee and donut at the Store the next morning. In the distance, gunfire echoed. The mountains were full of hunters at this time of year.

He made a wide detour around the old flower shop, fighting the urge to pop in and check on the progress of the library renovation. With every carpenter in Trout Run involved, the project had thirty chiefs and no Indians. Frank knew himself well enough to realize that if he went in to look, he'd be the thirty-first Sitting Bull.

He'd picked up plenty of scuttlebutt, though, at Malone's and the Store. Apparently Pete Ringold and George Feeney had almost come to blows over how to frame the checkout desk. Art Breveur, using Rollie Fister's power nailer for the first time, had attached his thumb to a stud. And, Penny, after approving what had been done so far, would be returning to the city on Sunday but would be back next weekend.

As he drew nearer to the Presbyterian Church, he could hear music in the air. The front doors of the church stood wide open on this Tuesday morning. No cars around—it couldn't be a funeral. Maybe Augie Enright was just releasing some heat. The handyman complained that once he cranked up the church's boiler in October, it couldn't be turned down until May. The music swelled and Frank stopped to listen. It was the organ, played in a way he'd never before heard in Trout Run. The piece sounded familiar, something Estelle used to play—Karg-Ellert, Bach? The notes boomed through the air, loud enough to shake the rafters of the little church.

He couldn't pass by without investigating the source of that marvelous sound. He entered the dimly lit narthex, passing by the ushers' table where Reid Burlingame and Randall Bixley oversaw the distribution of the bulletins on Sunday morning, and poked his head into the sanctuary. The organ keyboard occupied the left rear corner, with the pipes arrayed above and behind it.

Frank watched the long, slender fingers of the young man seated at the organ fly across the keys. One moment his head hunched over the keyboard, the next he flung it back, shaking his straight, dark hair from his eyes. Occasionally his right hand rose up to pull a draw knob or flip a coupler. At the same time, his feet, clad in thin-soled black shoes, performed an intricate dance across the pedals. A boy sat beside him on the bench and, without any cue from the performer, turned the pages of the sheet music. Fully focused on the music, they played on unaware of their audience.

The piece ended in a tremendous crescendo of the timpani and horn pipes. The sound ricocheted off the polished stone floor and the uncushioned pews on its way up to the vaulted ceiling, where it seemed to hang, almost palpable, for long seconds.

Frank had no desire to break the spell. The organist's head finally lifted after the last sound wave faded away. Only then did Frank applaud.

Two heads swiveled.

"It *is* Karg-Ellert," Frank said. "My wife loved to play that piece, but she claimed she wasn't fast enough to do it justice."

"Speed isn't everything." The organist smiled and extended his hand. "Oliver Greffe. And you must be Frank Bennett. I've heard about you, but not that you are a music fan."

"Oh, people often forget to mention my good qualities—they're so few and for between." Frank turned his attention to the boy sitting beside Greffe. "So, Matthew—I hear you're taking over as organist here. You might bring me back to church permanently."

Matthew Portman ducked his head and smiled. "Oliver—Mr. Greffe—is teaching me. I'm not too good yet."

"Don't believe him." Greffe patted Matthew's shoulder. "He's coming along marvelously. A natural talent." Matthew flushed under the praise, but Frank could see he enjoyed it. The poor kid had suffered a lot of bad luck in his short life. His mother had died last year in an accident on the Northway, his father struggled to support the family and care for the kids, and his older brother was mentally retarded. These lessons offered a break from the heartache at home. And Greffe didn't look more than twenty-two—he'd make a good role model for the boy.

"So what brought you to the North Country Academy, Oliver?" The young musician was obviously very talented. Why squander it teaching juvenile delinquents? "I imagine the students you teach there aren't quite as committed as Matthew."

Oliver smiled at his student. "Teaching Matthew is a real pleasure. My other students are a little more . . . uh . . . challenging. But I can't complain. The pay is great, and I'm not doing it forever."

Matthew suddenly looked forlorn. "Oliver got into a master's program to study the organ at the Curtis Institute of Music. He'll only be in Trout Run for a year."

"We can accomplish a lot in that time, Matthew." Oliver turned to Frank. "I want to devote myself entirely to music while I'm at Curtis, so I took the Academy job for a year to earn enough to cover my living expenses for next year. With the free room and board, I can save a lot of money."

So, Oliver could earn enough in one year at the academy to support himself for two. That was some teaching job. "And do you enjoy the work?" Frank asked.

"It's eye-opening. I'm realizing that I've led an awfully sheltered life. Ever since I learned to play the piano when I was four, music has been my whole world. These kids have problems I never even imagined, and they require a lot of patience."

Matthew jumped off the organ bench and began stuffing sheet music into a backpack, each page going in more forcefully than the last.

Oliver laid a restraining hand on his student's arm. "Hey, take it easy."

Matthew looked up with a scowl. "It's not fair that your have to spend so much time on those academy kids when they don't even appreciate you."

Oliver met Frank's eye over the top of Matthew's bowed head and smiled slightly. "I don't have a lot of free time, because even when I'm not teaching a class at the academy, I have supervisory duties. Matthew would like me to come and hear him play at the hymn sing next week, but I'm not sure I can get off. I'm going to try, though."

Matthew continued to sulk, and Oliver tried to jolly him out of it. He patted the boy's shoulder. "Hey, you should have been in my vocal class the other day. I had these four kids with tattoos singing 'Ave Verum Corpus,' and they sounded pretty good."

Matthew's head snapped up and his eyes flashed. "Yeah, I would love to be in your vocal class with only three other kids singing Mozart. But instead, I'm in Mrs. Fleischman's ninth-grade chorus, singing tunes from *Cats* with forty kids who would rather be in study hall."

Oliver looked like he had been slapped, but Matthew went on. "Those academy kids grew up with big houses and fancy cars, and all they can figure out to do with their lives is take drugs and shoplift. They don't deserve to study music with you." He grabbed his backpack and ran out of the church.

"Wow! Where did that come from?" Oliver asked as the outer door slammed.

"Oh, don't take it too seriously," Frank answered. "It's always hard to be fourteen, and Matthew's had a tougher ride than most. Probably next time you see him, it'll be like that never happened."

"I hope so."

"Is he right? Are all your academy students drug addicts and shoplifters?"

"I don't know each kid's history, but I don't teach the really difficult ones. Music classes are one of the privileges—the kids have to earn their way into them. You see, Mac really believes in the power of music, both positive and negative."

Mac? Frank couldn't imagine being friendly enough with MacArthur Payne to call him that.

"Most of the kids are fans of heavy metal, Goth, headbanger music. When they enter the school, Mac takes away all their CDs and iPods and they go completely silent for a while. Then gradually, they earn the privilege of coming to me. I get them singing in small groups—Mozart, Vivaldi, Tallis."

"They must just love that." Frank grinned.

"They start out sort of sullen," Oliver admitted. "But as I was telling Matthew, I had a group of them singing Mozart. I recorded them and played it back, and they all looked very pleased with themselves. I think I'm getting through to them."

"It sounds like you're doing a great job," Frank agreed. And maybe MacArthur Payne was, too.

A door in the front of the church opened and a tall man in a clerical collar came hurrying down the aisle.

"Fantastic!" Pastor Bob Rush started gushing before he'd reached the middle of the church. "I could hear you all the way back in my office. Who would've thought our little organ could even produce such amazing sound?"

"Actually, it's an Austin organ—a pretty fine instrument for a rural church," Greffe said. "But it hasn't been well maintained. I'm trying to avoid its weak spots, but that will be more challenging for Matthew. The organ could use a complete overhaul, if you can afford it."

"Whatever it takes." Bob's bright blue eyes glowed with enthusiasm. "Get me an estimate."

Frank glanced around. One pane of the leaded-glass window was still covered over with cardboard; the peeling choir loft cried out to be repainted. Hadn't Reid been complaining last week that the collection revenues were so sparse that Pastor Bob might have to forgo his last paycheck of the year? Not that Bob relied on the pittance he earned as a minister to support himself; he had family money to cover the breach. Maybe that's how he planned to repair the organ, as well.

Frank's negative thoughts seemed to draw Pastor Bob's attention to him. "Were you looking for me?"

An entirely neutral question, but Frank heard an underlying coldness. He and Bob had never really patched up their differences over the Janelle Harvey disappearance case.

"No, I heard Oliver and Matthew playing and came in to listen."

Bob's lips moved into a smile, but the effect wasn't too convincing. "I think it's best that Matthew's lessons not be interrupted. It's hard to learn in front of an audience."

Frank decided to turn the other cheek, mainly because he thought that might irritate Bob more than a protest. "Absolutely right. Nice to meet you, Oliver." He waved and sauntered out, but not before he heard Oliver Greffe say, "What a nice guy."

Bob didn't answer.

As Frank walked back toward the office, he saw Earl's little beige Escort shoot out of the parking lot and speed south on Route 12. Doris was standing in the doorway of the office. He broke into a trot.

"What's wrong? Where did Earl go?" he asked as he came up the steps.

"We got a domestic disturbance call from Peg Betz. Lorrie's over there making trouble."

"And Earl went to handle it on his own? Goddammit, he knows he's not authorized to do that!"

"I told him to go get you, Frank. Honest, I did."

Frank turned his back on the hand-wringing Doris and jumped into the patrol car. What in God's name had possessed Earl to go out on a dangerous call alone? Hadn't they been discussing how unpredictable domestic situations could be, when Earl was studying for the police academy entry exam? Just when he thought he was making some headway with that kid, Earl would let him down by doing something stupid.

Frank threw on the siren and raced toward Peg and Len Betz's home. They were Lorrie's in-laws, and everyone knew Lorrie's divorce from their son, Chuck, had been messy. Len and Chuck were both avid hunters, which made for a very real possibility that guns would play a part in this disturbance.

And there was Earl, heading into it with no more than a pen in his pocket.

Chapter 7

But when Frank screeched into the driveway, he saw Earl leading a teary-eyed Lorrie away from the house. She was as tall as he was, with an athletic build, but he had his arm around her shoulders and she was listening to him intently, nodding occasionally. Earl put her into the passenger seat of her car and got into the driver's side, choosing to ignore Frank's arrival.

Since the patrol car was blocking exit from the driveway, Frank postponed dealing with Earl and Lorrie and headed for the Betzes' front door. Len let him in and immediately started talking.

"Everything's okay now, Frank—we shouldn't have bothered you. You can get on back to your real work."

"Back up a minute, Len. You *did* call, and now I have to file a report. Tell me what happened." Frank looked over Len's shoulder into the living room, where two school-age kids, pie-eyed with all the commotion, sat silently on the sofa. Peg appeared in the doorway to the kitchen. "Go ahead and tell him, Len! Tell him what that bitch said!"

"Watch your mouth, Peg!" He turned to Frank. "Don't mind her—she's all wound up." With a glance toward the children, Len led Frank back onto the porch. "It was only a little disagreement over Lorrie's visitation with the kids. See, the judge was real specific about who has them when, but now that Lorrie has this new job, it interferes with some of her regular times. Peg told her if she wanted the times changed she'd have to take it up with the judge, and Lorrie flew off the handle. She started calling Peg names, then Peg called you to make more trouble." Len shook his head. "People say men are bad, but I tell you, women are spiteful. Purely spiteful." Len glanced over at Lorrie's car. "Earl, he did a real good job. He got Lorrie calmed down and out of the house. That's all we needed." He looked at Frank with mournful eyes. "Please don't file any kind of official report that will go on Lorrie's record, Frank. We got enough trouble as it is. This'll make things worse."

Frank eyed the other man for a moment. Certainly he wasn't hurt, and Peg hadn't shown any signs of injury, either. "It was simply a verbal argument?" he clarified. "Anything physical?"

"No, no—nothing like that. We're all okay, honest." Len took off his orange hunting hat and ran his hand over his thinning gray hair. "I'm too old for this. I wanted to start spending the winters in South Carolina, but now Chuck's got us dragged into the middle of his mess."

"All right, I'm going to bend the rules for you this time, Len. But I won't do it twice, understand? And I'll tell Lorrie the same thing."

"That's fine, Frank. I appreciate it. I really do."

Frank strode across the yard and yanked open the door of Lorrie's car. "Get back to the office, Earl. I'll talk to you later."

One look at Frank's face and Earl knew better than to argue. He left without a word.

Lorrie hung her head so her blond hair covered her high-cheekboned face. "Oh, God! Now I've got my cousin in trouble, too!"

"Earl's your cousin?" He hadn't known this but it didn't surprise him. Earl was like the Queen of England—related to everybody who was anybody.

Lorrie nodded. "He was trying to help me out. You won't fire him, will you?"

"Don't worry about Earl. You tell me what happened."

Lorrie repeated virtually the same story Len had related, except in her version it was Peg who had instigated the name-calling. After issuing her the same warning he'd given to Len, Frank backed out of the driveway and waited to make sure Lorrie drove home. Then he returned to the office.

"I can explain," Earl said before Frank even had his jacket off.

Frank turned on him. "No, Earl, you cannot explain. There's no good explanation for an unarmed civilian to put himself in the middle of a domestic disturbance call."

"It wasn't a domestic disturbance call. It was a family argument. My family's business."

"So you decided to ignore proper procedure?"

Earl shot him a look that said blood was thicker than water, and always would be.

Frank dropped into his chair. "I didn't know Lorrie was your cousin."

"Second cousin, actually. Her mom and my dad are cousins."

"So, tell me the whole story. Because I'm warning you, if we get another call from them, I'm writing it up." Earl began spinning a tale of woe that sounded like the lyrics to a Tammy Wynette song. Lorrie and Chuck had been high school sweethearts, Lorrie got pregnant and they got married young, and Peg had blamed Lorrie for ruining her son's life. After a second baby came along, Lorrie suspected Chuck of seeing another woman. One night she followed him when he went out, and when he was about to pull into the other woman's driveway, Lorrie cut him off, causing a crash that injured them both. After that, divorce was inevitable.

"Where do Peg and Len come into it?" Frank asked. "Didn't Lorrie get custody of the kids?

Earl squirmed in his seat. "This is the bad part. Can you keep a secret?"

Frank didn't deign to answer.

"Lorrie hurt her back real bad in the car crash. The doctor gave her these pain pills, and, well—"

"She got addicted."

Earl nodded. "One day Peg came to Lorrie's place and found her all spaced out, the kids running around half naked, and gas pouring out of the oven. She'd turned it on and never noticed it didn't light. Chuck got full custody by agreeing to live with his parents so they can watch the kids after school, and Lorrie only has visitation. It's really not fair. Lorrie's okay now, but she can't get the kids back because she hasn't had a good enough job to support them."

"Now she does—this job at the academy pays well, doesn't it?"

"That's just it," Earl explained. "Lorrie's been so excited about the job, she's been telling everyone she's going to get her kids back. Peg's not happy about it, so she's being real mean about the exact time when Lorrie can pick the kids up and drop them off. When Peg called about this so-called fight, I knew she was trying to make more trouble for Lorrie. That's why I went out there to calm things down."

"I see. But listen, Earl—Peg called the police, and she expected a response from the police. She didn't ask for Lorrie's cousin to come act as referee. If you're going to work for me, you have to learn to keep your job separate from your family loyalties, understand?"

Earl looked down and bobbed his head.

Frank considered continuing the lecture, but Earl seemed contrite. "Len said you did a good job. He doesn't seem to have any hard feelings against Lorrie."

"Nah, Len's okay. I think he wants out of the middle of this. That's why I told Lorrie to humor Peg for little while longer. Once Lorrie works her job for a few months and saves up some money, she can go back to the judge and ask for joint custody. Then all her problems will be over."

———— ◉ ————

ON SATURDAYS FRANK took an extended dinner break, then came back on duty to keep an eye on the town on the biggest social night of the week. At ten it was still too early for trouble at the Mountainside Tavern, so he figured he might as well cruise by the spot where the trespassers had entered the North Country Academy property and check for any new activity.

When he'd left the school grounds yesterday, Frank had easily spotted their path. Whoever it was made no effort at concealment: tire tracks on the shoulder of the road marked where their vehicle pulled off, and a fairly well beaten path led through the trees to the big flat rock beside the creek. Payne had posted a large no trespassing sign at the spot, obviously to no avail. The road curved right past this spot so Frank parked there, out of sight, to see if anyone would show tonight.

It was a nice night to build a little fire and hang out with your friends—crisp, and the sky ablaze with stars. He'd never known the night sky contained so many stars until he'd moved to Trout Run. He got out of the car and craned his head back, seeing how many of the constellations he remembered from his Boy Scout days. He never got tired of looking at them, although he supposed if he were seventeen, he might want a more exciting way to spend the evening. Eventually the cold urged him back into the car. An hour passed and only one car had gone by.

He checked his watch. Eleven-fifteen now, and no one had shown. He'd give it another half hour—kids wouldn't be out much later than that. The allotted time crawled by in absolute stillness, then he drove off to the last task in a long day.

Ten past midnight: the witching hour at the Mountainside Tavern.

The first lesson Frank had learned as police chief of Trout Run was how to read the mood in the town's only serious watering hole. Sure, the Trail's End served booze, too, but no one ever got ugly-drunk on amber ale and Celtic ballads. The Mountainside didn't encourage patronage from tree huggers and tourists. Working men went there to unwind, but on some Saturday nights, the winding turned back in the other direction. The tipping point came just after midnight, and Frank could usually tell as soon as he opened the door whether the crowd was building toward a fight or dissolving into booze-induced slumber.

Tonight, the difference between the sharp, clear night air and the smoky haze of the barroom smacked Frank in the face. A quiet, low-grade tension simmered, punctuated by harsh barks of victory from the pool table and dartboard, and occasional jeers at the wrestling match on TV. George, the bartender, greeted Frank with an uneasy smile.

George and Frank had a long-running disagreement over precisely how drunk a patron should be before he was cut off. Frank's arrival meant several customers' tabs would have to be tallied prematurely. On the other hand, George, too, could sense a fight brewing, and he preferred Frank to be on hand before glass started breaking.

The customers propped around the U-shaped bar all seemed mellow enough, so Frank forged his way through deeper clouds of smoke to the game area. There, Ray Stulke held court, talking loudly to a crowd of men as he lobbed darts at the board. He wore a black T-shirt with the sleeves hacked off, revealing biceps the size of Easter hams.

Frank leaned against an out-of-order pinball machine in a shadowy corner to keep watch.

"I just got back from Long Island this afternoon," Ray said as he landed a perfect bull's-eye. "You shoulda seen this spread. Freakin' garage was twice as big as my house. We backed the van right in there, and the kid's old lady let us in."

Frank listened with half an ear. Couldn't be talking about burglary if the homeowner had let him in. Ray's barroom tales were three-quarters fantasy, anyway.

Another dart flew from Ray's huge paw and hit the cork board. "We crossed over this shiny floor made outta the same stuff as gravestones, and went up a big curvin' staircase like in the movies. Go into the kid's room, haul his ass outta bed, and hog-tied him. His mom watched us carry him out of there like he was a sofa she didn't want no more."

A skinny guy with greasy hair took his turn at the dart board, but Ray continued talking. Frank was listening closely now. Who had he tied up? Did this have something to do with the traveling Ray claimed to do on his new job at the academy?

"Man, that was some trip home, though." Ray swigged from his beer and let out a colossal belch. "Traffic was so screwed up, took us nearly eight hours. And for the first three, the fuckin' kid never shut up. Drove me nuts."

"So whatd'ya do—put a gag on him?" someone on the sidelines asked.

"Nah, we're not allowed to do that. Once a guy stuffed a sock in some screaming kid's mouth, and he ended up chokin' on his own puke. We don't get paid if we deliver 'em dead." Ray brayed at his own wit.

Was this how kids arrived at the North Country Academy—bound and gagged? The tipping scale on which Frank measured MacArthur Payne crashed down again.

"Here's what I did." Ray lumbered over to the skinny darts player and put one massive hand around his neck, then lifted him a foot off the ground. The guy's face turned red and his legs kicked ineffectually as Ray held him off to one side. "I squeezed his neck like this 'til he turned a little blue, then I let him go." Ray dropped his darts opponent like a discarded toy. "That shut him up." The skinny man staggered backward, gasping, as two of his friends made ready to take on a grinning Ray.

"I think we've had enough fun for one night." Frank stepped forward and laid a restraining hand on one of the men. "Ray, I think you owe this gentleman an apology."

"The hell I do."

"Maybe you'd rather apologize to MacArthur Payne for demonstrating the abduction techniques you use in public," Frank said.

Ray glanced around nervously, as if realizing for the first time that he was playing to a full house. "I, I didn't mean nothin' by it. Just havin' some fun, tellin' some crazy stories, that's all."

"Apologize to the man, Ray."

"I, uh, I'm sorry." Ray spoke like a tourist reading from a foreign-language phrase book.

"You can leave, now, Ray," Frank said. "It's past your bedtime."

As he stood in the parking lot of the Mountainside, watching until the troublemaker's taillights disappeared over the horizon, Frank had to wonder about the reliability of any man who would hire Ray Stulke to work with children.

Chapter 8

B ear mania gripped Trout Run.

The bear on Corkscrew had apparently had his fill of bacon grease, because the trap the DEC set for him came up empty. With the rogue still on the loose, everyone who had ever hunted bear, chased bears out of their garbage, or just seen a bear minding its own business had developed a theory about what had prompted the attack. More worrisome, everyone seemed to have a defense plan involving heavy-duty firepower should the bear show its face on their property.

The fear surprised Frank. After all, these were Adirondackers, not suburbanites freaked out by a raccoon rummaging in their trash. But the general population didn't know about the bacon grease yet, so to them, the bear had violated all the normal rules of human-ursine engagement. Releasing the information about the bacon grease might calm people's fear of the bear, but it would start a second round of speculation about how the grease had gotten there. Until they were ready to say definitively either that the death was accidental or sabotage, Frank and Rusty had agreed to keep quiet about the grease.

Frank had slept in on Sunday and arrived at Malone's for breakfast as church was letting out. Caught in the confluence of the early breakfasters leaving and the late breakfasters arriving, he answered more questions about the bear than he would have if he'd been at work. His eggs grew cold as he counseled Vivian Mays not to buy a hunting rifle if she didn't know how to shoot, and Dee-Dee Peele not to organize a team of armed parents to sit outside the grade school, even though bears had occasionally been sighted in the woods near there.

During a lull, he propped a book up in front of him to ward off further bear theorists. So far *Jane Eyre* had driven off Augie Enright, Jack Harvey, and Bernice Mays, and Malone's had settled into silence. As he turned the page to read about the young Jane's arrival at Lowood School, a blast of cold air on his back and the sound of girlish squealing made him look up. A pack of teenagers had tumbled through the door and were now getting themselves seated in the largest booth.

"I'm not sitting next to Bra-ad, not after what he did to me on Friday."

"Lay off, Alison—you deserved it."

They piped down once the waitress went to take their order, and Frank returned to reading. But before long, the giggling and teasing escalated again. Frank glanced up and observed them in the mirror above the counter. Brad Fister, Rollie's grandson, sat in the middle of the crowd, with Alison Munro, despite her protests, right beside him. Rachel Portman, Matthew's older sister, sat on the other side, hemmed in by two boys whom Frank recognized but couldn't name. Across the table were Jessica Powers, and Kelly Davis, another cousin of Earl's. They were nice-looking, happy kids—not a tattoo or pierced eyebrow in sight. They must be sixteen or seventeen—the same age as many of the kids at the North Country Academy—but they seemed younger than the students Frank had met on that hike. Probably it was their innocence. The academy kids had all been around the block a few times, and it showed.

Gales of laughter rang out when Jessica dropped a French fry into Brad's Coke. It didn't take much to keep this group amused. Frank went back to reading and didn't look up again until Marge brought him his check. As he reached for his wallet, he heard Alison say, "No way, I'm not going back there again. Not with this bear on the loose."

"Don't be stupid," one of the boys answered. "The bear was on Corkscrew—that's nowhere near our spot."

"I don't care. I won't be able to relax. It won't be fun, like last week. Jessica doesn't want to go either, do you, Jess?"

Jessica gave an uncertain shrug. Frank smiled. He had a feeling that his opportunity to be ambassador for the North Country Academy had just presented itself. He left a five on the counter and paused by the kids' table on his way toward the door.

"Hi, guys."

They all greeted him politely, then silence descended on the table.

"I couldn't help but overhear your conversation. I think Alison is right. Better stay indoors at night while this rogue bear is on the loose." He smiled at them benevolently. "Where does everyone like to hang out these days?"

Everyone looked at Brad as if he were the only one qualified to answer. He rolled his shoulders in an elaborate shrug. "I dunno."

"You don't know?" Frank chuckled. "That must make it kind of hard to meet up."

"Sometimes down by the old covered bridge," one of the other boys volunteered.

"Oh, I haven't seen you kids down there since the middle of the summer. You must have a new haunt." Brad and the other boy exchanged glances.

"You ever go out to High Meadow Lane, near the North Country Academy?"

"No, huh-uh," Rachel and Alison said, too quickly.

"Listen, guys—do me a favor." Frank zipped his coat. "Stay away from the woods near the academy. The headmaster, Dr. Payne, doesn't appreciate your presence there."

"Why?" Rachel Portman sat forward. "We're not bothering anyone. After that first time, we've been real careful to pick up our trash."

"It's private property, Rachel. Dr. Payne doesn't want you there—you have to respect that."

Rachel took a breath, as if to argue, but Brad shot her a silencing look. Frank knew this argument didn't hold much water with them. Like most locals, they felt that you ought to be able to walk across anyone's property as long as you did no harm.

"He feels your being there is a distraction to his students," Frank explained. "They might want to come over and join you. And believe me, I don't think you'd like that any better than Payne would."

———— ◉ ————

FRANK HEADED TO THE comfort of his home, only to find the phone ringing and the answering machine full of bear reports. He changed the message on his machine to direct everyone to call the DEC with their bear problems, then drove over to the Iron Eagle Inn, where he could count on finding some rational conversation with its owners, his friends Edwin and Lucy Bates. And where he might also run into Penny Stevenson, who, according to Doris, was staying there.

He walked into the inn's wide entrance hall, which was empty except for the threadbare stuffed moose head that presided over the reception desk. A second later he heard footsteps coming down the stairs, and looked up to see a thin little girl with brown hair, dressed in a woman's heels, scarf, and sequined sweater and carrying a small wooden box.

"Hi, Olivia," Frank said. "Whatcha got there—a jewel box?"

"It's not a jewel box," Olivia said with the exaggerated patience children use when the adults in their lives say something incredibly stupid. "It's a reliquary."

"A what?"

"Open it up."

Inside, Frank saw a slightly charred splinter of wood that looked like it must've been pulled from the ashes in the fireplace.

"You know what that is?"

Fairly certain "a chunk of burnt wood" was not the right answer, Frank said, "No, what?"

"A piece of the one true cross. Today I'm a medieval queen. One of my knights brought this back for me from the Crusades." Olivia clomped off to the kitchen, the scarf floating behind her.

Frank followed and got there in time to see Edwin, his torso wrapped in aluminum foil, on his knees promising eternal loyalty, while Olivia dubbed him with an uncommonly long wooden spoon.

"You may rise, Sir Edwin!"

"Thank you, Your Majesty. Hey Frank, I didn't hear you come in."

"Probably the clanking of your armor drowned out my footsteps."

"Olivia and I have been playing Middle Ages all morning. Liv, why don't you go tell Lady Lucille that the roast mutton and mead is ready in the banquet hall."

"That's the page's job, not the queen's," Olivia complained, but she went.

Edwin smiled as he watched her disappear up the back stairs. "She doesn't miss a trick."

"So, she's doing well?" The lilt in Frank's voice gave away how badly he wanted to be reassured. He had put Olivia's mother, uncle, and grandfather in jail, and convinced Edwin and Lucy to take the little girl in as a foster child.

Edwin rocked his hand back and forth. "She has her moments. As long as we keep her distracted with games and reading and shopping, she's fine. But last weekend Lucy and I were busy with guests all evening, and when we went to check on her at bedtime we found her crying in her room. She asks about her mom a lot."

Frank knew his worry about the little girl must be written all over his face, because Edwin abruptly switched gears. "We have a full house tonight, very unusual for this time of year. Three sets of parents visiting the North Country Academy because they're thinking of sending their kids there. That place is going to be great for business."

"That's good." Frank accepted the distraction Edwin offered; worrying about Olivia wasn't going to change her situation.

Watching Edwin bustle around preparing for lunch had an oddly relaxing effect on Frank. Despite the five cups of coffee he'd drunk over breakfast, he almost felt he could drift off here in the inn's warm kitchen.

"Here—taste this," Edwin commanded, popping some unidentified morsel into Frank's mouth when his eyes had drooped shut for an instant.

"Aack! What is it?" Frank sat up, choking.

"Stuffed mushroom caps. Jen made them—what, are they awful?"

Frank chewed experimentally. "No, it's okay. Just not what I was expecting."

Mention of Jen Verhoef, the woman who helped Edwin part-time in the kitchen, woke Frank up.

"Jen's not going to leave you to work in the kitchen of the North Country Academy, is she? I hear they pay big bucks."

Edwin laughed. "No, Jen's too much of a smart aleck to succeed over there, and she knows it. From what I can tell, Payne hired the perfect person for his needs."

"Mrs. Pershing? You know her?"

"When I advertised for help here, I got applications from everyone in the North Country who ever boiled an egg. Helen Pershing applied and she did have experience working at the Sunnyside Cafe, but I didn't click with her. She was so timid. You have to be able to yell at each other to work together in a kitchen."

"I'd say you got what you asked for, in spades. Seems like Jen's always telling you that you don't know what the hell you're doing."

Edwin laughed. "She keeps me honest. I'm glad it worked out for Helen at the academy. When I told her I wasn't going to hire her, she burst into tears—she was so desperate for a job."

Frank felt an uneasy twinge. Edwin had verified what he suspected when he'd met Helen Pershing: She was too intimidated by Payne to speak openly in front of him. Maybe he should stop by her house for a chat before he finally signed off on Rusty's theory.

"So, are you excited about the new library Clyde is financing?" Edwin asked, as he dropped a handful of what looked to Frank like grass clippings into a big bowl of salad. "Clyde has asked me to be on the board of directors." Edwin had been an English professor before losing his tenure bid had forced him into a new career in innkeeping. He was constantly bemoaning the lack of a bookstore or library in Trout Run. "Penny Stevenson recommended me—you know, she's staying here the weekends that she comes up to help."

"Really?" Frank said. "She's here now?"

Edwin didn't seem to notice the hopeful note in Frank's voice. "No, she left a little while ago. Lucy had a long chat with her last night. Apparently Penny's not that happy in the city. She's working as a librarian in a big ad agency, helping the creatives and the marketers with their research. She thought it would be a good way to meet people, but she's says all the men are shallow and the women are catty."

Frank prowled around the kitchen, opening containers and jars in a quest for cookies. "Still, she can't possibly want to move back here?"

"Why not? The Adirondacks are full of people who've dropped out of life in the fast lane. I think she's testing the waters. And Lucy's scheming to entice her with eligible men."

Frank paused with a snickerdoodle halfway to his mouth. "Oh? Like who?"

Olivia chose that moment to bound back into the kitchen with Lucy. She plopped down at the kitchen table and began banging her plastic cup. "Where's my mead? I want mead!"

"Get it yourself, Queenie," Edwin answered. "The vassals have all gone back to the village."

Olivia got a big jug of apple juice from the fridge and lugged it back to the table, but it was too heavy for her to pour.

Lucy came up behind her and put her hands over Olivia's to steady them. Together they poured the juice, and after the cup was filled, Frank noticed Olivia sink back into Lucy's arms for a moment. Then she snapped back into character and raised her cup high.

"The finest mead in all the kingdom!"

Lucy surveyed the piles of chopped vegetables on the counter. "What's all this?"

"I'm testing the recipe for the soup you wanted for your dinner party—roasted red pepper and corn chowder with andouille sausage," Edwin said.

"Yuck!"

"Relax, Olivia, this dinner is for grown-ups only." Lucy assured her. "Edwin and I, Penny and her friend Janice, whom she used to work with at North Country Community College, Bob Rush, and you, Frank, if you're free. It's the Thursday after next."

"Sure, I'll come," Frank agreed. "I'm always up for a party." *Especially one with Penny.* But as he sat in the kitchen watching Olivia, Edwin, and Lucy continue their medieval drama, his contentment gradually ebbed away. Lucy hadn't recited the guest list in the proper order. The couples she hadn't specified were Edwin and Lucy, Penny and Bob Rush, himself and Janice. He and this friend of Penny's had been invited to make the Penny-Bob setup less obvious. He would have a ringside seat at Lucy's matchmaking extravaganza. He could hardly wait.

Chapter 9

"**A**re you *still* screwing around with those damn reports?"

It was the third time on this completely uneventful Monday that Frank had snapped at him, and even Earl's Zen-like patience had its limits. "How come every time you're in a bad mood, you yell at me for stuff that doesn't even matter?"

"I am not in a bad mood."

Earl turned his back and resumed his methodical typing.

Frank watched him. You had to admire Earl's absolute refusal to get into a pissing match. When he was right, he knew he was right, and that was enough for him. Frank would keep on arguing, even when the debate was entirely internal.

Which explained his foul mood. His bad temper had escalated every time he launched a new assault on the thorny issue of Edwin and Lucy's dinner party. The show in which he had a walk-on part as the elder statesman, the benign old uncle. The party that revolved around Penny and Bob.

Why did it bother him? Edwin and Lucy were always so generous—he should be pleased they included him in this gathering. And he knew they liked Bob Rush. Let Lucy play matchmaker if she wanted—why should it concern him? Penny was a big girl; she could make her own decisions. Not that she'd chosen very well the first time around...

That was it, he decided. He just didn't want Penny to be hurt again. The poor kid had been through enough. Could a romance with Bob Rush really lead anywhere? Sure, he was good-looking, and about the same age as Penny, and they'd both gone to Ivy League schools, but still, Bob was so, so ... so what? What the hell was it about Bob that he didn't like?

Other people, whom Frank liked, liked Bob—Reid, Edwin, even Earl. So why didn't he? The misunderstanding during the Janelle Harvey investigation—surely it was time to let go of that? He made up his mind. He would be nicer to Bob Rush. He'd start by going to the hymn sing next Saturday. He wanted to hear Matthew play, anyway, and he'd compliment Bob on it on the way out the door. It wouldn't kill him.

Earl crossed the room and silently dropped the completed reports in Frank's in-basket.

"Thank you, Earl."

Earl merely nodded.

Amends must be made. He began by telling Earl about the events of Saturday evening and Sunday morning—his reception at the North Country Academy, his encounter with Ray Stulke at the Mountainside, his talk with the trespassers. "So I'm wondering what Ray does at the academy," Frank said. "Do you think his job could possibly be bringing kids there by force, or was he blowing hot air, as usual?"

"I asked Ray what he would be doing there, but he wasn't too loquacious," Earl said.

"Too what?"

"Loquacious. That means talkative."

"I know what it means," Frank said. "I've just never heard you use that word before."

Earl pulled a paperback book from his desk drawer: *Pump Up Your Vocabulary in 30 Days.* "I'm using this to prepare for the vocabulary section of the police academy test. It's the only part that could trip me up. Every day I have to use five new words three times, to burn them into my memory."

"What are your other four words for today?"

"Culminate, penultimate, debacle, and lachrymose."

"Okay, repeat this three times: 'Doris's penultimate dye job culminated in a debacle that left her lachrymose.' "

"Wow, you're good, Frank. No wonder you passed your academy exam on the first try."

They were back on good terms. "Anyway, get back to telling me about Ray's job at the academy. Is he one of these so-called Pathfinders?"

"I don't think so—I think what he does is different from Lorrie's job. Lorrie says her job is to watch her group of five kids."

"Watch them do what?"

"Everything—eat, go to class, study. A staff member is with them every minute of the day. She says it's like being the mother of a toddler. You have to watch them constantly and correct them every time they do something wrong. That's why Mr. Payne figured she'd be good at the job. Because she has little kids."

"Yeah, but Lorrie's not so good at watching little kids," Frank said. "That's why she lost custody of hers. Does Payne know that?"

Earl waved away this objection to his cousin's competence. "Payne says she's been doing a good job keeping track of the transgressions and the points."

"What points?"

"Whenever the kids do something wrong, she writes them up in her book for a transgression. Then they lose points. They need points to work their way up to the next level. At every level, they get a few more privileges. Like on Level Two, you can get one call a month from your parents, and you can stay up an extra half hour to read. It's hardest to get from Level One to Level Two. Then when you get to Level Three, you become a Pathfinder yourself for a while, until you graduate."

"Sounds reasonable. But she must not be too popular with the kids."

Earl shrugged. "I don't know, but she and Ray both say they like working for Dr. Payne. And the pay is good, too—fifteen dollars an hour."

"Where does Payne get the money to pay everyone so well? Even fancy prep schools run on a pretty tight budget."

"Payne charges fifty thousand dollars a year for each student," Earl said.

"Get outta town! How do you know that?"

"Lorrie saw a stack of letters going out to parents who asked for more information."

"And how many kids are enrolled there?"

"A hundred and twenty-five right now, and more are due in this month. Lorrie says there's room for four hundred."

"That's twenty million dollars! My God, I didn't realize how much was at stake." Payne had a lot to lose if there was a taint of scandal around his school. But Trout Run stood to lose, too. If enrollment really did get up to four hundred, even more teachers and cooks and Pathfinders would be hired. And all those parents must come up to visit, which would mean rooms rented at the Iron Eagle and the Mountain Vista, meals eaten at Malone's and the Trail's

End. He was due to talk to Rusty later today, but the tenuous confidence he'd felt on Saturday was ebbing away.

"What do you think of this idea of Payne's that a previous camper dumped his bacon grease, and Reiger happened to pitch his tent over it?" he asked Earl.

"It's possible ..."

From the way Earl dragged out the word, Frank could tell he didn't think it was very probable.

"What makes more sense is that hunters dumped the grease there."

Frank sat up and paid more attention. "You ever hunt bear?"

"Once or twice, with my cousin Donald. It used to be a lot easier to hunt bear in these parts. Some hunters would hang out by the town dumps and pick off scavenging bears. It was illegal, but plenty of people got away with it. Now the open dumps have all been closed, so sometimes hunters resort to bear-baiting with bacon grease to increase their take." Earl held his hands up. "Not that Donald would ever do that."

Frank grinned. "Of course not." Suddenly he felt better. Earl's explanation made a lot of sense, much more sense than either Rusty's or Payne's. It paid to talk things over with the kid. He would bring this idea to his meeting with the DEC this afternoon. In fact, now that the initial shock of the attack had worn off, he wouldn't be surprised if Rusty and the other officers had already come to the same conclusion.

"I'm surprised people are that keen on hunting bear,"

Frank said. "What do you do with it after you've killed it? You can't eat bear meat."

Earl looked as if Frank had claimed the world was flat. "Of course you can—it makes real good chili. And there's a lot of fat on a bear. You can use that like Crisco. My great-grandma Gert fries up homemade donuts in bear fat."

Frank felt the morning's coconut cruller do a backflip in his gut. "What did your great-grandfather die of?"

"Stomach cancer. Why?"

"Never mind."

FRANK SET OFF ON THE morning patrol, turning right out of the parking lot on his usual loop: through the center of town, out to the Mountain Vista Motel, around through Crescent Ridge, past the lumberyard, and back down across Stony Creek.

Today he varied his route a bit, turning left, then right onto the Upper Crescent Road. He hadn't been up here in a while; he wondered if the McIlroys still kept their flock of sheep. Cresting the hill, he came upon a little country cemetery—twenty or thirty granite and slate headstones cocked at crazy angles by the passage of time. He slowed and looked out across the valley: In the foreground, a creek small enough to step across meandered through a rocky meadow. A few sheep, fat in their winter wool coats, browsed lazily. The outline of the Verona Range, hazy on the horizon, marked the boundary of this little world. Sometimes it seemed the best views in the Adirondacks belonged to the dead.

Down the road from the grazing sheep, an odd little house crouched. If the home had been situated on top of the hill, its occupants would have enjoyed the same stunning views as the inhabitants of the cemetery. Instead, Katie and Paul Petrucci had built their house into the side of the hill, with windows on only two sides. A sliding glass door faced south, but opened onto a six- foot drop. Obviously they'd never gotten around to building the porch it should have led to.

The place stood as testament to all Katie and Paul's enthusiasms. Two large black rectangles on the roof–solar energy collectors; a huge mound of leaves inside chicken wire with bits of banana peel and eggshell sticking out—the compost heap for the organic garden; a tall pole with a winged contraption on top—a windmill to generate electricity. And in the side yard, a monumental load of firewood, enough to heat the little house all winter with a wood-burning stove.

Frank caught a glimpse of something shiny moving up and down and realized Paul was outside splitting wood. He wondered why Paul wasn't at work, teaching at the North Country Academy on a Monday. On a whim, he pulled over.

Petrucci moved like an automaton, placing a log in position, bringing his ax down in one smooth sweep, tossing the split wood aside, and starting all over again. Wiry but muscular, Paul had wavy dark hair and a strong profile.

Easy to see why Katie Conover had fallen for him when they were both students at NYU. Harder to understand why they'd chosen to return to Katie's hometown to eke out a living and raise their kids in this rundown cabin.

"Looks like nice, dry wood," Frank said. "Where'd you get it?"

Paul dropped the log he'd been setting up and spun around.

"Oh, hi. I didn't hear you pull up." He surveyed his mountain of wood. "Bucky Reinholz delivered it."

"I need a small load for my fireplace, but I want it split and stacked."

"Bucky will do that for you, but it costs twice as much. I can't afford that service."

"Really? I keep hearing that working at the North Country Academy pays very well. You're not working today?"

"The pay isn't enough for the work Payne makes me do. And today, I finally have a day off."

Frank knew that Paul had taught at the academy for several years under the old regime. He fell into the "hippie intellectual" category in Frank's classification system, so it didn't surprise him that Paul and Payne hadn't hit it off.

"Are the hours longer, now that MacArthur Payne's running the show?"

"It's the way I have to fill them. Half the time I'm on guard duty."

"Can't take working with the kind of kids the academy attracts now?"

"The kids aren't a problem," Paul answered, leaning on his ax. "In fact, many of my students this year are highly creative. They just have trouble fitting in ... controlling their impulses."

Like an impulse to pour bacon grease over a sleeping teacher? The thought sprang into Frank's head even though he'd convinced himself the sabotage idea was crazy.

"Are any of them dangerous?"

Paul snorted. "They're simply rebellious kids."

"I hear Payne's hired some local people," Frank continued. "Ray Stulke, Lorrie Betz, Helen Pershing. Kind of an odd assortment, huh?"

"Not odd if you want to surround yourself with drones who will do your bidding without question." The ax fell again with a thud.

"Guess he'll have to do some more hiring, now that Jake Reiger died."

Paul paused. "Yes, that was a terrible accident."

"Did you know him well?"

Paul shook his head. "We've only worked together for a few weeks. He was one of the teachers Payne brought with him when he bought the school."

"So I guess Reiger shared Payne's educational philosophy, not yours. Did you get along?"

Paul kept his eyes focused on the next log to be split. "He was an outdoorsman. We had that in common."

"Was he popular with the kids?"

"None of us could possibly be well liked by the students, when we have to follow Payne's curriculum."

"But was Reiger more harsh than the other teachers?"

Paul seemed to sense Frank was on a fishing expedition, although he couldn't know why. "No, I wouldn't say so," he answered, then returned to his chopping with greater vigor.

Frank stood around a while longer, but Paul seemed to feel no compunction about ignoring him. As he was about to leave, the door of the house banged open and a little girl came tearing down the hill toward her father. Paul, who had his back to her, pulled his ax back for another swing.

Frank intercepted the child and swept her up in his arms. "Whoa, there, missy—don't get too close to that ax."

She squirmed away from him. "My name's not Missy, it's Deirdre."

Katie appeared right behind her daughter. A pretty woman, she succeeded in making herself look frumpy by yanking her hair back in a tight ponytail and wearing clothes that might as easily have belonged to her husband. "Deirdre, haven't we spoken about how inappropriate it is to approach Daddy when he's using a sharp tool?" she said in a patient voice.

Frank tried not to roll his eyes. Definitely inappropriate to get your head split open like a cantaloupe. But he was glad Katie had shown up—he had a feeling he could push her buttons well enough to learn a little more about the North Country Academy.

"Kids—they charge ahead without thinking, don't they?"

"Yes, I'm afraid teaching them that actions have consequences is a long process," Katie said. Paul held Deirdre in his arms, where she hid her head on his shoulder.

"That's sort of what MacArthur Payne's trying to do with his students, isn't it?"

"Harsh punitive measures are counterproductive, isn't that right, Paul?" Katie always spoke in declarative sentences, never bothering with "I think" or "in my opinion."

"Usually they are." He set Deirdre down and encouraged her to carry some of the split wood over to the stack he had started between two trees.

"Some of those kids are pretty wild, though, aren't they?" Frank asked.

"They're wild because most of them have parents who aren't qualified to raise gerbils, let alone children," Katie said. "Like that poor Heather LeBron."

"I think she was one of the girls on the campout with Jake Reiger." Frank said. "I got the impression that even the other kids considered her a trouble-maker."

"Heather is in Paul's English class," Katie said. "Tell Frank what she's like, Paul."

Paul had picked up his ax again and answered them with his back half-turned. "I could tell from reading her essays that she was a deeply troubled girl, full of pain and rage. I'm trying to reach out to her, but she's been reject-ed so often, she's terribly wary."

"Rejected?"

"Her parents are divorced and both remarried," Katie said. "Apparently neither couple wants Heather living with them. She's been farmed out to nan-nies and boarding schools for years."

"So why is the North Country Academy any different than what she's used to?" Frank asked.

"It's precisely the wrong environment for her," Katie said. "She acts out because she's starved for love and attention. Paul told Mac that her behavior would improve if they could find some positive outlet for her emotions."

"I want to give her the lead in a class play I'm planning," Paul said, leaning on his ax. "But Payne insists she has to earn the right to even a walk-on part by jumping through all his behavior modification hoops. And she can't do it—she keeps seeing the prize move further and further away with every transgression." Transgression—that word again. It had such a Bible-thump-ing sound to it. "But surely you shouldn't reward bad behavior?" Frank said.

"No, of course not. But in Heather's case, I feel that giving her a chance to be the center of attention in a positive way might allow me to break through to her. But Mac is adamant: no exceptions, everyone toes the line. It drives me crazy."

Paul was on a roll now. "And another thing—I don't even have control of my own classroom. There's always one of these Pathfinders sitting in the back, writing bad reports on the students in a notebook. How can they feel free to express themselves in an atmosphere of fear?"

"It's ridiculous," Katie chimed in. "Paul is far more qualified to know what teaching methods will work with these children."

"Payne does have a PhD," Frank reminded her.

Katie's mouth twisted in scorn. "A PhD in *motivational science* from someplace called the Institute for Human Potential. Paul has a master's in education from NYU—he didn't send away for his degree from the back of a cereal box."

Frank smiled at the fact that a woman who lived in a house without central heating could be capable of elitism. "This disagreement over teaching methods must make it hard for you to keep working at the academy, Paul."

Paul bent and set up another log to split.

"Yes." Katie's voice had an edge of stridency. "Paul won't compromise the educational principles he believes in. But we both feel he can be a more effective force for change if he continues working there than if he quits."

A force for change, maybe. A force for keeping a roof over his head was more like it.

Paul's ax fell with enough force to send the two halves of the log flying across the yard.

Chapter 10

Frank walked into the DEC field office a few minutes past their scheduled meeting time and found Rusty, Rusty's boss, Howard Norvin, and State Police Lieutenant Lew Meyerson all waiting for him.

"Sorry I'm late."

"No problem—we all just got here," Howard said genially. He opened a file in front of him. "I understand Rusty has some concerns about the death of the teacher over on Corkscrew. Lew, what can you tell us about the lab tests your boys did on the tent and the sleeping bag?"

"Rusty was right. The substance he detected on the bag was definitely bacon grease."

"About how much would you say was on there?"

"There were only scraps of the bag recovered, so it's hard to say."

"What about the tent?"

"Grease was detected on the bottom of the tent, but again, the fabric was shredded and not much was recovered."

Rusty sat forward eagerly in his chair. "Just like I said—it's consistent with grease being poured—"

Howard held up his hand for silence. "Let's hear what everyone has to report before we start analyzing. Frank, you spoke to Dr. Payne to find out who had access to the camping gear and the kitchen?"

Frank reported what he'd learned from Payne: that only Reiger and Payne had keys to the equipment room and only the cook and Payne had keys to the kitchen. "The kids don't have much freedom of movement on campus," Frank added. "Someone's watching them twenty-four/seven. I don't think they would have the opportunity to procure the grease."

"So we can be fairly certain the grease attracted the bear," Howard said. "Now the question is, how did it get there? Rusty?"

Rusty took a deep breath. "I believe that it had to be intentionally poured on him as he slept. I feel the ferocity of the attack indicates a significant quantity of grease. The fact that very little was left of the sleeping bag and tent bottom supports this. If the grease had been on his bag from a prior use, Reiger would have noticed it when he pitched camp. He was an experienced camper—he would have understood the danger. It had to have been put on as he slept—he told me he was a heavy sleeper."

Howard nodded but didn't react. "Your thoughts, Frank?"

"As I pointed out, it would've been hard for the kids to get the stuff. Plus, I don't really see them as having a motive. I spoke to two teachers who both seemed to feel these kids are just rebellious teenagers. Maybe a little more difficult than most, but not violent. And Payne says he won't take kids with a history of violence."

"And you believe him? Take him at his word?" Rusty burst out.

Frank was startled by Rusty's accusatory tone. He'd always gotten along well with him. "I didn't tell him what you suspected. He had no reason to lie."

Howard nipped the exchange. "Lew, tell us what you think."

"I'm with Frank—I don't see motive or opportunity among the students, although it is puzzling how the grease got there."

"I have a theory given to me by someone who understands hunters. Tell me what you think of this." Frank explained Earl's idea that hunters had disposed of the grease and Reiger had had the misfortune to pitch his camp near the spot.

"I had a similar thought myself, and shared it with Rusty earlier," Howard said. "It *is* the most popular spot to camp on that trail. And we do have problems with hunters setting bait. Not very sportsmanlike, but when they come up here for a hunting weekend, they don't like to go home empty-handed." Howard turned to his colleague. "You've gotta admit, that theory holds water, Rusty."

Frank felt reassured that Howard, an officer with twenty-five years of experience, had independently come up with the same idea as Earl.

"There was a lot of grease! How could he not notice something like that on the ground?" Rusty protested, but he sounded less adamant than he had previously.

"You told me the kids said they pitched the tents under Reiger's supervision," Howard reminded him. "Part of their training, right? Most of these kids are city dwellers. What would they know?"

"It makes sense to me," Lew agreed. "For that matter, if they're city kids, how would they even get the idea for this type of sabotage if they don't know about bear behavior?"

"But if the grease was on the ground, how did it get on the bag?" Rusty asked. "If they pitched the tent over it, it would've only been on the tent bottom."

"They could've dropped the sleeping bag on the spot first," Frank said. "Some of the bags I returned didn't have covers—they were rolled and tied."

"I think we have a reasonable explanation, Rusty," Howard said with an I've-indulged-you-enough finality. "I'm sure if anything else turns up, Frank and Lew will let us know."

Rusty said nothing, just looked down at his boots. The older men exchanged glances.

Surprisingly, the tension breaker came from Lew. "Did I ever tell you about one of my first cases when I got assigned to the Ray Brook Barracks twelve years ago? I had worked in Rochester when I first became a trooper, and I didn't know the Adirondacks at all. One day I got a call to investigate a break-in at a summer cottage. Thief sliced through a screen to gain entry while the homeowners were out. The place was trashed. Kitchen completely ransacked—drawers pulled out, contents of the cupboards thrown on the floor. First thing I think—the thief is looking for cash, because people often hide cash in the kitchen. Then the homeowner shows me the bathroom—medicine cabinet ripped clean off the wall. Aha, I think—looking for prescription drugs. Thief left by breaking through the bedroom window—must've been surprised by someone's approach, I figure."

By this time, Howard's shoulders were shaking with silent laughter. "I remember this case! *You* were the cop?"

Meyerson, normally so hard-nosed, cracked a smile. "I got teased about it for years—I can't believe I'm bringing it up again. So anyway, I filed the report, say we're on the lookout for a violent burglar, possibly with a drug habit. The next day, the homeowner calls to say that while they were cleaning up the mess, they found a big pile of shit in the closet and it didn't look human. Oh, and that maybe he'd forgotten to mention that his wife had baked an apple pie before they'd left the house that night, and they found the empty pie pan under the bed."

Frank was laughing and even Rusty had to smile. Lew rose and clapped the young ranger on the shoulder. "The moral of that story is, even if it looks like a crime, even if it sounds like a crime, it might just be a bear with dinner on his mind."

Chapter 11

"Who the hell's that?" Frank asked as he looked out at the green where a knot of people had gathered around a blond woman in high-heeled boots and a long wool coat. Augie Enright gestured toward the church and the green, while the woman took notes.

"A reporter for the New York *Beat*," Doris said. "I wouldn't be surprised if she's on her way over here."

"Why?"

"She's doing a story about Jake Reiger getting killed by the bear."

"Why would a paper like the *Beat* care about that?" Frank asked. "I thought they specialized in stories about rock stars and politicians caught with their pants down." Sure enough, Augie's parting gesture was a finger pointing out the town office, and the reporter crossed the street, heading in Frank's direction.

In Kansas City, all inquires from the press were referred to the public affairs officer. So often had it been beaten into their heads that talking to a reporter was the surest way to screw yourself, your case, and the department, that they all came to regard reporters as the Antichrist. In Trout Run there was no public affairs officer to palm the reporter off on, so Frank braced himself for an ordeal. Say as little as possible, that much he knew.

"There's a Dawn Klotz here to see you," Doris announced as she held Frank's office door open. The look on her face could not have been more astonished if she had ushered a crowned princess into his presence.

A cloud of expensive perfume drove out the usual smell of stale coffee and damp wool that pervaded Frank's office. The reporter had somehow made it through the mud in the green, despite boots that looked like they were made for prancing down a model's runway. "Dawn Klotz, New York *Beat*," she said, as if all of it were the name she'd been christened with. "So, you're in charge of the investigation into Jake Reiger's murder. What have you learned about how that bacon grease got on his sleeping bag?"

Frank felt his mouth opening and closing like a goldfish. "I... who ..." He got a grip on himself. "There is no active police investigation into Jake Reiger's death." But Dawn had noticed his floundering surprise. "Why not? Are you trying to hush this thing up? I understand that students from the North Country Academy are the only people who would've had access to the sleeping bag. Is that true?"

"No, I'm—"

"Really? Who else had access?"

"I meant, no, I am not trying to hush anything up."

"So, the students *were* the only ones with access to the bag." The entire time he spoke, Dawn kept scribbling in her notebook.

"No!" Frank felt his temper flare—he was used to being the questioner, not the questioned. "Who said anything about there being bacon grease on the sleeping bag?" So far as he knew, he and Earl, Rusty, the state police, and Payne were the only ones aware of the bacon grease. Surely the troopers and Payne wouldn't have told this woman anything. Was leaking the information to the press Rusty's way of forcing an investigation?

"I can't reveal my sources," Dawn replied. "So, you're confirming that someone did place bacon grease on the bag, is that right?"

"No, I'm not confirming anything!"

"Is it true that a murderer is loose and people from this community are terrified?"

"That's ridiculous. People are a little jumpy about the bear, but—"

"I understand that some people around here are willing to overlook anything to keep that school in business. Would you say that MacArthur Payne has undue influence over the political leaders of Trout Run?"

The sudden change of tack left Frank floundering again. "Undue influence? What are you talking about? And what are you writing in that notebook? I haven't told you a thing."

"Actually, Chief Bennett, you've been quite helpful. Thanks for your time."

An uneasy silence settled over the office after Dawn Klotz left, persisting until a torrent of acorns and leaves hit the window an hour later. The lights flickered.

Earl looked out. "Man, that was the wind. A front's moving in from the west. The temperature's supposed to drop into the teens tonight, and they're predicting snow."

"I knew the nice weather couldn't last." Frank walked over to the window to scrutinize the sky. "If this wind keeps up, we'll have broken branches bringing the power lines down."

As he returned to his desk, the phone rang. He listened carefully, taking notes. After he hung up he said to Earl, "Get the gear. A hiker from the North Country Academy is lost on Lorton."

EARL PEERED UP THROUGH the windshield as they drove toward the tallest peak in the Verona range. Thick, steel-gray clouds had erased the morning's bright blue sky. "She picked a bad day to get lost. It sure looks like snow."

Frank glanced at the dashboard clock. "Yeah, and we have less than three hours to find her before it gets dark." According to the call from the DEC dispatcher, the missing hiker was Heather LeBron, fifteen years old, five foot seven, one hundred forty pounds. She'd become separated from her group of ten hikers and one teacher as they descended the Lorton trail. For some reason, no one noticed she was missing until they reached the trailhead parking lot and prepared to get in the van to go back to the academy.

Frank knew Heather was the girl who'd jumped on the boy's back when they were carrying Jake Reiger off the mountain after the bear attack. She must be terrified now. She sure wasn't a natural outdoorswoman.

They arrived at the trailhead amid a cacophony of barking dogs, complaining teenagers, and shouting adults. Rusty was trying to outline the search strategy to five ECOs and ten civilian volunteers. Among them were Ray Stulke and Oliver Greffe. MacArthur Payne stood beside Rusty, and from the look on Rusty's face, things weren't going well.

"... and John's group will take the south trail. Please stick together and follow the orders of your party leader. We don't need searchers lost, as well. I'm sure I don't have to remind you that with the temperature dropping and sunset at 5:10, time is of the essence." Rusty scowled at MacArthur Payne. "I only wish we had been notified sooner."

"I still think you're overreacting," Payne said. "I know Heather and she's either hiding in those woods to call attention to herself, or she's trying to run away. We'll probably find her hitchhiking on Route 73."

"You have expressed your opinions and they are duly noted," Rusty said. "Now let's begin the search."

A split second of silence descended, as everyone waited to see Payne's reaction to his dismissal. After a slight hesitation, the headmaster fell in behind the conservation officer assigned to lead his group, and the search teams fanned out.

"Where do you want Earl and me, Rusty?" Frank asked.

"Huh?" Rusty seemed a little rattled, as if he'd surprised himself by winning that battle. "You two can work with me. I've only got Roger, and that thin fellow there, a teacher at the academy who came over to help search—Oliver Something."

Rusty gathered them together. "We're going to drive around to the west side of Lorton and take a secondary trail up the mountain. It's steeper and rougher than the trail the kids went up on. If she wandered off the main trail, there's a chance she's worked herself around to this one. We'll go up on the trail, then bushwhack our way down, covering the area between the two trails. Sam here will be searching for signs of her scent."

Rusty held out a dirty sock to a medium-sized brown and white dog. The dog sniffed and cocked his head, his intelligent brown eyes looking eagerly at his handler. Frank had worked with Sam before. If anyone could find Heather, this little mutt could. They set off up the trail.

A sharp blast of wind cut through Frank's jacket. He wished he'd worn his heavier coat, but it had been twenty degrees warmer when he'd left the house this morning. "Geez, the temperature's dropping like a stone. We'd better find her quick."

"It's worse than you think," Rusty told him. "Because it was so nice this morning, the hikers all took off their jackets and left them at the lean-to halfway up the main trail because they were overheating. They picked them up again on the way down—we found Heather's still there."

"You mean the kid's out here without a coat?" Frank asked. "She could die of exposure."

"The situation is very serious," Rusty agreed. "I tried to make that clear to Mr. Payne, but he didn't seem to understand. He kept saying, 'This experience will test her resourcefulness.' Well, let me tell you, all the resourcefulness in the world isn't going to save you when you're wearing jeans and a cotton sweatshirt in an Adirondack snowstorm."

"How come when they all picked up their coats at the lean-to, no one noticed one was still there?" Earl asked.

"That's what I'd like to know." Rusty paused and looked up the trail. "Heather obviously got separated from the group somewhere above the lean-to, yet no one noticed she was gone until they got all the way out to the trailhead. How can that be?"

"I think I might be able to answer that," Oliver said from behind them on the trail.

They all stopped and turned to look at him.

"Heather hasn't adjusted very well to the routine at the academy. She has a bad habit of not only getting herself in trouble, but also pulling other students into it with her. I think many of the kids avoid her because they don't want to risk losing points."

"That seems kind of mean," Earl said. As the youngest in the group, he had the clearest memory of the pain of high school.

"You mean you think the other kids noticed she was missing but didn't say anything?" Rusty asked.

"Oh, I'm sure it wasn't intentional," Oliver said, but Frank thought the expression on his face wasn't as certain as his words.

"Heather might have been trailing along behind because she didn't like being on the hike and no one wanted to walk with her," Oliver continued. "So they probably thought she was right behind them and would pick up her coat when she got to the lean-to."

Frank didn't comment. No point in speculating how it had happened; the bottom line was, the kid was lost. But he didn't like the feeling he was getting that some of the other searchers from the academy might not be that motivated to find her. A few fine flakes of snow drifted down, the advance troops for the invading army.

The trail was now steep enough to make conversation a waste of energy. They scrambled up a bare outcropping of rock, and the trail leveled out for a bit. The dog had been trotting along beside them, staying on the trail and showing no signs that he had scented anything. Occasionally Sam took a detour out into the brush, but he always returned promptly. Now, as they paused to take a drink, Sam lay down and stared at his handler hopefully, as if to say, "You promised me a better outing than this."

"She hasn't been through here," Rusty confirmed. "We're about a half an hour from the summit. Once we're there, we can cross over to the main trail. I want to go partway down that way to a spot where the trail's a little ambiguous." They slogged on, their hard breathing leaving puffs of vapor in the air.

A small cascade of rocks skittered down the path as Earl stumbled and went down hard on one knee. When Frank offered him a hand up, he realized Earl had no gloves and had been walking with his hands in his pockets. His skin was red and chapped, the nailbeds white with cold. "Here, Earl, wear my gloves for a while until your hands warm up," Frank offered.

"Nah, I'm okay."

Frank pulled his gloves off. "Do it. That's an order."

Earl accepted the gloves, and within ten minutes Frank began the feel the effects of his generosity. Even when you weren't using your hands to climb the rocky outcroppings of the trail, it was difficult to keep your balance with them in your pockets. More than once he teetered and caught himself by grabbing at an overhanging branch with his numb fingers.

"The summit is just past these rocks," Rusty said. "We can't bushwhack here—it'll be easier to cut across the top and come down a way on the other trail. Be careful. This is slippery."

Frank looked at the huge gray rock, worn smooth by centuries of wind and rain, looming above him. If this was the easy route, he didn't want to think about the hard one.

Rusty scaled the rock first, effortlessly finding hand-holds and toe-holds in the slightest indentations. Oliver went next. Thin but agile, he climbed the rock quickly, slipping only once. Sam took a long detour through some scrubby evergreens and found an easier way up for a creature with four paws.

Earl handed him the gloves. "You go next, Frank. Then you can toss them back down to me."

Frank suspected the worried look on Earl's face had nothing to do with the missing girl. Probably figures he'll have to shove me up this thing from behind, he thought as he began to climb. The fine, icy snowflakes glazed the rock with a slippery film. Earl had been right to give him the gloves—getting a grip would be impossible without them. He could see Oliver's and Rusty's boots a foot or so above his head when his left leg slid out from under him. He scrabbled desperately to keep from falling. Earl gasped, but Rusty remained calm. "There's a foothold for your left foot about six inches up from where your right foot is," he directed.

Frank found it and pushed himself up. Oliver and Rusty grabbed his arms, and he landed on the summit with all the dignity of a wide-mouthed bass flopping on the dock of a fishing cabin. Christ, he was getting old! Looking down at what he had just climbed made him a little queasy, and he stepped back as Earl made the ascent.

The force of the wind whipping from the west brought tears to his eyes, and he turned his back to the view of Lake Placid that would lay in that direction. There was nothing to see from the summit now. The gray sky had descended over Lorton and they stood within the clouds.

They crossed the summit, found the main trail, and headed down. "Look there," Rusty said after they'd been going downhill for ten minutes. "When you're coming down the path and you look ahead, you see the trail marker on that birch down there."

Frank could barely pick out the round blue disk with adk printed on it that indicated this trail was maintained by the Adirondack Mountain Club.

"But," Rusty continued, "if you're tired and looking down at your feet, you see how the rocks come together to form a natural pathway that steers you over to the right. It's possible Heather could have gone off the path here, and by the time she realized it, she couldn't find her way back to the marked trail." Rusty called to Sam and offered him another sniff of the worn sock belonging to Heather that had been provided to the searchers. Sam refreshed his memory and took off down the unmarked path. But within a minute he had circled back, his head cocked expectantly.

Rusty shrugged. "I guess I was wrong—he's not catching her scent down there."

Frank hesitated. Rusty's theory had a lot of merit. The false trail seemed more natural to follow at that point than the marked trail, and the marker, so far down the path, would be easy to overlook. But Sam didn't scent her, and Frank knew from experience that the dog couldn't be fooled.

"Let's start bushwhacking between this trail and the trail we came up on," Rusty directed. They walked another fifteen minutes, as the sky grew darker and the air grew colder.

They crashed through the underbrush, regularly calling Heather's name, until they reached the secondary trail, then they slowly worked their way down and across to the other trail.

On their third switchback between the two trails, Earl shouted, "Hey, there's the lean-to." They all sat down on the edge of the platform and drank from their water bottles. Sam made a disinterested circuit of the lean-to, then drank eagerly from the collapsible dish Rusty had brought for him. He flopped down and rested his head on his paws.

Rusty stared at the dog.

"What's the matter?" Frank asked. "He's not giving out on us, is he?"

"Look at him. He's totally relaxed. He's not showing any sign that he scents Heather. And we know she was in this spot—she left her jacket here. Her scent should be strong."

A few months ago, Frank would have assumed the dog was unreliable. But Sam had proved his mettle on another investigation, and that forced Frank to look at the facts from a different perspective. Fact one: Heather had been here. Fact two: Sam wouldn't miss the scent he'd been asked to follow.

"Give me that sock," Frank demanded. He turned it over and found two small black letters, a laundry mark, on the sole. "MT," he said. "This isn't Heather's sock."

"MT would be Melissa Trenk, Heather's roommate," Oliver said. "She didn't come on the hike."

Frank threw the sock down. "Jesus H. Christ! We wasted nearly two hours sending that dog tracking the wrong person."

Rusty immediately got on his walkie-talkie to confer with the other searchers. While he talked, Frank quizzed Oliver. "Who gave Rusty that sock?"

The young teacher paused to think. His soulful brown eyes and earnest expression unconsciously mimicked Sam the dog. "I guess it must have been Mac, or maybe Steve Vreeland. He's one of the Pathfinders. There was a lot of confusion when we left the academy—assembling the search party, finding the articles of clothing, running back for water bottles."

Rusty signed off and outlined the new plan. "The team who took the westernmost side of the mountain was also using one of Melissa's socks. But the team on the main trail was using Heather's coat. Unfortunately, the dog on that team was the least experienced of the three. His handler said he seemed to pick up Heather's scent right at that spot above us that I pointed out. They followed it for a while, but lost it at a little stream.

"They're going to head back up the trail with the coat," Rusty continued. "Sam and I will go down to meet them. You guys go back to the spot in the trail where she seems to have wandered off and follow it to the stream. Take the radio—we'll stay in touch and meet there."

Frank tramped wearily back up the trail, letting Earl take the lead. His feet were freezing; with every step he felt a hot stab in his thighs. He'd been climbing much faster than he would on a recreational hike, trying to keep up with the younger men. To take his mind off the pain, he asked a question.

"Oliver, Heather was one of the kids on the camping trip when Jake Reiger was attacked, wasn't she?"

"Yeah, it's like she's a bad-luck magnet. I've heard the other kids are somehow blaming her for that." Oliver shook his head. "Ridiculous."

"I noticed when we were bringing the campers down that Heather had hardly any hair. If she's recovering from chemotherapy, it's going to be even harder for her to survive this cold."

"Chemotherapy? Oh, no—Heather didn't lose her hair to cancer. Mac made her shave it off."

"Why?" Frank and Earl asked in unison.

"It's part of the treatment that all the kids have to give up their outrageous fashion statements—take out the nose rings, get rid of the hot pink hair."

"So if a girl has her hair dyed a crazy color, Mac shaves her head?" Frank was appalled. Caroline had once poured peroxide on a big chunk of her dark hair.

She looked like a skunk, and Estelle had cried, but Frank had just laughed. It was only hair, and it had grown out. Some things weren't worth fighting over.

"No, he makes them dye it back to a normal color. But Heather came to the academy with dreadlocks," Oliver explained.

"But she's white."

"Well, she has this frizzy kind of hair and she was trying to get it to form dreadlocks, but it turned into a big matted lump," Oliver explained. "There was no way to comb it out, so they shaved her head."

Frank glanced at Earl to gauge his reaction. He looked distinctly unconvinced. Oliver must have noticed their expressions.

"I know it sounds harsh, but her hair really was pretty disgusting. And Mac's been letting her wear a hat, even in class, until it grows back in."

"She better have that hat on now," Frank said, as another gust of wind blew sharp ice particles into his face. Now that they were lower down on the mountain, the temperature must be right at the freezing point, making the precipitation neither rain nor snow, but an icy sleet. The thick clouds and the dense canopy of balsam and pine had chased off the last moments of daylight.

Not yet pitch-black, but dark enough for Frank to pull out his flashlight as they searched for the false fork in the trail that Heather must have followed.

"I think this is it." Frank used the flashlight beam to point out some rocks that formed a natural staircase leading off to the right. The three of them followed it, making their way toward the creek that they could hear but not see.

Before long, the false trail disappeared, and they were dodging between trees and rocks. What lay ahead looked the same as what lay behind; easy to see how Heather had gotten confused.

To Frank's left, Earl tripped, and the steepness of the mountainside kept him stumbling forward with gathered momentum. Frank could hear him crashing through the brush, then Earl yelled, and the sound of running stopped.

"Are you all right?" All they needed now was a searcher with a broken ankle. Frank played his flashlight beam through the trees until he finally picked out Earl lying on the ground with his arms wrapped around a bent sapling.

"I'll be right down to help you," Frank said.

"No! Don't!" Earl held up one hand while clinging to the tree with the other. "I'm at the edge of a rock ledge here. I almost went over." He leaned forward gingerly. "It's about a thirty-foot drop. I can't see the bottom too good, but the stream's down there. I'm going to work my way across to where it's less steep. Shine the light down here."

Frank and Oliver watched from above as Earl edged his way across on all fours until he reached ground level enough to stand on.

"Do you think Heather could have gone over that?" Oliver asked.

"I think we better get down below and check the area very carefully."

"I see a way down," Earl shouted, "and I think I hear the dogs."

Frank radioed Rusty as he and Oliver picked their way down to Earl. Together, the three of them made it to the creek bed as Sam came tearing into view. Nose down and tail up, Sam shot past them, baying in excitement.

He headed straight for the base of the cliff.

Chapter 12

For the second time in a week, Frank found himself helping Rusty Magill carry a stretcher through the woods.

They had discovered Heather slumped at the foot of a large boulder, where she'd gained some meager protection against the biting wind. A purplish bump distended her forehead and scratches covered her face and hands. She probably had tumbled down from the ledge. Her skin was gray and clammy, her pupils dilated, and she muttered incoherently. Hypothermia had definitely set in—they had found her just in time and began treatment immediately. Another hour and it would have been too late.

As they loaded her into the ambulance, the paramedic temporarily removed the oxygen mask. The blue had receded from Heather's face; a healthy pinkness edged back. Her gray eyes, more alert now, looked straight into Frank's, and she spoke: "The bastards left me. They left me on this damn mountain to die."

Then the stretcher was hoisted inside, the ambulance doors slammed shut, and Heather was whisked away.

The DEC team had dispersed to their various vehicles, packing up dogs and equipment. Rusty stood still among all the activity, his gaze on the receding ambulance lights. Frank stood beside him, contemplating a tire track, bracing for the inevitable. He didn't have long to wait.

"I suppose you're going to tell me this was a coincidence." Rusty spoke without moving his eyes.

Frank felt a weariness entirely unrelated to all his climbing. It was that all-pervasive enervation that comes from knowing an impossible task lies ahead, and you have no choice but to take it on.

"No, Rusty. You know I always say I don't believe in coincidence. I'll go over to the hospital later and talk to Heather. Then I'll go back to the academy tomorrow to see what MacArthur Payne has to say." Frank crammed his hands in his pockets. *And get myself crucified for my trouble by everyone who wants to make sure the North Country Academy stays in business.*

"I'M SO GLAD YOU CAME by this afternoon." MacArthur Payne stood at the door of his office, beaming at Frank like a maître d' greeting a valued customer.

"Wanted to update you on the trespassing problem. I think I may have solved it." Frank wondered how long this pretense of charm and civility would last once the real reason for his visit became apparent.

"Wonderful. Let's take a stroll around the grounds and you can tell me about it."

Frank reported on his encounter with the teenagers in Malone's, and told Payne he'd continue to cruise by on the weekends to be sure the kids followed his directive.

"Excellent," Payne said. "Eliminating this problem is one of my top priorities. That, and hiring a replacement for Jake Reiger. By the way, what's become of Jake's camping gear?"

"The state police lab still has it. Why?"

"I like to have these things ... accounted for."

"I'll keep you posted."

Payne took a breath, as if to continue arguing, then let it drop. They walked along in silence for a while.

"How is Heather LeBron feeling?" Frank asked. "Recovered from her hypothermia?"

"Much better. I think her experience on Lorton was instructive, both to her and the other students. She learned the necessity of cooperating with the group."

"When we found her, she seemed convinced the group had intentionally abandoned her. I wanted to talk to her about it, but the doctors wouldn't let me see her last night, and when I went back this morning, she had already been released."

"Nonsense!" MacArthur Payne didn't seem the slightest bit cowed by the suspicion in Frank's questions. "Heather has been manipulating people with her skillful lies for so long, she's come to believe her own stories. If she hadn't alienated herself from the group, she would never have gotten lost."

"I understand she kicked up quite a fuss about coming back here when she was released from the hospital this morning. Said you were trying to kill her."

Frank thought this information—brought to him via Earl, whose aunt was one of the nurses at the hospital—would put Payne on the defensive, but he grinned broadly.

"Of course she did—she had a whole new audience of doctors and nurses to play to. That child could give Meryl Streep a run for her money. But I've seen a definite improvement in her attitude since she's been back. She's reconciled herself to the work that lies ahead. As I said earlier, she had to accept the impossibility of running away."

Frank looked at Payne, swaying slightly with his muscular arms folded across his chest, the snow-dusted peaks of the Verona Range unfolding as his backdrop. If ever there were a man in control of his fiefdom, Payne was it. Maybe Heather's attitude change had come from knowing her only chance of rescue had slipped away.

"I find it a little odd," Frank continued, "that the only student to be on both the Reiger campout and this hike was the one who got lost."

A spasm of annoyance creased Payne's face. "I fail to see the connection. The last time you were here, we agreed that Jake's death was an unfortunate accident. I don't see how what happened to Heather changes that." Frank wasn't sure he saw it, either. All he knew was that he wanted to talk to Heather to be certain the two events weren't linked. "I'd like to talk to Heather while I'm here."

Payne's blue eyes stared ahead without blinking for an inordinately long time. "Fine," he said. "I'll have to go back to my office and check the schedule to see where she is at this time of day."

Payne pivoted and began to march back toward the administration building. Frank had to hustle to match his long strides.

"So, how are all your new employees from Trout Run working out... Lorrie, Ray?" Frank hoped a little conversation might slow the man down.

"Lorrie is developing into a marvelous Pathfinder. I'm very pleased with her work. She sets an excellent example for the students." The irritated set of his shoulders relaxed a bit and he slowed to a more leisurely gait.

"Glad to hear it," Frank answered, trying not to sound breathless. "Uh, what about Ray—he's not a Pathfinder, is he?"

Payne chuckled. "I should hope not. He's on the transportation team."

"Transportation team?"

"He picks up new students from their homes and escorts them to the academy. We need someone strong— and how shall I say?—not too squeamish for the job." Again, that jovial smile.

So Ray's description of how he'd brought the boy to the academy had been accurate, yet Payne seemed completely open about it.

"Let me get this straight." Frank stopped on the path. "Parents agree to have their kids brought here by force?"

"Sometimes it's the only way. I can't emphasize enough how troubled these kids are, Bennett. In many cases, their families are afraid of them. You can't expect them to arrive in the family station wagon as if they're headed off to Harvard."

Payne wagged an instructive finger in Frank's direction. "Take Heather LeBron's family, for instance. They've been through hell the past three years. Heather has run away from home or from her school five different times. She's crashed the family car, driving drunk and without a license. All they want is for her to be in a safe, secure environment, but Heather resists all their efforts. They had no choice but to bring her here under duress."

Payne gestured toward the cluster of buildings that lay ahead of them. "It's a dirty job that I do here, Bennett, but it's work that has to be done. Yes, it seems harsh that some of them come here with their hands tied. But if they weren't coming to me, they'd be coming to you and your colleagues. You'd be handcuffing them and hauling them off to prison. Isn't this a better alternative?"

Frank offered a reluctant nod. He wasn't at all certain that someone from the academy might not yet be led off in handcuffs.

WHEN THEY RETURNED to Payne's office, the headmaster checked a schedule and told Frank that Heather was currently on an outside work detail on the west side of campus. "It will be quicker if you drive there," Payne said. "I'll phone ahead to let them know you're coming. Take the access road off the main drive."

Frank did a three-point turn to get out of the parking area. As he slowed to turn left on the access road, he felt a thump from the back of the patrol car. Glancing up, he saw a bald head framed in his rearview mirror.

Heather LeBron crouched on the trunk like a large alley cat. She must have leaped out of the shrubs that lined the road. He got out of the car and walked up to her, and before he could speak, she had her arms around him.

"Take me with you, please!"

A strong girl, Heather had a grip that was hard to break. Frank pulled her off the car and disentangled himself.

"You've got to save me! They're trying to kill me here."

"Now, Heather, calm down. Tell me what the problem is."

Her eyes opened wide in panic. "There's no time for that—get in the car and drive! I'll explain on the way."

"I can't take you away from your school, Heather. I need to—"

She lunged forward and pummeled his chest with her fists. "I'm assaulting a police officer. Arrest me!"

Frank grabbed at her flailing arms and caught the right one. With her left, she struggled to get at his service revolver.

With one deft move, Frank flipped her against the patrol car and pinned her arms behind her back. "Enough! What the hell are you trying to prove?"

She twisted her head sideways to look at him over her shoulder. Tears streaked her face and white showed all around the irises of her eyes. "I'm so afraid," she said between rasping breaths. "Someone else is going to die. I think it might be me. But even if it's not, I don't want to be here when it goes down."

"What—?" Frank began.

"Heather! What are you doing away from your work detail?" Steve Vreeland was approaching from across the lawn.

Heather slid out of Frank's loosened grasp and straightened up as the young man drew closer. "Nothing," she said with remarkable casualness. "This is the policeman who found me when I was lost on the hike. I was just thanking him again."

Seeing Heather and Steve together, Frank was struck by how close they were in age. He couldn't be more than three years older than the girl, yet Steve spoke in a steady, low voice of absolute authority, his eyes focused unblinkingly on Heather. "You did not have permission to leave the work detail."

"I'm sorry, Pathfinder Steve. I should have asked permission." Heather continued to recite woodenly, "This is an example of the impulsive behavior I must learn to control."

"This transgression will be written up in your book," Steve said. "You can expect repercussions. Now, let's go back to the work detail." He jerked his head toward a group of kids trimming hedges at the rear of the main building.

Frank felt a prickle of fear for Heather. As she turned to leave, he caught her hand. "I came to talk to Heather. I'll walk her back over there when I'm finished."

Steve stood his ground. "That's not possible," he said in a level tone. "Heather has not earned the privilege of unsupervised visitation."

"Go ahead and call Payne—he'll give you the go-ahead."

"No!" Heather yanked her hand away from Frank. "Let's go," she said to Steve, and strode away without a backward glance.

Frank trotted after her. "Heather, wait!"

But she never slowed her stride.

Chapter 13

The last glimmer of daylight faded as Frank drove back to the center of town. The mountains gradually disappeared, enveloped by the absolute darkness as he drove down the lonely stretch of road between the academy and the village. With no view, his ride was consumed by an uneasy internal debate.

Had Heather been acting, or was she truly frightened? Was she scheming to get released from the school, or was something dangerous really going on there?

When Frank had gone back to Payne, told him what had happened, and insisted on having Heather brought to him, Payne had acquiesced with an I-told-you-so smirk.

"This is textbook behavior, Bennett. Classic stuff. Create a scene, and when that doesn't work, pretend it never happened. I'll get Heather for you, but I guarantee she'll have nothing to say to you."

Sure enough, when Heather was led into an empty classroom to talk to Frank, she had sat sullenly and refused to speak. He'd assured her that they were alone and that she could confide in him, but she answered with just one sentence: "Can you get me out of here?"

"Heather, I can't take you away without any evidence that you're in danger or have been mistreated. Tell me everything that happened on the hike. Why do you think you were intentionally abandoned?"

But Heather had turned her head toward the blackboard and refused to answer. No matter how he phrased the questions, no matter how he tried to probe what had happened on the campout with Reiger and the hike on Lorton, Heather met his persistence with an implacable stare. "Can you get me out of here?" she'd ask occasionally. And when he said, "No, not without cause," she resumed her glowering pose.

Payne said nothing when Frank gave up and left. He would've liked to wipe the smug smile off the headmaster's face by putting Heather in the patrol car and driving away with her, but he had no legal standing to do so. Her parents had entrusted her to the North Country Academy and presumably that's where they wanted her to stay. He wondered if they knew about the bear attack and the hike where Heather had been lost. Would that change their opinion of the academy?

No point in asking Payne; of course he would claim they had been told. Tomorrow he would call the hospital and inquire if Heather's parents had been notified of her hospitalization. Surely they would have to know, if their insurance was covering her treatment. Having a plan of action relaxed him a bit as he pulled into the center of town and surveyed the peaceful scene.

The early dinner crowd filled the window tables at the diner, and the Store was doing a brisk business in last-minute dinnertime necessities. The trucks that had been parked in front of the old flower shop all day had departed, but Frank could see a light burning inside, a bare bulb that cast a harsh glow on the partially finished walls. No doubt the last person working on the library project had failed to turn off the light. He decided to check to make sure the door was locked. And maybe take a peek through the window to see how the work was coming along.

Frank parked the patrol car and trotted up the steps. To his surprise, the doorknob twisted to the right although it took a hard push to get the warped old door to open. He hadn't really expected it to be unlocked, and his cop's instincts made him wary.

Frank stepped into the front room, breathing in the smell of freshly sawn two-by-fours and something vaguely flowery. The studs for a half-wall separated this space from the area in the back, where the bare light-bulb dangled. A shadow moved across the floor.

"Who's there?" he barked, his hand instinctively moving toward his sidearm.

A decidedly feminine shriek answered him, and Penny Stevenson poked her head around the corner. "Geez, Frank—don't shoot. It's only me."

Pleasure replaced tension as he saw her familiar teasing smile. "Sorry, Penny. Old habits die hard. I saw the light on but no cars parked outside, so I came over to check."

"I left my car parked over by the Store. Edwin wanted me to pick up nutmeg for something he's making for dinner tonight, but of course they didn't have any."

"I'm sure Edwin can improvise," Frank said. "So, what do you think of the job they're doing here? Are they following your specs?"

"I'm so bad with spatial relationships—I couldn't visualize what it would look like. But now that the partitions are up, I can picture it better." She grabbed his hand. "Come here—look at this."

Her fingers felt cool and smooth grasping his. She couldn't know that his heartbeat had quickened at her touch. If she did, she'd probably be horrified. He allowed himself to be led into the back room. In the far corner, three broad tiers of plywood formed what looked like big steps to nowhere.

"See—it's like a mini-amphitheater," Penny said. "We'll carpet the platforms and get some big squishy pillows. The kids can snuggle up there for story hour—" she made a broad gesture with her right arm, where some bracelets jangled "—while I sit down here in the middle—" she positioned herself to demonstrate "—reading the book, so everyone can see." She looked up at Frank, her eyes shining with enthusiasm. "Isn't that neat?"

"It's terrific," Frank agreed. Penny's zeal was infectious, but her words puzzled him. Surely she wasn't planning on running the little library after she got it set up? "I didn't realize you intended to be the librarian here."

Penny glanced away. "Well, I meant whoever's reading the story would sit here," she said softly. Then she brightened up again. "But I sure plan to do it at least once—for the grand opening." She made a trumpet sound through her fists.

Frank laughed. "And when's that going to be?"

"Who knows? The guys change the date every week. They seem to have hit some snafu with the plumbing." Penny put her hands on her hips. "You're handy. How come you haven't been over here helping? With the way you love to read, I thought you'd be our biggest supporter."

"I'll be a loyal patron when it opens, I promise, but I'm leaving the construction to everyone else." Frank scuffed his toe through the sawdust on the floor. "You know me, I'm not really one of the guys."

Penny took both his hands in hers. "I think most people in this town feel safer, knowing that you're not."

Compliments and hand-holding—was she flirting with him? Yeah, right—in his dreams. She was just being Penny, full of dramatic gestures.

The sound of the door being wrenched open again drove them apart.

"Penny, are you in here?" a male voice called, and Pastor Bob came around the corner. He nodded to Frank. "No problems, I hope."

"No, I saw the light on and stopped to check. Penny is showing me around."

"The men are doing a wonderful job." Bob shifted his brilliant blue gaze to Penny and smiled broadly. "I think Penny's weekly inspections keep them motivated."

Bob stepped across the room to look more closely at the seating area, coming between Frank and Penny as he did so. "Say, the reason I tracked you down—my car won't start and I wondered if you'd give me a ride over to the Iron Eagle. I called Edwin and he said you were probably here."

"Sure," Penny answered. "I didn't know you were coming to dinner tonight, too." Then she turned to Frank. "Why don't you join us, Frank? There aren't any guests eating there tonight, but you know Edwin always makes enough to feed an army."

So, Lucy was speeding up the matchmaking process. Frank glanced at Bob. Part of him dearly wanted to accept the invitation, just to see what the other man's reaction would be, but he shook his head. "No, Friday night is a work night for me. You two enjoy your dinner."

"Thanks, I'm sure we will," Bob said as he ushered Penny out the door.

Frank watched them cross the green as he locked the library door. He hoped whatever Edwin was making would be inedible without nutmeg.

———◦———

THE EVENING PATROL took him past the Stop'N'Buy, which had a few customers, and the Mountain Vista Motel, where the vacancy light was on, up to the Trail's End. Bursts of music could be heard whenever the door opened, but the crowd didn't look too big. Frank looped back down through the valley, passing the darkened buildings of Stevenson's Lumberyard, and crossed the bridge over Stony Brook. On the other side, a car was pulled onto the shoulder with its hazard lights flashing.

Frank pulled up behind the vehicle and approached the driver's side as cautiously as he had been trained to years ago in Kansas City. The driver's door opened and a tall thin man jumped out. Frank tensed for a moment, then relaxed when he recognized Oliver Greffe.

"Hello, Oliver, what's the problem?"

"Hi, Frank." Oliver ran one hand through his shaggy, dark hair. "Maybe you can tell me. I'm hopeless with cars."

Raising the hood and shining his flashlight inside, Frank immediately he saw the problem—the timing belt had snapped. The car would have to go to Al's Sunoco, probably for the better part of a week.

Oliver shrugged at the news. "No great loss. There's no place to go around here, anyway."

"Getting a little cabin fever over at the academy?" Frank asked they waited for the tow truck.

"Yeah. I went over to the Trail's End tonight to listen to the band, but—"

"But what?"

"Nothing."

"They were no good, huh?"

"Terrible." Oliver shuddered. "I shouldn't be so critical. Other people seemed to be enjoying them."

"I understand. My wife could never sit through a bad performance, either."

"You've mentioned your wife before. She's a musician? I'd love to meet her."

"Was. She died before I came to Trout Run."

Oliver looked down and fiddled with the zipper of his coat. "Oh, I'm sorry. I didn't realize ..."

"Actually, she would have loved meeting you. She would've been so impressed that you're going off to study at Curtis. She never had an opportunity like that—she married me instead."

Oliver studied him with serious brown eyes. "If you were happy together, then I don't think she missed her opportunity," he said softly.

"Here comes Al!" Frank said, with more enthusiasm than was normally warranted by the arrival of the tow truck.

Al checked the engine and confirmed Frank's diagnosis. He handed Oliver a clipboard. "Fill out this form so I know how to get ahold of you."

Frank watched as Oliver filled in the blanks with meticulous printing. "You could never be a doctor," he joked. "Not with handwriting that neat."

Oliver smiled. "I never considered any career other than music. My mother encouraged me from the time I was in kindergarten. I'm an only child."

"Looks like her efforts paid off," Frank said as Al pulled away with the little Toyota hitched to his truck. "C'mon, I'll take you back to the academy."

They drove in silence for a while until Oliver spoke. "Do you ever feel like there's a big party going on and you're watching it from the other side of a locked glass door?"

Frank wanted to answer, "Every day," but instead he said, "What makes you ask that?"

Oliver shifted in his seat and looked out the window at the pitch-black forest rolling by. "I'm afraid I don't fit in too well at the academy. The other teachers and the Pathfinders are so gung-ho about the *mission* of the school. We have these meetings where Dr. Payne leads us in discussing the precepts of the academy, and everyone else gets all charged up. I guess it's like a football coach psyching up his team." Oliver laughed. "Not that I'd know anything about that. Hell, I only signed up to be a music teacher."

"You didn't know what kind of school this was when you took the job?" Frank asked.

"I knew in a theoretical sense. I guess I didn't understand what that would mean day in, day out—that I would be expected to take part in all this discipline and regimentation. I'm not much of a tough guy."

"So why did Payne hire you?"

"He's a huge music fan. He attended a concert I gave and came up to me afterwards to talk. He was so enthusiastic about my playing, so complimentary. Then he offered me this well-paying job, the answer to all my money problems. It dropped in my lap—how could I say no?" Oliver sighed. "I guess I should have been a little more cautious. Now I'm stuck. I signed a contract, and I don't think Dr. Payne would let me out of it without a fight."

Frank could tell from the tone of Oliver's voice that the kid wouldn't dream of crossing swords with MacArthur Payne. Who could blame him? He didn't relish it himself. "He is pretty demanding."

"Whenever I'm alone with Mac, just he and I and we're talking about music, I like him fine. But when he's in his official 'headmaster' role, he's like a different person."

"What is it that bothers you about him?"

Oliver thought for a moment before answering. "I guess it's the way he's always so sure he's *right.*"

Words of agreement were on the tip of Frank's tongue, but he changed them to a noncommittal "hmm." "I understand Payne never makes exceptions to his rules. Paul Petrucci was telling me he wanted to get Heather LeBron involved in his class play, but Payne said she hadn't earned enough points."

"Yes, Paul and I have talked about Heather. Apparently she likes to sing, too, but she hasn't earned the points to take my classes, either."

"Are the other teachers, uh, nervous, after what happened to Jake?" Frank asked as he turned the car onto High Meadow Road.

"Well, the ones who lead the hikes and the rock climbing and stuff are a little anxious because that bear still hasn't been caught. Mac has suspended overnight camping, but the other outdoor activities are still on. He says they're too important to the program to cancel."

"You're never involved in the wilderness outings?"

"No way!" Oliver held his hands out in front of him. "I can't risk injuring my hands. Mac accepts that."

"So who does them?"

"Randy Ohlandt, Paul Petrucci, and Steve Vreeland."

"Steve must really be nervous, having such a close call."

"No, just the opposite. At our first meeting after Jake's death, Steve volunteered to lead the next hike. He'd do anything for Mac. Steve's one of his"—Oliver made quotation marks in the air—"success stories."

Frank pulled up at the gates of the North Country Academy. The guard emerged, looking very puzzled to see the patrol car there. Oliver leaned out the window to tell him about his car troubles, and the guard waved them on. Frank followed the road to the dormitory that Oliver pointed out as his residence.

He put the car in park and turned to face his passenger. "Tell me, Oliver—do these kids ever scare you?"

Oliver undid his seat belt and looked Frank in the eye. "Back when I was in high school, it was the jocks who scared me. I crossed the street when I saw the football players coming. These kinds of kids—the stoners, the freaks—they never bothered me. They just seemed sort of sad and lost. They still do."

Chapter 14

"Frank! How did this happen?" Reid Burlingame bustled into Frank's office minutes after his own arrival and dropped a newspaper onto his desk.

GRUESOME DEATH CASTS SUSPICION ON TACTICS OF TOUGH-LOVE ACADEMY

Special to the New York Beat

By Dawn Klotz

(Trout Run, NY—November 11) Citizens of this bucolic Adirondack hamlet were shocked five days ago when a teacher leading a school camping trip was mauled by a black bear. Now, shock has turned to terror as the teacher, Jake Reiger, has died from his wounds, while local police are attempting to cover up the possibility that the attack may have been instigated by students at a local boarding school, the North Country Academy.

According to Trout Run Police Chief Frank Bennett, "There is no outstanding police investigation into the death." But local outdoorsmen and hunters wonder why not.

"The word is out that Jake Regier's sleeping bag was soaked in bacon grease. Everyone knows bacon grease is a lure for bears," said William Nestor, who was hunting yesterday near Corkscrew Mountain. "It looks to me like someone set the guy up."

Frank paused in his reading. "Who the hell is William Nestor?"

Reid and Earl both shrugged. "Keep reading," Reid directed. "It gets worse."

Chief Bennett did confirm that grease was found on the sleeping bag and that North Country Academy students were the only people who would have had access to it.

Bennett characterized as "ridiculous" the community's concerns that the attack on Reiger could be the portent of more violence to come.

The article went on, with more description of the rigorous treatment students at the academy received. The next paragraph began with a quote.

"Lots of people been getting jobs over there. The pay's real good," said Augie Enright, a lifelong resident of Trout Run. "As long as they keep those kids locked up away from us, we like the school fine."

Chief Bennett denied that the town leaders were pressuring him to look the other way in matters concerning the North Country Academy. "There is no undue influence," he said.

Frank stopped reading when he was certain his name wasn't mentioned again.

"This is bullshit! I never said any of this!" Frank protested.

"Well, then, where did she get those quotes if she didn't talk to you?" Reid asked.

"I did talk to her, but this is not what I said." Was it? Frank rubbed his temples, trying to recreate that crazy interview in his mind.

"But what about this theory that the sleeping bag was sabotaged? Is that true?' Reid asked.

Frank couldn't meet Reid's eyes. "I don't know," he said, and then told Reid about the state police report and Rusty's concerns.

"Why didn't you inform me of this right away?" Reid demanded. "Don't you think I have a right to know, as chairman of the town council? Really, Frank, I'm quite disappointed in you."

"I wanted to look into it myself before I got everyone all worked up."

"Well, they're certainly worked up now. This looks bad, Frank. The article makes it seem like we're trying to shield the North Country Academy at the expense of our citizens' safety. At the same time it makes the academy look bad, even though the students are blameless. They are blameless, aren't they? Frank?"

Frank jerked to attention. "Yes. Yes, of course." But as his mouth uttered platitudes of reassurance for Reid, his mind followed a different track, determined to find out more about Heather LeBron and Jake Reiger.

Frank finally succeeded in shuffling Reid out the door and returned to his desk to call the hospital. After some wrangling with the nurse in charge of the emergency room, Frank succeeded in getting Heather LeBron's mother's phone number. When he dialed, the phone rang endlessly. He was about to hang up when a hoarse voice muttered, "Hullo?"

"Mrs. LeBron?"

"Not anymore, thank God. Who's this?"

Of course, the parents were divorced so the mother's name would be different. "This is Police Chief Frank Bennett in Trout Run, New York. Are you Heather LeBron's mother?"

"Oh, Christ! What's she done now? Dr. Payne assured me she couldn't get out of that place."

Obviously, Heather's mother was no stranger to phone calls from the police. "Heather's not in any trouble, ma'am. I wanted to be sure you were aware that she was lost on a hike two days ago and had to be hospitalized briefly for hypothermia."

"Oh, yeah. I got a message about her being treated in the emergency room. It sounded like something minor."

So *you didn't even bother to call back and find out?* No one would accuse Heather's mother of being overprotective, that's for sure.

"What do you mean she got lost on a hike?" the woman continued. "She tried to run away again, didn't she?"

Had she already spoken to Payne, or had she leapt to that conclusion independently? "Have you heard from Dr. Payne or Heather since she's been at the academy, ma'am?"

"Payne e-mails me once a week with a progress report. He says Heather's adapting slowly to the program. She not allowed to talk to me until she reaches Level Two." "And you're all right with that?"

"It's what I expected. The program was fully explained to me when I signed the contract. The kids all plead to come home by claiming they're being abused. It's easier on everyone if they can't talk to their parents. Frankly, I'm glad that's the policy. It's been quite peaceful around here without Heather's daily drama."

"Did you know about the bear attack on the camping trip Heather was on?"

"Bear attack?" For the first time in their conversation, Frank detected a note of concern. "Heather was attacked by a wild animal?"

"Not Heather. The teacher leading the trip. He was killed, in fact."

"Come to think of it, I think Payne mentioned some unfortunate accident in last week's report. What's that got to do with Heather?"

"She was there when it happened. I think she was quite traumatized by what she saw."

"Traumatized? Heather? Well, that would be a first! Usually she's the one dishing out the trauma. Like the time she nearly pushed her little brother out a second-floor window. And the time she drank a pint of rum. And the time when she loaded all the guests at her fourteenth birthday party into her step-father's Lexus and crashed into a tree."

Frank felt that the condition of the Lexus, or maybe even the tree, was the family's primary worry. But probably he was being too judgmental. Living with a kid like Heather couldn't be easy. "I understand she can be difficult, ma'am. It's just that I'm worried about her, and I wanted to be sure you were fully aware of everything that's happened to Heather since she's been at the North Country Academy."

"Fully aware? Oh, I'm fully aware all right. I'm fully aware that this is the last stop for Heather. I can't have her back here terrorizing our family. There are no other schools that will enroll her. Payne says he can straighten her out." She took a long breath. "It has to work at the North Country Academy. It just has to work."

FRANK STARED AT THE phone after he hung up with Heather's mother, thinking back on his daughter's teenage years. Caroline had given them plenty of anxious days and nights—hitchhiking, using a fake ID to get into raunchy clubs on the Boulevard in Kansas City, climbing out her bedroom window when she'd been grounded. All his law enforcement horror stories about murdered hitchhikers and drugged and raped girls fell on deaf ears. Caroline at fifteen had been determined to experience all the excitement that lay beyond the shelter of their placid suburban neighborhood.

Any of her stunts could've gotten her killed, of course, and that's what had kept him and Estelle up pacing the floor whenever Caroline was out. But he'd never felt she was totally out of control. She must have sampled booze and drugs, but he was so attuned to the symptoms of regular use that he knew she'd never had a problem with the stuff. All Caroline's antics were pulled off while staying a straight-A student, running track, and playing cello in the school orchestra.

What would they have done if she'd been a danger to other people, like Heather, or an addict and thief like Steve Vreeland? Would they have sent her away as a last resort, a desperate gamble? He couldn't imagine it, if for no other reason than it would seem like admitting utter failure as a parent.

But if your child had pushed you to the limit, if he was destroying the rest of your family, would a school like the North Country Academy seem like a logical choice? Or maybe these parents were simply unwilling to deal with the mess of their children's lives any longer and jumped at the opportunity to dump them in the lap of someone like MacArthur Payne.

Impulsively, he reached for the phone and dialed Caroline's number.

"Hi, Daddy! What's up?"

"I'm just sitting here thinking about the time you told us you were spending the night at Jennie Roth's and instead you hitched to St. Louis for a rock concert."

Caroline laughed. "U2—an awesome performance! What put that in your head?"

Frank told her about the North Country Academy and his anxiety over Heather LeBron.

"Wow, that puts my day in perspective. I'm sitting here worrying about Ty and Jeremy waving sticks on the playground. You don't think that's an early sign of delinquency, do you?"

"No, I think it's a sign of being three-year-old boys. How's Eric?" Frank continued in the most casual tone he could muster. His son-in-law had briefly moved out of the house, but supposedly their marriage was now on the mend.

"He's fine. We both really like this new therapist we're seeing. We go once a week together, then once a week alone to work on issues we each brought to the marriage."

What issues? he longed to ask. Issues created by your inept parents and your traumatic childhood? Or issues of being a person with flaws and desires and needs that your husband never noticed over the long candlelight dinners of your courtship?

"But you're working things out?" he prodded gently, hopefully.

"Yes, Daddy. Don't worry."

Don't worry—as if that could ever be possible, as long as they both walked this earth. Worry began at the moment of conception and it seemed to him it never let up, only changed form. To stop worrying about his daughter would be to stop loving her. Maybe that's what had baffled him about Heather's mother. It seemed that Heather had pushed the woman to the absolute limit of worry, and she had to shift the burden to MacArthur Payne or be crushed by it. It seemed cold at first glance, but it didn't necessarily mean she didn't love her daughter.

———◉———

"BENNETT!" HIS OWN NAME thundered through the telephone receiver and ricocheted around his head. Frank didn't have to ask who was calling. MacArthur Payne had obviously read the New York *Beat*.

"I need to talk to you about this newspaper article. There are some things going on here that you clearly don't understand."

First Reid, now Payne. Frank was angrier at himself than at either of them, but he couldn't find a way to keep the frost out of his voice. "What might that be?"

"I'm not going to discuss it on the phone. Do you want me to come there, or will you come out here?"

Frank took a deep breath; this was his penance. "I'll be right over."

The rapport of their last visit—whether it had been forced or sincere—was banished today. Frank sat in the low-slung visitor's chair, designed for intimidation, while MacArthur Payne loomed over him, lecturing.

"You have been sadly misled by a number of people here, Bennett."

"Oh?" was the best that Frank could manage as a sarcasm-free response.

"First, this notion that academy students sabotaged Jake Reiger's sleeping bag is ludicrous. I told you that the camping gear is kept under lock and key and that the students would have no access to the kitchen or any food supplies."

"I didn't tell the reporter that I believed the students did it. She drew that conclusion herself."

"No, she did not." Payne jabbed a long index finger in Frank's direction. "I'll tell you why she wrote it, Bennett. Because she's got an anti-academy agenda. Someone's been poring vitriol in her ear, and I'm quite sure I know who."

Frank was getting weary of the pauses for dramatic effect. He stared at Payne silently until he spit it out.

"Paul Petrucci. He's a thief and a liar."

Frank sat up straighter and Payne continued, looking gratified. "When I took over the academy and did an audit, I discovered funds missing from a student activities account that Petrucci had access to, not to mention valuable video equipment and cameras that had somehow walked away when Petrucci mentored the photography dub."

"You reported this to the police?"

"I didn't have enough evidence, but when I confronted Paul, he couldn't explain what had happened. He became very defensive and contradictory. So I warned him that I would be keeping an eye on him."

"If you think he's stealing from you and spreading stories, why don't you fire him?"

Payne pursed his thin, nearly colorless lips. "I can't afford to lose another staff member right now. I'm expecting five new students this week who will need close supervision. I'm already stretched thin with Jake's death. And Petrucci has solid academic credentials that enhance the academy's prospectus, I'll say that much for him. He's hard to replace on short notice. But he can see he has no long-term future here. This stunt with the reporter is his parting shot."

Payne dropped into the second visitor's chair beside Frank and leaned across to face him. "I'm at a critical juncture here, Bennett. I can succeed with these kids, but if I don't *appear* to succeed, it's all for naught. Get it?"

Frank drew back.

"Public perception is as important as reality," Payne continued. "Even if nothing is ever proved regarding this bear incident, the school is condemned, because the academy can't function under a cloud of suspicion and doubt. We won't be able to make the claim that troubled students are transformed into productive citizens under our care. Enrollment drops, the doors close, the jobs evaporate."

Frank's eyes locked with Payne's and he received the message: If the academy closed due to rumor and innuendo, it would be laid at his feet. On the other hand, if any of this stuff were true and he appeared to be hushing it up, as Dawn Klotz implied, he'd be doubly screwed. His neck muscles felt as stiff as oak boughs; he could feel the seeds of a colossal headache sprouting. "I'll get to the bottom of all this."

"I'm glad we see eye to eye."

Chapter 15

Frank had intentionally avoided discussing Heather LeBron with Payne. Heather's mother had verified everything that Payne said about the girl, but it couldn't hurt to check up on the kid. Now, standing in the hallway outside Payne's office, Frank looked up the wide staircase at the numbered rooms that lined the second-floor hallway. She was most likely in class right above him; he headed up to look. It was always easier to apologize than to ask permission.

Each closed door had a window that framed an amazingly similar scene: a small group of students sat with their eyes focused directly ahead on their teacher or directly down on their desk. No one slumped or sprawled, no one looked out the window or up at the ceiling. No one looked at the door, so no one noticed him. In the third room he checked, he found Heather, her close-cropped head bowed over a notebook as she wrote steadily.

Frank tapped on the door, then walked right in. "Excuse me for interrupting, but I need to speak to Heather LeBron, please."

The teacher hesitated, but Frank's uniform and the confidence of the request seemed to reassure her that Frank's presence was sanctioned. She nodded at Heather. "You may go."

Heather walked toward Frank, as wide-eyed as if the tooth fairy had come for her. Before she left the room, she glanced back at a boy who was watching the proceedings intently.

"What are you doing here?" Heather asked when they were alone in the hall.

"Just thought I'd check on you. You were a little wound up the last time I saw you."

She jerked her head toward the lower level as they walked toward a bench at the end of the hall. "He knows you're here?"

"He knows I was here. He may believe I've already left although I didn't tell him that."

"Oh, Christ! You're going to screw me over."

"Your teacher gave you permission to speak to a police officer. I fail to see how you can be blamed for anything."

"That's the problem—you fail to see a lot of things."

Frank put his hands on Heather's shoulders and looked her in the eye. "Well, then, why don't you set me straight? And no bullshit."

Heather slid away from him and sat on the bench, her eyes cast down. His willingness to listen had taken the wind out of her sails, and Frank wondered if she knew how to communicate with someone who wasn't an adversary.

"Let's start with the camping trip when Mr. Reiger was killed. Is there anything, uh, worrying you about that?"

Heather's eyes glittered with unshed tears and her breathing quickened. "I have nightmares... *nightmares...* about him being eaten alive."

Questioning Heather was going to be a little trickier than anticipated. Obviously if he put the slightest suggestion of sabotage in her head, she would run with it. "How was the camping trip going before the attack? Any problems?"

Heather heaved a huge sigh. "It was *so* hard. Hauling all that heavy shit up the mountain, trying to put up those *dumb* tents with all those *stupid* poles. And Mr. Reiger wouldn't help us. He said we had to figure it out ourselves. Like I could do that—I've never camped in my life! Good thing Justin was there—he was the only one who could do it right."

So much for the sinister aspects of the camping trip. He moved on.

"Tell me about the hike when you got lost," Frank prompted. "You said they intentionally left you behind to try to harm you. Tell me why you think that."

Heather stretched the sleeves of her green sweatshirt over her hands. "Well, um ... I told Steve that my boot was giving me a blister and that I couldn't walk that fast, and I swear they speeded up until I lost sight of them. That's when I went off the trail."

"Maybe you thought that if you fell behind, you could find another way down to the road and hitchhike away from here."

Heather gave him that disgusted eye roll that every teenager has perfected. "Yeah, *right.* Like I would even know what direction to look for the road. I grew up in New Jersey—if it's not an exit on the turnpike, I can't find it."

It was hard to picture Heather as an intrepid bushwhacker, but desperation could drive a person to take chances. "We probably would have found you much sooner, except the search-and-rescue dog was following the wrong scent. Did you know we'd been given your roommate's sock, not yours?"

"Really? That figures—the bitch hates me."

"So you think Melissa herself would have done that intentionally?"

She hunched her shoulders up to her ears, glowering at him like a snapping turtle.

"What about when I was here the other day—you told me someone else was going to get hurt. What did you mean?"

Heather scuffed her sneaker against the bench. "The way they treat people here, something's bound to happen sooner or later. Probably sooner. That's why I want out."

"You've been at a lot of schools, haven't you?"

"This one is the *worst.*"

"Why? What makes it so terrible?"

"Every single person is awful." She paused. "Well, except for Mr. Petrucci—he's okay. And there are so many rules, and everyone's watching me, just waiting for me to fuck up. Not only the teachers and the Pathfinders, but the other kids, too. They rat each other out."

"Why?"

"So they can get ahead—earn points to get privileges, like calling home; earn more points and you finally earn your way out of here. Except I'll never get out. I'll never get enough points so that I can even call my mom." Her voice got shriller. "I can *never* get ahead, because someone's *always* turning me in for some stupid *infraction.* I'm always at rock *bottom.*"

She was winding up to the drama queen routine again. "It's a school, Heather, not a prison. Even if you never earn any points, you still get out when you're eighteen."

"Eighteen! That's three years—I'll *die* before then! Don't you see, when you're like me and you have no points to lose, they have to find another way to punish you."

Was she going to claim they beat her? Because surely any signs of physical abuse would have been apparent when they treated her at the hospital for hypothermia.

"How do they punish you?"

"They put me in the isolation room, and I can't *stand* it." She reached for a strand of hair to fiddle with, forgetting that she no longer had that prop, and ended up tugging on the tiny tufts available.

"The isolation room?"

"It's this white tile room, totally empty." Her eyes opened wide and her lip trembled. "They put you in there naked. It's freezing and there's no place to sit, nothing to look at, nothing to hear. They won't give you any food or water because they won't even let you out to go to the bathroom. You either hold it in or go on the floor. The first time I was in there for three hours; the second time it was a whole day.

"You're in there all alone and there's nothing but your thoughts ... terrible, terrible thoughts. That's why you've got to get in touch with my mom and tell her about this place." Heather leaned forward and grabbed Frank's hand. "She didn't realize it was like this when she sent me here. If she knew, she'd get me out."

"I did talk to you mother today, Heather. She seems pretty committed to having you stay here."

Heather shoved his hand away and shrank into the corner of the bench. He knew he'd taken away her last shred of hope, so he decided to give her one more chance to convince him.

"Back up a minute. You were put in this room naked? You had no food or bathroom for twenty-four hours? Who took away your clothes?"

Heather gnawed on a fingernail that was already bitten to the quick. "One of the new Pathfinders—I forget her name."

"Describe her."

Heather squirmed into the corner of the bench. "Uh, kinda tall, with stringy blond hair."

"Lorrie Betz?"

Heather stood up and backed away from him. "Look, there's no point in asking her about it—she'll deny it. Just let me call my mom."

"I need to know—"

"Oh, forget about it!" Heather hunched her shoulders and folded her arms across her chest.

"You're describing physical abuse—I can't forget about it. I need to know the truth. What other students have been put naked into this isolation room? They can verify your story."

"No, they won't! Look, no one else thinks it's as bad as I do. I guess I, I—exaggerated a little."

Only her pathetic, cowed expression kept him from a sarcastic response. "How so?"

"I wasn't naked, but I only had on a T-shirt and jeans, and it was cold and they wouldn't give me a sweater. And I told them I had to go to the bathroom, but they wouldn't let me out."

"Did they make you go on the floor?"

She shook her head.

"Were you really in there for twenty-four hours?"

"Well, it seemed like it," she said in a small voice. "But I guess it was less."

"How long?"

"Four hours, maybe. See, I knew you wouldn't understand! It's awful! I can't bear it! I won't *survive* if they send me there again." She began to cry noisily, but when a teacher stuck her head out of a classroom door. Heather turned off the display as if her tears were controlled by a switch.

Frank was beginning to understand how Heather's family had come to send her to the North Country Academy. Dealing with this hysteria, on top of the drinking and wild behavior, would wear a person down.

Frank laid his hand on the girl's shoulder. "I'm sure you don't want my advice, but I'm going to give it to you anyway. If you don't like the isolation room, try not to do anything to get yourself sent there. Follow the rules. Study hard. And no tall tales." He gave her shoulder a little squeeze. "You'd better get back to class."

She trudged down the hall, then turned and shot one last sullen look at Frank.

"Stop playing the victim, Heather," he responded. "You may find this place does you some good."

GREAT-GRANDMA GERT Davis's ninetieth birthday bash was in full swing when Frank arrived after work. The birthday girl was dancing to a Dwight Yoakam tune with one of her many grandsons, a hip replacement waiting to happen. Earl played disc jockey while his mom and aunts buzzed around the buffet table.

Earl's family threw these huge parties for most significant life events, and every single death. Frank had only attended one other—the annual Davis Fourth of July picnic—mainly to prevent Earl from blowing his hand off with illegal fireworks. But no matter how many times Frank politely declined the invitations to these family gatherings, Earl continued to ask him. He had planned to pass on Great-grandma Gert's birthday too, but Earl had begged him, saying that Gert had asked for him specially.

She was a feisty old gal and Frank got a kick out of the way she said whatever she pleased right to people's faces. That was one perk of old age he was looking forward to. So here he was at the site of all the Davis hoedowns: the huge garage/workshop Earl's uncle Mike had built behind his house.

After offering his best wishes to Gert and chatting with Earl's mother, Frank scanned the room and quickly spotted Lorrie. Even in a room full of her own relatives, Lorrie looked bereft, sitting at a picnic table eating with her two kids. The children were obviously losing interest in the meal, and she paused periodically to exhort them to eat, without much success. Soon they scampered off to play with the others of their generation, leaving Lorrie smoking a cigarette and staring into space.

Frank saw an opportunity to find out a little more about the workings of the North Country Academy. In an unguarded moment, Lorrie might drop some information he could use as he struggled to decide whether he should be protecting the academy from a smear campaign or launching a murder investigation.

Frank loaded up on chicken, potato salad, and green bean casserole, carefully avoiding the bubbling Crock-Pot that he suspected of holding bear-meat chili. Thus armed, he dropped onto the bench across from Lorrie.

"Mind if I join you?"

"Go ahead." She looked surprised that anyone would want that seat if others were available.

"Your great-grandmother sure is enjoying herself." The music had stopped and Gert now sat in the middle of a circle of admirers, tearing open her presents with the gusto of a five-year-old.

Lorrie's eyes flicked in that direction, then resumed their blank stare. "Yeah, I guess."

Frank sized up Lorrie. She had many of the attributes of a pretty woman—long blond hair, a good figure, clear skin—yet he didn't find her very attractive. Some aura of damaged goods clung to her. At ninety, Gert possessed a youthfulness that had already been snuffed out of her great-granddaughter.

"So, Earl tells me you like your job at the North Country Academy."

She brightened a bit. "Yeah, the pay is good."

Just once, he'd like to hear someone say they found fulfillment in helping troubled kids. "So, what is it that you do over there, anyway?"

"I'm a Pathfinder," she said, as if this were as self-explanatory as "I'm an accountant" or "I'm a chef."

Frank didn't think she was being intentionally uncommunicative; she just seemed to have lost the art of conversation. "So tell me about it—what's your typical day like?"

For the first time, Lorrie's eyes focused on him with interest. "Earl told me you were nicer than most people think."

Frank accepted this with a gracious nod. A compliment was a compliment, however backhanded.

"Dr. Payne's a good boss. He really knows what he's doing. He's taught me the system of infractions and points—says I'm doing a good job carrying it out."

"But I guess writing kids up for infractions all day doesn't make you the most popular lady. Kind of like being a cop."

Lorrie ground out her cigarette in the remains of her potato salad. "They hate me. But I don't care. They're all such spoiled little rich brats. They don't appreciate any of the things they've been given. They don't appreciate that Dr. Payne's trying to save their lives."

Frank didn't like the hard set of her mouth. He'd seen it in too many cops who'd grown so bitter and angry from dealing with bad guys that they couldn't see the good in anyone anymore. He wondered how spending eight hours a day in a state of constant antagonism with these kids could do them good. Wasn't there any upside to their regimen?

"Is it all about not losing points, or is their some way to win points?" Frank asked.

"Yeah, you can work your way out of the hole." Lorrie flipped her hair back and reached for another cigarette. "Fifty push-ups earns you one point. Or you can volunteer for dirty jobs—cleaning toilets, mucking out the horse stalls, scrubbing floors. And the teachers give out points." She smiled and for a moment Frank saw the glimmer of a pretty girl. "Especially Paul and Oliver—they're both soft touches." Then her face hardened again. "Those kids don't realize what good teachers they have. But their favorite way to earn points is to rat each other out."

That verified what Heather had said. "If one kid tells on another, he earns points for that?"

Lorrie nodded. "They make sure I don't miss anything. Little bastards."

Lorrie certainly held a dimmer opinion of her charges than Paul Petrucci or Oliver Greffe. It must be a class thing—maybe she resented them for having parents who could afford to spend so much money on their care, when she lived such a hardscrabble life. He wondered where Jake Reiger fell on the spectrum. Had he actively disliked his students?

Lorrie might be able to provide some useful insights, now that he had her in such a chatty mood.

"How well did you know Jake Reiger?" Frank asked.

Lorrie stiffened; the hand that held the cigarette trembled slightly. Frank watched her with carefully guarded interest.

"I was the Pathfinder in his classes sometimes."

"How did he get along with the students?"

"He was experienced. He knew how to handle them—there was never any trouble." Lorrie stood up. "Tiffany!" she screeched, "Leave your cousin alone!" Lorrie's daughter came skating up the table and grabbed her mother's hand. "C'mon, Mommy! Grammy Gert's going to blow out her candles!"

There was no excuse to miss the climax of the party. Frank gathered around the massive cake with all the other guests and watched while three relatives armed with butane lighters ignited ninety candles. With so much heat, they sang quickly. Gert, assisted by a dozen puffing, spitting children, blew out the candles.

Frank's pumping session with Lorrie was over. She stood chatting with another woman as she ate her cake. Her daughter, having gobbled hers down, leaned tiredly against Lorrie's leg, while Lorrie absently ran her fingers through the little girl's hair.

The cake was damn good, and Frank worked his way through the crowd to pay his compliments to Aunt Sally, the baker in the family. As he passed the buffet table he heard raised voices by the door and the sound of a chair hitting the floor.

He spun around to see Chuck Betz squared off in front of Lorrie. "The time!" he bellowed, tapping the watch on his big, hairy arm. "Look at the time, Lorrie. You were supposed to have those kids back to my house forty-five minutes ago."

Now both kids were clinging to Lorrie, their eyes riveted on their father's red, sweating face.

"It's a party, Chuck. They wanted to stay for the cake."

"They can get all the damn cake they need at my house. The deal is, you get them home by eight o'clock on a school night. I'm telling the judge about this!"

"No! You are *such* an asshole." Lorrie's voice spiraled up the scale. "I hate—"

Earl stepped forward and laid his hand on her arm. "Lorrie, don't," he said quietly. He turned toward Chuck. "Take it easy, Chuck. It's Grandma Gert's ninetieth birthday. Don't ruin it for everyone."

"I don't give a shit about whose birthday it is in your crazy family. She's broken the rules again, and she's going to pay. Come here, kids."

The children remained frozen to the spot.

"I said, get your butts over here!"

"You're scaring them, Chuck," Earl said. "Let Lorrie bring them home."

Chuck shoved Earl. "Get out of my way. You think you're hot shit because you work for the police department. You're not a real cop, you're an errand boy."

Frank thought Earl had been doing a very good job, but now he felt compelled to step in. "Earl may not be a real cop, but I am." He put his hand on

Chuck's shoulder and turned toward Lorrie. "You take the kids home now, Lorrie. Chuck, you go over there and sit for a while until you calm down."

Chuck pulled roughly away from his grasp.

"I'm warning you, Chuck," Frank said. "The judge won't be impressed with an arrest report for disturbing the peace."

Reluctantly, Chuck headed for the far corner of the room, while Lorrie and the children gathered their things and left under the silent gaze of all the Davises. Before the door shut behind her great-granddaughter, Gert spoke.

"That girl has had her own personal rain cloud following her all her life."

Chapter 16

"That was some party last night," Frank said as Earl sat down at his desk.

"Yeah, it was fun. At least until Chuck showed up. I don't know how two people who used to be in love could be so mean to each other."

Frank smiled. "Then you must never have been in love."

"Guess not," Earl agreed. "And if that's what it brings you, I'll stay solo."

"What about that girl who works at the pharmacy in Verona—aren't you still seeing her?"

"Nah—too possessive. She kept calling me all the time, checking up on me. Who needs that?" Earl peered intently into a file folder. "What about you and Penny?"

"Penny? There's nothing between me and Penny." Frank shut his desk drawer more firmly than necessary. "She's too young for me. She's only five years older than my daughter."

"I guess someone oughta tell her that because she keeps looking at you and asking about you."

"Asking about me? When?"

Earl looked up with a grin. Christ, he had fallen right into the kid's trap.

"The other day, she asked me if you always had to work on Friday and Saturday nights. Sounds to me like she's fishing for a date. I told her you're the boss, you can take off when you want to."

Frank felt a pang that he reluctantly acknowledged as disappointment. "Oh, she was asking that because Lucy's arranged a dinner party to set Penny up with Bob Rush and they want me for some friend of Penny's from the community college. That's all."

Earl said nothing, but a sly smile played on his lips as he went about his filing.

Frank raised a piece of paper. "Here's a guy who was unlucky in love: Jake Reiger. MacArthur Payne told me he left his last job to get a fresh start after some trouble with a woman. I'm going call his sister in Utah and see what she can tell me about him."

"Why?"

"As many times as we've gone around and around on this bear attack, we've never looked very closely at the life of the victim," Frank said. "What do we really know about the man? Why would someone want to kill him?" What he didn't add was that Lorrie's reaction last night to his questions about Reiger made him wonder if the man had once again gotten involved with a colleague at work. Could Reiger have seduced and dumped Lorrie in the two months they'd worked together? Could the bacon grease on his sleeping bag have been her retaliation? It certainly gave a whole new twist to "hell hath no fury like a woman scorned." As a local girl, Lorrie would know that bacon grease was a lure for bears. If they were lovers, she might know what a sound sleeper Jake was. She could have followed the campers up the trail and planted the grease. He certainly didn't see Lorrie as a cold-blooded killer, but it might have been a cruel retribution that went too far. Earl would be appalled if he knew such ideas had crossed Frank's mind.

"Payne gave you the sister's number?" Earl asked. "I thought he was mad about this idea of Rusty's that the bear attack wasn't an accident."

"Now he thinks someone's intentionally spreading rumors about the academy. My new assignment is to put an end to that." Frank kicked a file drawer shut. "Of course, if the truth I uncover happens to be unpleasant, I'll be screwed for that." He glanced at his watch. "It's barely seven in Utah—maybe I can catch the sister before she leaves for work."

Kathy Reiger answered on the first ring, sounding frazzled. "Who is this again?" she asked after Frank identified himself. "What do you want?"

Frank introduced himself again, then asked, "Had you heard from your brother since he started teaching at the North Country Academy? Was he happy there?"

"He called me when he got there. Said the setting was beautiful and he could hardly wait to get out and explore. He sounded happy. Jake was a free spirit—he always liked the beginning of a new adventure."

But not the end. "Was he experiencing any problems with the students?" Frank asked

"No—he knew what to expect from them."

"Did he mention a new woman in his life?"

Kathy Reiger snorted. "There was always a woman in Jake's life. I didn't bother to keep track. Why are you asking me these things?"

Frank hesitated. "There's a remote possibility that your brother's death was not entirely accidental."

"How could a bear attack not be an accident?"

"That's what we're trying to determine. Look, we're probably wrong, but if you could clarify a few things about your brother's life, it would help." When she didn't protest, Frank forged ahead. "How did he happen to get this job at the North Country Academy?"

"Well, he got romantically involved with another teacher at his last job, and it didn't work out. So when MacArthur Payne called, he decided to make a fresh start." That confirmed what Payne had said. "And he knew Payne from this previous job?"

"Not the one he just left, the one before that. Jake used to work at the Langley Wilderness School—that's why I was surprised—"

Frank could hear a car horn honking repeatedly in the background. "Surprised about what?"

"Look, I can't talk anymore now—my carpool is leaving. But you can read all about it. The Langley Wilderness School was all over the papers out here last year." She hung up.

It didn't take Earl long to search the Internet for the news articles Reiger's sister mentioned. He handed Frank the printouts and stood reading over his shoulder.

"God—one of their students died of heat prostration and dehydration on a fifteen-mile hike in the desert. Couldn't they tell the poor kid needed water?"

"Does it mention Jake Reiger's name anywhere? Was he the one leading the hike?" Earl asked.

Frank shook his head and reached for the next article in the pile, headlined "Langley School to Close Amid Controversy."

"Battling charges of egregious safety violations, the Langley Wilderness School defended its controversial disciplinary practices," Frank read the lead. "Egregious—know what that means?"

Earl looked as if he were in the final round of *Jeopardy!*. "Uhm, like out-standingly bad?"

"You're getting to be a regular Webster," Frank said as he continued to scan the article. "Whoa, here we go," he read aloud: " 'In an effort to avoid an investigation by the state department of education, the co-owners of the Langley Wilderness School have closed their operation and sold the property. "In the current climate of finger-pointing and assigning blame, we feel we cannot get a fair hearing," said one of the partners, MacArthur Payne.' "

"So Payne ran one of these schools out in Utah and had to close it because some kid died," Earl said. "No wonder he's so sensitive about bad press. Now the same thing is happening here."

"Yes, but a teacher died here. And no one's saying it was because of lax safety standards."

"Yeah, but these rumors are worse. They're saying it was murder."

———————◉———————

"CHIEF BENNETT? I NEED your help."

Frank's bedside clock read 2:20. The voice coming through his phone was hoarse and breathless but sounded familiar.

"Who is this?"

"Can you get out to the North Country Academy right away? Don't use the siren." The voice spoke softly but urgently. He couldn't be sure if it was a man or a woman.

"What's the problem?"

"I can't talk. You'll see when you get here."

Chapter 17

The floor and walls of the white-tiled room were smeared with streaks of brilliant red blood. It seemed to be everywhere, yet the heavy metallic scent of it was not in the air, as it was at crime scenes where the victim had bled massively. There were no pools of it on the floor. Except for the blood, the room was entirely empty.

Frank had arrived to find the front gate wide open, people with flashlights combing the grounds, and MacArthur Payne in a state of wide-eyed panic. No one that he encountered would acknowledge having placed the call. At first Payne had seemed alarmed to see Frank there, but he'd suddenly changed tack, grabbed him by the arm, and led him wordlessly to this room on the second floor of the main building where they now stood.

"What happened?" Frank asked him.

"We're not sure. Ray Stulke found it like this at midnight. We've been searching ever since."

"Searching for who?" Frank asked, but even as the words left his mouth, he anticipated the answer.

"Heather LeBron."

"This is the isolation room, isn't it?"

"Yes, how did you—"

"She obviously attempted suicide," Frank said. "She's bleeding heavily; how hard could it be to follow her trail?" But when Frank looked out into the hall, there was no trail of blood leading from the room.

"I think ... I'm afraid ... it's more complicated than that," Payne said. "Two other people are unaccounted for as well—Lorrie Betz, one of our Pathfinders, and Justin Levine, a student, are also missing."

Frank turned on his heel and headed toward the stairs.

"Where are you going?" Payne asked.

"To call the state police."

"No! No! I only want *your* help—if the state police come, the media will be right behind."

"You think this is just a little image problem that can be swept under the rug? Open your eyes, man! A crime has been committed here." Frank continued toward the stairs, with Payne trailing after him.

"But—"

Frank stopped and put his hand on Payne's shoulder. He spoke slowly and patiently, in the tone doctors use to explain a particularly unpleasant procedure they're about to perform. "This entire school is to be considered a crime scene. You will round up every student and employee and put them all together in the gymnasium. When the state police get here, we'll start interviewing them."

"But shouldn't we continue searching?" Payne protested. "Someone's been gravely hurt."

"The state police will search," Frank answered. What he didn't add was "until they find a body."

⬤

BY TEN A.M. FRANK HAD already put in a full day of work.

Ceaseless activity—briefing the state police crime scene team, coordinating efforts with Lieutenant Meyerson, interviewing witnesses—was the only way to keep at bay the terrible fear he felt for Heather LeBron. The child had warned him that she was in danger, that something terrible was going to happen, and he had written it off as teenage melodrama. He'd allowed MacArthur Payne to convince him that nothing was amiss at the school, despite the rumors and freakish accidents. Payne wouldn't talk his way out of this, but that was small consolation to Heather.

Establishing a few definite facts helped him feel more in control. At dinner, Melissa Trenk, Heather's roommate, had received the last serving of lasagna. Heather, right behind her in line, had been forced to take pot roast, which she disliked. When they sat down, Heather's milk spilled onto Melissa's lasagna, ruining it. Melissa maintained, and the others students at the table backed her story, that Heather had done it intentionally. Heather claimed it was an accident and became hysterical when the others accused her of spoiling her roommate's meal. Lorrie Betz, the Pathfinder on duty in that half of the cafeteria, had decreed that Heather must spend five hours in the isolation room. Heather refused to go quietly, and Ray Stulke and Lorrie had dragged her there and locked her in.

What happened next was anybody's guess.

Under intensive questioning from Frank and Lieutenant Lew Meyerson, Ray Stulke had insisted that he'd followed isolation room procedures to the letter. He'd unlocked the room and checked to be sure it was totally empty, while Lorrie had taken away Heather's belt and shoes and emptied her pockets. But Ray admitted that Heather had been struggling the entire time, so it was possible that Lorrie had missed something. *Like a big knife,* Frank thought.

Ray explained that he had to help Lorrie pry Heather's hands off the door and slam it quickly. Then Lorrie had locked the door and double-checked it. They'd each gone their separate ways, Lorrie with the key.

Heather's session in the isolation room had been set to end at 11:30 p.m. Since Lorrie had been the one to send her there, it was her responsibility to let Heather out, and everyone assumed she had. At midnight, prior to locking the outside door, Ray had been making one final patrol of the main building when he saw the light on and the door open to the isolation room. He'd discovered the blood, notified MacArthur Payne, and they'd both gone to look for Heather and Lorrie. But not before each of them had stepped into the isolation room, thoroughly contaminating the crime scene. Not only had they not found the women, they'd discovered that Justin Levine was also missing.

Now Frank and Lew sat in a classroom on the second floor that they had commandeered for their interviews. They'd already spoken to all the students and half the staff. A team of state troopers was searching the academy grounds, while another pair had been dispatched to Lorrie's home in Trout Run.

Frank rubbed his bloodshot eyes. "What do you think, Lew?"

"Let's start with the most obvious scenario. This kid Justin decides to spring Heather from the cell. He jumps Lorrie for the key; she gets stabbed trying to resist, they get rid of the body and take off."

Frank stood up and paced the room while he played devil's advocate. "Why should he take such a huge risk for a girl he barely knows? None of the other students said Justin and Heather were special friends."

Lew knew Frank was thinking out loud, and let him continue.

"Second, how the hell would they carry a woman Lorrie's size down the hall, down the stairs, and out the door into the grounds without getting any blood on the floor and without anyone noticing? Why move the body at all? Why not just run?"

Lew shook his head. "The other possibility is that Heather did try suicide, and Lorrie feels responsible because she overlooked the weapon Heather must have had on her."

"If Lorrie ran off in a panic, where's Heather?" Frank objected. "Lorrie couldn't move Heather any easier than Heather could move Lorrie—they're about the same size. And another thing that doesn't make sense: What made Ray and Payne both go into that room?"

"Ray's a moron, but you'd think Payne would have more sense," Lew agreed. "Why walk into that blood when you can see everything there is to see from the doorway?"

"Unless you wanted to pick something up," Frank said. "Like a weapon. Or a body."

"Why—"

Lew was interrupted by a tap on the door as Trooper Pauline Phelps appeared. "Got the lab results on the blood in the room—type O positive. Also tracked down the medical records of all three missing persons. Heather Le-Bron and Lorrie Betz are both O positive." Frank's eyes met Lew's. "The truth is, we can't be sure who the victim is here."

⟢ ◉ ⟣

THE DOOR SHUT BEHIND another staff member. They only had a few more left to interview, and Frank still hadn't learned who had placed the call that had brought him to the academy last night. The students had quickly been eliminated as possibilities—access to the phone was so tightly controlled that it seemed virtually impossible for one of them to have called.

Payne had insisted that he had been about to call when Frank had arrived, although Frank doubted it. Payne would have kept this mess hushed up as long as possible. One of the staff must have become uneasy about the cover-up and called anonymously. And now that person was afraid to own up to it, for fear of losing his or her job. Frank had been listening closely to each staff member they interviewed, trying to place that breathy voice.

Oliver Greffe entered the room next, looking bewildered.

"Hi, Frank. What in the world's going on? I can't get a straight story out of anyone here."

Frank nodded a greeting—he couldn't afford to treat Oliver any differently than the other staff members.

"Heather LeBron, Lorrie Betz, and Justin Levine are missing. One of them has been injured. I need you to recount for me everything you did last night, from dinnertime forward."

Oliver's mouth dropped open slightly and he nodded, taken aback by Frank's unaccustomed severity.

"Were you present at dinner when Heather was taken to isolation?"

"Yes, poor Heather. I felt so bad that she was in trouble again."

No one else had expressed much sympathy for Heather. Frank looked more closely at Oliver. "Did you go to check on her in the isolation room?"

Oliver cocked his head. "Check on her? No, what could I do? I went back to the boys' dorm after dinner. I was on duty in the recreation room until lights-out at nine-thirty."

"Was Justin in the rec room?"

"He came in for awhile—watched us playing cards. Then he went back to his room."

"You didn't see Justin after that?" Frank asked.

Oliver paused to think. "He might have come back in again later, but he didn't stay long. At nine-thirty the boys all went to their rooms and I locked their doors. Then I went to my room and read until I dozed off."

"What time was that?"

Oliver shrugged. "Ten-thirty, maybe. Next thing I knew, it was one a.m. and all hell had broken loose. Dr. Payne and Ray Stulke came to the boys' dorm and discovered Justin was gone. I heard them say something about Heather, but I couldn't piece together what they meant. They told me to stay awake and keep watch in the dorm." He yawned. "I've been up ever since, but no one ever came back to tell me what was happening."

"There's a phone in the boys' dorm, isn't there?"

"Yes, in the office."

Frank leaned forward slightly. "Oliver, did you place the call to my home last night requesting my assistance here?"

Oliver blinked his bloodshot eyes. "Me? Call you? No, of course not. Wasn't it Dr. Payne who called?"

Frank listened to Oliver's voice, clouded with exhaustion and confusion. He was pretty sure this was *not* the voice he'd heard last night. "Thanks, Oliver. You can go.

"Who's left?" Frank asked Meyerson as Oliver left the room, casting a perplexed look over his shoulder.

"Steven Vreeland. Roster says he's a Pathfinder. He wasn't on duty in the cafeteria last night—worked the early shift. But he lives here on campus."

"Ah, Pathfinder Steve. I think he and Heather have a little history."

The door opened and Steve Vreeland walked in. He looked only slightly older than most of the kids here, but he possessed an entirely different bearing. All the students they had interviewed had fallen into two categories: sullen or scared. Steve presented himself as the ultimate in clean-cut confidence. He met their eyes, shook their hands firmly, and sat facing them with a look of eager attentiveness. Frank could sense Meyerson relax a bit.

Frank led off. "So, Steve, you're a Pathfinder here, just like Lorrie Betz?"

"Yes, sir, that is correct."

"How did you find working with her? Did she do a good job?"

"Lorrie has the potential to become an outstanding Pathfinder. She hasn't mastered all the procedure yet."

"I see. How does one go about mastering the procedure?"

"It comes with experience." Steve stared unblinkingly at Frank, yet his focus seemed to be a little off-center.

"You're pretty young, Steve. What—eighteen, nineteen? How have you managed to become such an experienced Pathfinder?"

"I'm nineteen. I am a graduate of the Langley Wilderness School. I accepted this job out of gratitude to Dr. Payne for saving my life."

"You started out like some of these kids and Mr. Payne's program turned you around?" Meyerson asked.

"That is correct. I was on a self-destructive downward spiral, and by following the procedure I have been returned to a productive life." Despite use of the first-person pronoun, Steve seemed to be speaking about some other young man of his acquaintance.

"You're living proof that it works, huh?"

"I am."

"How about Heather? Was the procedure working with her?"

"She was extremely resistant, as they sometimes are. Always looking for a back door, a way to avoid taking responsibility for her choices. We needed to break down her barriers."

"By putting her in the isolation room?"

"She had no points available. The isolation room was our only recourse." Steve spoke with the certainty of a mathematician proving a quadratic equation.

Frank wanted to say "Even though you knew it might make her crazy enough to kill herself?" but that was an issue to take up with Payne, not his foot soldier. "Have you had occasion to send Heather to the isolation room?"

"Yes. Twice."

Frank studied the young man's emotionless face. He was certainly a good-looking guy—even features, straight teeth, wavy hair—if you could get past that blank expression. Surely it wasn't wise to put someone like this in a position of authority over young women.

"And did she do anything to try get out of that punishment?" *Like offer you a quick fuck.* He could imagine Heather that desperate. Would Steve be immune?

"It's not punishment. It's the repercussion for inappropriate behavior. And there is no way to get out of it. It's mandated by the procedure."

Frank studied the young man's resolute face. He wondered what it was like to go through life never having any doubts that you were doing the right thing. He wasn't likely ever to find out. "Thank you, Steve. That's all for now. We may need to speak to you again later."

"What d'ya make of him?" Frank asked as the door closed behind Steve. He suspected Meyerson approved of Steve's tale of redemption through adherence to the rules. But Lew surprised him.

"I think if someone pulled his system software, he'd crash."

"TWO OF MY MEN HAVE found Justin Levine," Meyerson said, coming back into the interview room after a break.

Frank looked up. He didn't have to speak the words "dead or alive?"

"Standing outside the Noonmark Diner in Keene Valley, waiting for the Trailways bus."

"Well, that's the best news we've had today. They're on their way here?"

"They'll be here in twenty. No point talking to anyone else until we hear what Justin has to say."

"Let's see if we can scare up some coff—" The phone rang, and Frank eyed it warily.

Meyerson picked it up, listened briefly, and handed it over. "Earl. Says it's important."

"This better not be another bear sighting, Earl," Frank said before Earl had uttered a word.

"No, that reporter's here, Frank. I know you're busy. If you want, I can—"

"No!"

That's all he needed. Bad enough that damn woman twisted him in knots. He could only imagine the job she'd do on Earl. No surprise she was on to the story. With so many state police cars cruising through Trout Run, he was amazed it had taken her this long to show up.

"Listen, Earl—I need time to think before I talk to her. Tell her we've had a break in the case, and if she can be patient for an hour, I'll have a statement for her. Let me know if she's okay with that."

Frank stretched in his chair and stared at the ceiling while he waited for Earl to come back on the line. He wasn't going to take the rap for giving this Klotz woman information that she could inflate into some salacious story. He would have Reid Burlingame right beside him while he talked to the reporter. After all, Reid was a politician—he ought to know how to beat the press at their own game.

Earl's voice brought him back to the here and now. "She didn't look real happy, but she said she'd be at Malone's waiting for your call."

As soon as he hung up, two burly state troopers escorted a skinny, foot-dragging teenager into the room. He plopped into a chair and stared at Frank through heavy-lidded eyes.

"Justin Levine?"

"No, Michael Jackson. I just flew in from Neverland."

Frank leaned across the table that separated them and spoke softly. "Look, son, I'm sure you've made a specialty of the wise-guy rebel routine, but we're going to put that away today. I want straight answers."

"What's the big freakin' deal? I ran away, you found me, I'm back. End of story."

"*You're* back. Where are Heather LeBron and Lorrie Betz?"

"Huh?"

Meyerson slammed his hand down on the table, taking on the bad-cop role. "I'm not screwing around with pot-smoking and shoplifting, boy. Someone's been badly hurt here and I want to get to the bottom of it. So let's talk."

Justin looked from Frank to Lew in confusion. "Who's hurt? Why are you asking me about Heather?"

"You ate dinner in the cafeteria last night?" Meyerson asked.

"Yeah."

"Then what?"

"Went back to my room."

"And ... ?"

Justin folded his arms across his chest. "I'm a minor. You can't question me without a parent present. And mine are both in Europe. At least, that's where they were last time anyone checked."

Nothing like an experienced felon to know his rights, backward and forward. He'd overlooked one loophole, though—and Meyerson knew it, too. "You're at boarding school. Mr. Payne is *in loco parentis*. Do you want me to call him in to be present during the interview?"

Justin sat bolt upright. "No! No, ask me what you want to know."

"How did you get out of your room last night?"

Justin sighed. "It was such a good system, I hate to give it up. But I guess it wouldn't work again anyway. I kept a piece of plastic wrap from my lunch when we were hiking a couple of weeks ago. I put it over the latch in my door—it kept it from locking, even though the doorknob wouldn't turn from the outside, so it looked like it was locked. Then I waited for the right night."

"Which was last night, because Heather was in the isolation room," Meyerson said.

Justin glanced at him in annoyance. "I don't know why you keep bringing up Heather. It was the right night because of who was on duty in the boys' dorm."

Frank was instantly alert although his face remained impassive. "Randy Ohlandt," Frank prompted. He had been on duty watching Justin and the other boys confined to their rooms, and he swore he'd locked Justin in and never left his post. Obviously, he was lying.

"It was the combination of Randy and Oliver together that I had to wait for," Justin explained. "See, whenever Randy worked, before lights-out he always headed into the bathroom—with a magazine, if ya know what I mean. And the person watching the rec room was supposed to cover the main hall while he was in there. But whenever Oliver worked the rec room, he always played cards with the guys. He was the only staff member who did. So, when Randy was in the can and Oliver was playing blackjack, I slipped out and headed through the woods for Keene Valley."

"Very clever. Now back up and tell us how you got Heather out of the isolation room. Does the plastic wrap trick work there, too?"

"Nah, you can't use the plastic there—door's got a double dead bolt." Then Justin's eyes widened as the full import of what Meyerson had said sunk in. "You mean Heather got outta isolation somehow? And you think *I* helped her?" Justin pushed back from the table.

"I was looking out for me, not leading the Great Escape. If Heather got out of isolation, it's because she worked her own deal."

"Worked a deal? With whom?"

The boy rolled his shoulders. "Chicks. They have their ways. Know what I mean?"

Chapter 18

Frank drove back to Trout Run for his appointment with Dawn Klotz and Reid Burlingame, enjoying a few minutes of peace in the patrol car. The day of interviewing students and staff at the academy had turned up many facts, but he hadn't been able yet to organize them into a coherent picture of what had occurred at the school last night. He hoped he could dispense with the reporter quickly and regroup with Meyerson's team to analyze the information they had so far. If they couldn't figure out what had happened to Heather and Lorrie, at least the brainstorming would prepare him for a second round of interviews at the school.

He had been too busy all day to really think about Heather herself, but in the solitude of the car, her image loomed: her frightened face when she'd told him someone else was going to die; her forlorn slump when she admitted she'd been exaggerating. What the hell was the truth? Should he have known she was in danger? Should he have acted to get her out of there? But who was he to intervene in a treatment plan that Heather's parents had set up willingly with MacArthur Payne?

Or was that angle entirely wrong? Had Heather "worked a deal," as Justin implied?

Which brought him to Lorrie. From what he'd seen of her so far, she seemed more a victim than a perpetrator. But getting kicked around by the strong brought out the worst in the weak—he'd seen it time and again.

The lights of Malone's came into view as he approached the green, but they didn't convey their usual cheery welcome. Frank drove on by and went to pick up Reid at his home. He spent a few minutes bringing the lawyer up to speed on the investigation, then they headed out to meet Dawn Klotz.

The reporter sat in the back booth of Malone's, furiously tapping away on her laptop. Her eyes never left the screen as Frank and Reid dropped into the seat across from her. Her fingers continued to fly across the keyboard until, with a grunt, she punched one final key and looked up.

"Sorry. I'm on deadline." She extended her hand to Reid. "Dawn Klotz, New York *Beat.*"

"Pleased to meet you," Reid said graciously.

Frank felt like telling him not to bother. The woman would only regard civility as a sign of weakness. He stared at Dawn impassively, waiting for her to make the first move.

She obliged. "So, have you determined if Heather LeBron is a suicide or a murder victim?"

Reid adjusted his tie. "My dear woman! There's no conclusive evidence that anyone has died. The girl is simply unaccounted for—"

"But there are signs of foul play at the school, are there not?"

"It appears someone may have been injured," Frank said.

"And Lorrie Betz, who would have been the last person to see Heather alive, is also missing, right?" Dawn started pounding her keyboard again.

"No ... uh ..." Reid stammered.

Dawn's keen eyes peered at Reid over the computer screen. "So, someone else *did* see Heather LeBron after Lorrie Betz put her in the isolation room? Who?"

Frank laid a restraining hand on Reid's arm. He didn't want the chairman of the town council to get screwed by Klotz; he just wanted him to understand how impossible this woman was to deal with. "We have spent the day interviewing the students and staff of the North Country Academy to establish the chain of events last night. We are receiving their full cooperation."

Dawn shifted her gaze to Frank. "Has the school informed you of Heather LeBron's history of suicide attempts?"

Reid's and Frank's stony-faced silence was as good as an answer to Dawn. "The girl twice tried to overdose on pills at the last school she attended. Did the North Country Academy have any procedures in place to safe-guard her?"

"I'm not in a position to answer that," Frank said. "You'd have to discuss it with MacArthur Payne."

"I would, but he refuses to take my calls. Is it true that Payne tried to conceal the girl's disappearance and that it was only revealed when an anonymous caller alerted you, Chief Bennett?"

Frank refused to register surprise again. "I was called as soon as the school was aware they had a problem." How the hell did she know the call had come anonymously?

"Did Dr. Payne place the call?" she persisted.

"The call woke me from a sound sleep. I'm really not sure who placed it," Frank answered. He, too, suspected Payne of a cover-up, but he was damned if he'd let this woman put those words in his mouth.

"So, what's the big break in the case your assistant told me about?"

"We found Justin Levine."

"Who?"

"The third person who was missing." Frank could see that for once, he'd caught her off guard. "He's a student at the academy and apparently chose last night to run away. He was found today in Keene Valley, waiting for the bus. At the moment, it appears that his actions were unrelated to Heather's and Lorrie's disappearances."

Dawn studied Frank's face intently for a moment, then abruptly turned her attentions to Reid. "If this tragedy forces the North Country Academy to close, what will that mean to the town of Trout Run, Mr. Burlingame?"

"It's quite premature to be predicting tragedy, Ms. Klotz. I'm confident that Heather and Lorrie will turn up unharmed."

"Really? Considering that the person responsible for Jake Reiger's death still hasn't been apprehended, I find your optimism rather surprising."

"An *animal* was responsible for Jake's death. And who says there's any connection between the two events?" Reid demanded.

Dawn merely raised her eyebrows.

Reid rose from the booth and stood glaring down at the reporter. "No wonder the *Beat* has been involved in so many lawsuits—the paper clearly sanctions the reporting of unsubstantiated gossip. I'd verify my sources very carefully if I were you, Ms. Klotz."

"Will do." She flipped her blond hair away from her face and went back to typing.

"That woman is maddening!" Reid said as they walked down the steps of the diner.

The "told you so" didn't need to be spoken.

Frank focused on the state police cars parked in front of his office. It was time to review all they had and plan the next move.

Chapter 19

"Did you know that Heather LeBron had suicidal tendencies?" After brainstorming with the state police the evening before, Frank had decided his approach should be to come down hard on MacArthur Payne and try to scare him into being more forthcoming. Consequently, he had gone on the offensive the moment he walked into Payne's office this morning.

"Suicidal tendencies? Where did you hear that?"

"I understand that she tried to take her own life twice at her last boarding school. Were you doing anything to safeguard her?"

"At St. Bridget's, she swallowed five over-the-counter sleeping pills. I don't call that suicide, I call it a very long nap. Heather was constantly looking for ways to draw attention to herself. I suspect this is just another one of her stunts." The bright morning sunshine seemed to have restored Payne's confidence. Instead of the jittery and panicked man of yesterday, Payne now strode around the office with his customary arrogance.

"Shedding your own blood hardly seems like a stunt, Dr. Payne."

"What if she didn't actually *shed* it, Chief Bennett? What if the blood in that room was menstrual blood—have you considered that?"

Frank recoiled in his chair. Menstrual blood? How had Payne come up with that? And yet, he might actually be right. It would explain the fact that the blood in the room was smeared, not spattered, and that there was no trail of blood down the hall. But if the forensics team hadn't come up with that theory, how the hell had Payne?

"Forgive me, Bennett; I'm getting ahead of myself. You see, I've been up half the night thinking about this and I finally had an epiphany. I'm quite sure I know what happened here on Thursday night."

"Well, I'm glad someone knows." Frank stretched out his legs and crossed them at the ankle. "Don't keep me in the dark."

Payne perched on the edge of his desk, swinging his foot so that the tassel on his highly polished loafer danced. He leaned toward Frank. "The first thing you have to understand, Bennett: I have enemies."

"Oh?"

"I used to own a school in Utah called the Langley Wilderness School."

"So I've heard."

"So then you know it closed amidst a scandal."

Payne had these moments of disarming honesty that threw Frank. Maybe that's why he had accepted Payne's explanations for what went on at the school—because when you most anticipated a lie from the man, he blurted out the truth.

"I had a partner in that school. His name is Glen Costello. We parted on bad terms. I blamed him for the catastrophe of that boy's death. Now he's started a new school in Mexico, where he can get away with substandard conditions. He's trying to compete with me; he can afford to charge less because his overhead is lower. But the one thing he can't deliver is results. His students aren't transformed; he doesn't save lives. So he's trying to drive me out of business the only way he knows how: by creating another scandal that will shut me down."

"Very interesting, Mr. Payne. Has your former partner been seen around Trout Run?"

Payne held up a long finger demanding silence. "I believe he has planted a spy—an operative—inside the academy." He said this with all the drama of James Bond revealing some diabolical plot, and Frank took it about that seriously.

"And that spy is Heather LeBron?"

"Of course not. Heather is just a tool. What does that girl want more than anything else in the world?

"To get out of here?"

"Exactly. So she is persuaded to stage this stunt in return for her freedom. She waits until she has her period, she dumps her milk on another student's dinner, knowing she'll be put in isolation, she defiles the room with her menstrual blood, and she is liberated."

"Wait a minute," Frank said. "How did you come up with this? Why would Costello ask a young woman to smear her menstrual blood around a room? I mean, that's ... gross."

Payne smiled slightly. "I suppose it does seem like a bizarre concept to you, but Glen and I think alike from spending so many years working with troubled teens. Using body, er, excretions is a very common way for these kids to act out. I can't tell you how many messages I've found written in feces. Believe me, the menstrual blood wouldn't be a stretch for him."

Payne paced in front of Frank, elaborating on his theory.

"Costello has probably given her enough money that she can hang out with drug addicts in some big city until she poisons herself with the stuff. And it looks like something terrible has happened to an academy student and I'm trying to cover it up. I can only imagine what filth he's feeding to that *Beat* reporter—today's paper will be full of it."

Frank was never one to subscribe to elaborate conspiracy theories, but if ever there was a time that he wanted to believe Payne, it was now. If the headmaster was right, Heather LeBron was unharmed and would stay that way as long as they tracked her down before she ingested too many drugs.

"What about the attack on Jake Reiger? Is that part of this plot, too?"

"I've been thinking about that, Bennett." Payne tilted his head and pursed his lips. "I'm not sure, but it's possible, isn't it? You see, when the boy in Utah died on the backpacking trip that Costello was supervising, I blamed him for not making sure everyone had enough water, and for not having first aid equipment to treat heatstroke. His defense was that nature is unpredictable—he couldn't have known that the temperature would shoot up to ninety degrees in April. Staging this bear attack might have been his way of proving to me the unpredictability of nature."

"Killing Jake Reiger is a pretty harsh way to prove that lesson."

"Costello couldn't have meant to kill him. Jake worked for us in Utah and got along with us both. No, it must be that Costello thought up the plan, but it was carried out wrong."

"By Heather, since she was on the camping trip, too?"

"Exactly."

"And you think Lorrie is Costello's spy, the one who put Heather up to this? She certainly needs money."

"Lorrie? No, she's not smart enough. The spy is Paul Petrucci."

"So, what do you make of that theory?" Frank asked Meyerson.

"It does explain a few things, but not everything. It's worth running a test on that blood—I'll get the lab right on it. How does Payne account for Lorrie's disappearance?"

"Says she freaked when she saw the room bloody and empty, and ran so she wouldn't be blamed."

"You want to talk to Petrucci now?"

Frank shook his head. "We have nothing on him—he wasn't even on duty the night Heather disappeared. Might as well wait for the blood test results to come back. In the meantime, let's do a little background check on Costello. And I want to talk to everyone who was on that camping trip with Jake Reiger."

<hr />

IN ADDITION TO HEATHER, there had been five other students on the camping trip, as well as the Pathfinder, Steve Vreeland. Frank called them into the interview room one by one. The answers given by the first three were all the same: they had no access to the kitchen or the camping equipment; aside from their toothbrushes, journals, and clothes, Mr. Reiger and Pathfinder Steve had packed everything and distributed items for each of them to carry. Mr. Reiger had chosen the spot where they would pitch their tents, but the kids had set them up. No one could remember who had pitched Reiger's tent; some said Steve, another speculated it might have been Justin. Everyone agreed Heather had been hopelessly inept with tent poles. They had gone to sleep after dinner and heard nothing until they were awakened by the sound of the bear attacking. They hadn't noticed anything unusual about Heather's behavior. She had complained the entire time, but that was par for the course for Heather. All of them had been forthcoming but ultimately unhelpful.

Melissa Trenk, Heather's roommate, was the fourth student to be interviewed.

"Melissa, are you happy here?" Frank led off.

The girl pulled back in her chair, as if the question were a large, ugly insect that had flown into her face. "I wasn't sent here to have fun. I came to confront all the bad things I've done in my life and learn to accept accountability for the pain I've caused others." Her eyes didn't meet Frank's as she spoke; she seemed to be looking right through him.

What bad things had she done, what pain had she caused, Frank wondered? "How old are you, honey?"

"Sixteen."

"Why did your folks send you here?"

"I was drinking, spending time with older kids who were a bad influence, not paying attention in school," Melissa recited.

"Some of the same reasons Heather was here, right? But you didn't seem to get along."

"Heather didn't embrace the program. She was resistant to change. Worst of all, she tried to ruin it for the rest of us. I'm trying to attain a Level Three, and Heather didn't respect that."

"Heather was very troubled, Melissa. Did you ever try to reach out to her, help her?"

"We all tried to help Heather in Group Encounter, by pointing out all the issues she needed to confront. But she refused to participate in a constructive way."

"Tell me more about Group Encounter. How does it work?"

"I'm not in a position to explain the program. I haven't completed it yet, so I don't fully understand it."

"So, describe a group encounter session. What happens?"

Steadfastly, Melissa shook her head. "That would be taking one element of the program out of context. You should ask Dr. Payne these questions."

"All right, I will. Thank you, Melissa, you may go." Frank waited until she got to the door. "One more thing, did anyone here *like* Heather?"

Melissa's eyes narrowed. "I hated her. She wanted to keep me from attaining my goals. Most of the others felt that way, too. Except maybe ..."

"Who?"

"Justin."

JUSTIN LEVINE WAS THE fifth student to be interviewed. He slouched into the room and splayed himself across a chair, looking up at Frank with an expression finely crafted to conceal any glimmer of interest.

"So, Justin, let's talk about the night Jake Reiger was attacked by the bear."

For a split second the boy seemed curious, then he pulled his ennui back into place and drawled, "Talk away." Frank led him through the same questions he'd asked the other students and got the same answers.

"Did you set up Jake Reiger's tent?"

Justin shrugged. "I might have helped. I got mine up right away, then I helped the others. I like setting up the tents—reminds me of building with Legos when I was a kid."

Frank observed Justin closely. His helpfulness provided a great opportunity to spread the bacon grease, but he didn't seem the least bit nervous about admitting he might have handled Reiger's tent.

"Did you notice anything unusual about Reiger's tent?" Frank asked. "Was it stained in any way?"

Now Justin seemed more alert, although his nonchalant pose hadn't changed. "I said I wasn't sure if I put up Reiger's tent. I know I put up one yellow one, and his was yellow, but so were two others."

Frank nodded and moved on. "And how did Heather behave on the trip?"

"God, she never stopped bitching and moaning. It was so irritating, especially since she wasn't even supposed to be on that trip."

"She wasn't?"

"She wasn't scheduled to go until two weeks later. But the campout earns you five points, and she needed points to be able to audition for that play. So Mr. Petrucci finagled it so she could be on the earlier trip."

"Heather told you this?"

"Nah—I overheard Petrucci and Reiger making the deal. Petrucci had a thing for Heather."

"What kind of *thing?*"

Justin waved his hand. "Not a sex thing. He just fell for her 'I've had a pathetically deprived childhood' routine, that's all."

"Was Heather a special friend of yours?"

Justin looked as if he'd caught a whiff of something rotten. "Hardly."

"Some of the other kids seem to think you were close."

"Well, Heather might have considered me her special friend, but the feeling wasn't mutual."

Another rejection for Heather. Frank continued asking questions about the position of the campsite and how much of the attack Justin had seen. The boy was sitting up straighter now, and Frank saw shrewd intelligence in his eyes.

"You think there's a connection between what happened to Jake Reiger and what happened to Heather, don't you?" Justin asked.

"Do you?"

"I don't know. But now I really wish I'd made it onto that bus in Keene Valley."

Chapter 20

Although the long day of interviewing hadn't produced any concrete results, Frank left the academy feeling slightly optimistic. It was possible that Heather had been encouraged to pull a stunt in the isolation room, and that Lorrie was either in on it or had fled in a panic. If so, the whole mess would be resolved sooner rather than later, because he didn't think either one was clever enough to remain on the lam for long.

Frank decided that attending tonight's hymn sing and pie social was the best way to project an air of confidence that the problems at the academy would be cleared up shortly. He arrived in time to see Matthew Portman's siblings, Rachel, Clarice, and Ernie, file into the Fellowship Hall. Their father, Henry, was nowhere in sight.

He chatted with a cluster of men at the back of the hall, made sure Reid and Ardyth noticed his presence, and followed Mary Bixley into the kitchen to find out exactly where she planned to place her pie on the buffet table. On the way out of the kitchen, he eavesdropped on Bernice and Helen Meisterson.

"That Lydia has her nerve. She's in there barking out orders like the kitchen belongs to her alone. Imagine telling me my lemon meringue doesn't need to be in the fridge!"

"Calm down, Bernice. You can't really blame her. Ardyth is busy out front, and Lydia took up the slack."

"Humph. I tell you, we wouldn't have these power plays if Pastor Bob would just get married. It's the minister's wife's job to be in charge of all the social events."

"So true. But Bob's been here for three years, and he hasn't shown the slightest interest in any local girls."

Bernice scowled. "Mighty slim pickins there. But you know who would be perfect.." She leaned toward her friend and whispered.

Helen's face lit up as Frank slipped past them. "You're right! Penny Stevenson would be marvelous for Pastor Bob!"

So, even the old biddies saw Penny as the perfect match for Bob. He must be the only one who couldn't make the connection. He shook his head. Penny pouring tea at the annual Presbyterian women's luncheon—that, he'd pay money to see.

Suddenly the lights flickered and the fluorescent tubes on the right side of the Fellowship Hall ceiling went out, while the adjacent kitchen was plunged into total darkness. After a split second's stunned silence, a high-pitched cacophony broke out.

"Oh, no!"

"Who plugged both coffeepots into the same outlet?"

"Lucille, why did you turn on the microwave when the coffee was still perking?"

"I didn't know that I shouldn't."

"Everyone knows!"

Frank unclipped the flashlight from his belt as he made his way to the basement stairs. Passing the kitchen, he called to the ladies to unplug the coffee. As he made his way across the dank basement toward the circuit breaker, he could clearly hear the ladies above, still clucking.

"What was the big rush to warm up that apple crisp? The coffee needs to finish first. I told her ..."

The breaker box was on the far wall. He soon passed all the way under the kitchen and the ladies' voices receded. He shone his light ahead and saw the box, with two circuits tripped. He flipped them back and waited for a second to make sure they wouldn't trip again. As he stood in the absolute silence of the basement, two new voices began speaking above him.

"Tell Dad he can relax. We don't need the money anymore," a woman said.

The voice, young and edgy, was familiar, but he couldn't place it.

"What do you mean? You're not going to give up and let the bank take the house, are you?"

"Don't worry, Mom, we're not moving in with you." The note of bitterness was unmistakable.

"Katie! That's not what I meant. I told you we'd try to help you, but things are tight for us, too, right now. I sure don't want you to lose your house."

"I know, I know. But Paul says he's worked it out. We don't need to borrow anything from you."

Frank looked up at the floor joists, through which the sound of the voices traveled. Katie and Paul—it must be Katie Petrucci talking to her mother in the little back hallway that ran from the kitchen to the bathrooms. It seemed the bank was threatening to foreclose on Katie and Paul's house; he hadn't realized their money problems were so serious.

"But how did Paul work it out?" Katie's mother asked. "You said the bank wouldn't budge."

"Look, he got the money and we don't need a loan from you. That's all that matters, isn't it?"

<hr />

BOB RUSH HAD SWITCHED on the microphone at the podium on the stage and was urging people into their seats. Frank headed down the main aisle but discovered that the only seats were either all the way in the back, or in the front row next to the three Portman children. A tough choice. A seat in the back would allow him to slip outside after a while until the pie appeared. On the other hand, he honestly wanted to see Matthew play. He took a deep breath—in for a penny, in for a pound—and sat down in the front-row seat next to Ernie.

Easily six-foot-three, Ernie had huge hands and feet. He turned his head toward Frank and studied him without reservation. Apparently Frank passed muster. Ernie grinned broadly. "Hi, I'm Ernie. That's my little brother up there." He pointed to the stage, where Matthew had taken his place at the piano. Ernie waved, but Matthew looked over the heads of his family in the front row, scanning the crowd. Frank guessed that he must be looking for Oliver Greffe. He hadn't noticed the music teacher in the hall, and with his car in the shop, it seemed unlikely that he would make it to the hymn sing.

Ernie elbowed Frank. "What's your name?"

"Frank."

"Okay, Frank, you have to promise to be real quiet while my brother plays, okay?"

"All right, I will."

But Ernie couldn't heed his own advice. He chatted loudly with Frank throughout Pastor Bob's introduction and welcome, until his sister, Rachel, leaned across Clarice, tapped Ernie on the knee, and held her finger to her lips.

"Yeah, right," Ernie said. "We have to be quiet," he told Frank.

The hymn sing started out quietly, with "Be Thou My Vision." Frank helped Ernie find it in the hymnal, but after singing the first familiar line with gusto, Ernie's voice petered out. When Frank glanced over at him, Ernie was holding his hymnal in front of his face, but peering up at the ceiling. Could he read? Maybe a little, but probably not well enough to follow the lyrics, Frank suspected.

The folding chair was hard, the hall was stuffy, and Ernie continued to fidget. Bob announced another hymn from his spot at the podium. This event needed Billy Crystal as emcee, and Bob was more like Al Gore. Frank began to regret not taking the seat in the back.

But then Pastor Bob made a quip about Martin Luther, and a few people laughed. Emboldened by his success, he disconnected the mike from the podium and started strolling around the stage, bantering with Matthew as he introduced the next hymn.

Before long, Bob had tapped his inner Jay Leno. He called the little children in the audience forward to sing "Jesus Loves Me" and cheerfully let them upstage him. He rounded up a crew of foghorn baritones to sing the refrain in "I Wanna Be a Christian." And he brought down the house when he hand-selected the primmest Presbyterian ladies and got them to sway and clap their hands to "Ride the Chariot in the Morning."

Against all odds, Frank found himself having fun.

But Ernie, who'd been so affable when Frank had first sat down, now grew cranky. He pulled his hymnal away from Frank and refused to let him help find the hymns that Pastor Bob announced. He shuffled loudly through the pages and dropped his hymnal with a clunk several times. Finally Rachel switched places with her younger sister to try to settle Ernie down, but he pulled away from her, too.

"And now," Bob said, "let's join together on number 181, 'When I Survey the Wondrous Cross.'"

"No!" Ernie leaped to his feet. "No, I don't want to sing that one. I don't like that song." Rachel tugged at her brother's sleeve, but he shook her off. "I want to sing 'Amazing Grace.' Play 'Amazing Grace,' Matthew— that's my favorite."

Matthew sat with his fingers frozen above the keyboard, looking frantically from his brother to Pastor Bob. Although startled, Bob recovered quickly. "You're right, Ernie. 'Amazing Grace' is one of my favorites, too, and we've waited too long to sing it. Let's all turn to number 154 now—'Amazing Grace.'"

Ernie sat down with a satisfied thump. After a slightly shaky intro, Matthew launched confidently into the melody. Ernie made no effort to open his hymnal, but for the first time that evening, he sang.

Amazing Grace, how sweet the sound,
that saved a wretch like me.
I once was lost, but now am found.
Was blind, but now I see.

He had an amazingly resonant baritone. By the end of the first verse Frank stopped singing so he could hear Ernie more clearly.

Whatever musical gene had touched Matthew had also been bestowed on Ernie. His voice rang out clear and perfectly on pitch. Soon, other people around him had stopped singing also, and Ernie's voice rose above those at the rear of the hall. He had every word of the hymn memorized and never missed a beat. He sang with pure, unbridled joy.

Pastor Bob watched Ernie in wonder. As Matthew neared the end of the fourth verse, Bob approached the piano and whispered something in his ear. Matthew finished the verse and stopped playing.

Ernie took a breath to launch into the fifth verse, then paused in confusion. "Hey—there's more to sing!" Pastor Bob walked up to Ernie and led him onto to the stage. "I don't know how well those of you in the back could hear Matthew's brother, Ernie, singing this hymn. But he has a beautiful voice and I'm going to ask him to sing the last verse of "Amazing Grace" as a solo with his brother to accompany him."

A big grin spread across Ernie's broad, blank-eyed face. He looked at Matthew for approval, and Matthew smiled back in encouragement. They launched into the fifth verse in perfect synchronicity.

"When we've been here ten thousand years..."

If there was a dry eye in the house after the last note faded away, Frank didn't know what heartless soul it belonged to. There clearly could be no more singing after the showstopping performance, so Pastor Bob escorted Ernie and Matthew off the stage and signaled the ladies to bring out the pies.

Frank made a beeline for the strawberry rhubarb and snagged a big wedge, then sat in companionable silence with Randall Bixley and Art Breveur, whose wives were both behind the serving table. Contentment washed over him. He owed Ardyth and Reid a thank-you for pressuring him to come. There was nothing like loud singing of familiar tunes with a great accompanist to pick up your spirits. And who would've thought ol' Bob had it in him to be such a showman?

Across the packed room, he spotted a familiar profile. A young woman much taller and slimmer than the two ladies she chatted with lifted her head and looked toward him. Her face lit up, she waved, and began working her way through the crowd. Frank rose to meet halfway—she must have arrived after the singing had begun. But before he could move, she sidestepped the last cluster of pie eaters blocking her path and headed straight for Bob Rush.

———◉——

MOST OF THE HYMN SING crowd had driven off when a loud, mournful wail cut through the night air, interrupting the final good-byes spoken on the church steps.

The siren calling together the members of the Trout Run volunteer fire department echoed against the mountains in a long steady crescendo, tapered off, and began its climb again. Within minutes, pickup trucks were racing down Route 12 to the fire station. Frank jumped in the patrol car and followed them.

A fire, especially one beyond the reach of the ten hydrants on the town water system, almost always resulted in a total loss of property. The town had one tanker truck, but it didn't hold enough water to put out more than a small kitchen fire. If the burning house was located near Stony Brook or a pond, enough water could sometimes be pumped to put out the fire before the building was consumed, but usually the members of the fire department could do little more than stand alongside the despondent owners and watch the structure burn.

Frank arrived as the ladder truck was pulling out of the firehouse, and he followed it as it sped out of town, past the Stop'N'Buy and the Mountain Vista Motel. In his rearview mirror, Frank caught the occasional flashing light of the pumper truck following them. Soon the lead truck careened to the right, down High Meadow Lane, and within minutes, Frank could smell smoke. He knew where the truck was headed.

The gates of the North Country Academy were already wide open and the procession sped up the long driveway. A cluster of people stood outside the main administration building, watching smoke billow out the second-story windows. As Frank got out of the car, he saw MacArthur Payne speak briefly to the fire chief, Andy Kubash, before the firemen adjusted their oxygen masks and charged into the building.

The people surrounding Payne were all staff members; at this hour the students were presumably all safe in their beds. "The building is empty?" Frank confirmed as he walked up.

"Yes, Ray was doing his final check when he smelled smoke, then saw a cloud of it in the second-floor hallway," Payne answered.

"You're sure no one's in the isolation room?"

A spasm of irritation crossed Payne's face, but he answered levelly, "All the students are in their dorm rooms. They've been counted twice."

Payne winced at the sound of shattering glass as a fireman broke a large window and signaled to the crew below to direct the water there. Several of the men were unrolling long lengths of hose to reach the stream that bordered the property. Flames were briefly visible in the room with the broken window, but after about twenty minutes the clouds of smoke started to thin out. Soon, a sooty Andy emerged from the building.

"Think we got it under control. Most of the fire damage seems to be confined to two rooms at the end of the hall. 'Course you'll have smoke and water damage throughout, but that can't be helped. Lucky this old building is mostly stone and solid plaster—the fire didn't spread too much."

"Any idea what started it?" Frank asked.

Andy grimaced. "Can't be positive—we should get the experts in—but I'd say an accelerant was used."

Payne's gaze flicked rapidly from Andy to Frank. "Surely not. Surely it was just faulty wiring. The building is so old—"

"Definitely not electrical," Andy said. "I've seen enough of those in my time." Then one of the other firemen called to him, and Andy went back into the building.

Frank watched Payne, who was swallowing hard as if fighting off nausea. Oliver stepped forward from the crowd of school employees milling around anxiously.

"Come on, Mac," he said gently. "There's nothing else you can do here tonight. Why don't you go back to your house and try to get some rest. There will be a lot of work in the morning."

Payne looked at the music teacher for a moment, as if trying to place who he was. Then he nodded and allowed himself to be led away.

The firemen were starting to roll up their hoses, so Frank assumed it must be safe to enter the building. The big stone-floored foyer was undamaged except for water and streaks of soot. He made his way up the granite staircase, sidestepping puddles. At the end of the upstairs hall he could see the worst of the damage: two classrooms whose wooden doors were now charred skeletons and whose plaster walls were blackened.

Frank followed the sound of voices and found Andy and another fireman in the last room on the right. Andy was in the far corner pointing something out.

"You see this?" He pointed to a scorch pattern on the floor. Then he looked behind him to a wall that, unlike the others, had buckled and seemed close to collapse.

"This wall is made of Sheetrock, not plaster," Andy said. "Looks like they built a new interior wall here at some point—there's space behind this." He motioned to the other fireman. "Better knock this down so we can be sure there's nothing smoldering back there."

The fireman swung his ax at the charred and soaked wallboard, which crumpled inward between the two studs. A terrible smell rushed out at them, entirely separate from the acrid scent of smoke.

Frank's stomach lurched as he stuck his head through the opening and looked down.

The blank, distended eyes of Heather LeBron stared back up at him.

Chapter 21

MacArthur Payne sat on a wine-red leather wing chair, cradling his shaved head in his hands. His face drained of all color, the veins crossing his temples stood out like roads on a map. "My God, I never thought Glen Costello would go this far to get back at me. To kill a child ..." His voice cracked and he twisted away from Frank.

Frank watched him in a cold fury. He remembered Payne dismissing Heather's pleas for help as an Academy Award-winning performance. Well, who was acting now? He'd never believe another word this man said.

But what was the point of raging against Payne? He had no one to blame but himself for what had happened. He could've prevented Heather's death if only he had listened to her, asked more questions, believed in the poor kid.

Heather's body had shown no cuts or wounds of any kind, although there had been blood on her clothes. When Dr. Hibbert, the medical examiner, noticed bruising around the neck and broken blood vessels in the eyes, he had offered an unofficial pronouncement of the cause of death: strangulation. There was no doubt about it— Heather LeBron had been murdered.

MacArthur Payne had been flattened by the news Frank delivered, but now he seemed to be pulling himself together. "Have you made the arrest yet?" he asked.

Frank noted the odd choice of words: "the" arrest, not "an" arrest. "No, why—"

Payne sprang out of his chair. "Good Lord, man, what are you waiting for?"

Evidence seemed the obvious answer, but Frank refused to spar with this man anymore. He wouldn't give him the satisfaction.

"Dr. Payne, the idea that Paul Petrucci is somehow involved with your former partner is a just one lead that we'll have to follow up on."

"Lead? It's a fact—I'll give you proof!" Payne started ticking off points on his fingers. "Petrucci wasn't on duty the night Heather was killed. He sneaked back on campus, killed her, and hid the body behind that new wall. He's worked here longer than anyone else. He was here when the previous owners did that remodeling project. He's the only one who would've known about that little space."

Payne paused and glared at Frank, whose face must have been etched with skepticism. "You don't believe me! You don't believe someone from your precious town could do such a thing. Take off your blinders, man! Petrucci is desperate for money. Costello probably offered him thousands—people have killed for far less."

Frank took a deep breath. "Dr. Payne, sit down, and let's go over this calmly and rationally." Payne opened his mouth, but Frank cut him off "I'll lay out what we know—hear me out.

"Jake Reiger was killed in a bear attack that may have been intentionally provoked. He worked for both you and Glen Costello previously. Heather was present when Reiger was killed. Next, Heather gets lost on a school hike and claims she was abandoned, that someone was trying to kill her."

"That's ridic—"

Frank held up his hand for silence. "Let me finish, please. Heather confides in me that she can't bear being sent to the isolation room, yet she does something— intentionally, if the other students are to be believed— that gets her sent there. According to Ray, she is locked in the empty isolation room. Lorrie is supposed to let her out at ten, but we don't know if she ever did that. Ray discovers the bloody room at eleven and calls you. Lorrie Betz, Justin Levine, and Heather are all discovered to be missing.

"Now, you believe that Heather smeared her menstrual blood around that room to make it look like she had attempted suicide, and that Paul Petrucci slipped back onto campus, supposedly to release her and get her off campus. Instead, he strangles her and hides her body in a crawl space created during remodeling that you claim no one else knew existed. Are you with me so far?" Payne nodded.

"All right, let's ask ourselves...Why? You claim your ex-partner wants to destroy your school with a scandal and gain a competitive advantage. Now, why would he choose a bear attack on a teacher to do that?"

"Glen knows that a hallmark of my program is the emphasis on strenuous outdoor activity—hiking, climbing, camping, boating. I'm sure he's trying to undermine parents' confidence that these activities are safe and well supervised. The Web site for his new school in Mexico shows sunny, sandy beaches, but I've heard the place is on a godforsaken, snake-infested patch of real estate in the Yucatan. But this is his ploy—asking parents if they want to send their kids to a place where they can frolic in the surf, or to a school where they'll be attacked by wild animals."

Frank remained stony-faced. There was always a certain logic to Payne's explanations; that's how he reeled you in. "But why sabotage a teacher's sleeping bag— wouldn't it have been more effective to attract the bear to a student's tent?"

Payne stretched his long legs out in front of him and studied his shoes, as if the answer could be found in their glossy surface. "Perhaps," he said finally, "Heather was reluctant to set the bear upon one of her friends."

"Heather didn't seem to have any friends—the other kids all shunned her."

Payne's thin lips drew down in exasperation. "An unstable young girl was recruited to do the dirty work, Bennett. You can hardly be surprised if the plan didn't come off without a hitch."

"Okay, let's move on to what happened in the isolation room. Earlier today you said the blood was just a hoax to make it look like something terrible had happened—"

"You've got me there, Bennett. Obviously, something terrible *did* happen."

"Yes, but if the intention was to kill Heather, why smear the blood, why hide the body? Why not strangle her and leave her there? You can't ask for a greater scandal at a school than the murder of a student. Why would your ex-partner and his ally—whoever it is— want to conceal it?"

For the first time, Payne looked nervous. "I-I don't know."

"You put forward the idea that the blood in the room was a hoax, and that Heather had been given her ticket to freedom. I might have believed that, if the body had never been found. If, perhaps, it had been moved to a temporary hiding spot until it could be safely removed from the school and—just theorizing here—buried somewhere on the two hundred fifty acres out back."

"What? What are you implying? That *I* had something to do with that poor child's death?"

"I'm not sure who killed her, Dr. Payne. Although I don't see why, if she and Paul Petrucci were working together, he would want to kill her. All I know is, you're the one with the best motive to keep her murder hidden."

Chapter 22

Frank stumbled out of the county morgue Monday morning, gulping in the fresh cold mountain air with the greediness of a drowning man. He knew if he could see his own face it would be as green as a Martian's. He'd never been good at autopsies. As a rookie, he'd humiliated himself by fainting dead away the first time he'd seen an ME crack open a murder victim's ribcage. Over the years, he'd learned to hold nausea at bay by filling his gut with saltines and rubbing his nose with Vicks, but it was often touch-and-go. He was out of practice now—it had been more than three years since he'd had to attend an autopsy. And Heather LeBron's had been particularly bad.

But he'd learned three things. Heather had died on the night she'd been put in the isolation room, although the pathologist couldn't pinpoint the time any closer than a range of six hours. The marks on her neck were not consistent with manual strangulation. Heather's neck had been crushed by the pressure of an arm around her neck in a chokehold. And at the time of her death, Heather LeBron had been menstruating.

Frank got into the patrol car but didn't start the engine. Operating on only a few hours' sleep, he felt the information he'd gathered at the autopsy grind slowly through the gears of his mind.

Despite Payne's explanation, it bothered him that the headmaster had been right on the money about the menstrual blood. Maybe because he had some part in creating the bloody scene. But why would he do it?

And the chokehold grip that had killed Heather—was Lorrie powerful enough to apply that kind of pressure? Lorrie was a strong, solidly built woman, but so was Heather. Or, had whoever killed Heather killed Lorrie as well? Had the killer hidden the bodies in separate locations, and they just hadn't discovered Lorrie's yet? But why? None of it made sense.

He thought of Ray Stulke that night in the Mountainside—the way he had lifted his darts opponent up by the neck, the way he'd boasted of choking the resistance out of one of the students he'd transported to the academy. Ray would have to be interviewed again.

Frank turned the key in the ignition, and the surge of gas to the engine seemed to energize him as well. Meyerson said he planned to spend the morning at the academy with the arson investigators—he would compare notes with the trooper there and plan his next move. As he drove, he radioed the office to check in with Earl.

"Anything to report?" he asked, after the connection had been made.

"Nothing much, except Rollie Fister came over looking for you. But he says it's not urgent—he knows you're busy."

"Okay, hold down the fort. I won't be back until late afternoon."

When Frank arrived at the academy, the school grounds seemed to be crawling with troopers.

Meyerson spotted Frank and started speaking the moment he stepped out of the Trout Run patrol car. "Jason Levine is missing again. Discovered it in the morning head count."

Frank's hand tightened on the car door, frozen in the act of slamming it shut. "What! Payne told me that all the students were accounted for when I arrived at the fire last night."

"They were—as of ten p.m., we have three witnesses that place Levine in his room, with the doors locked. He disappeared sometime between then and this morning at seven."

"Any sign of foul play in his room?" Frank asked.

"None. They found clothes rolled up under the covers to make it look like the bed was occupied. He ran again, but he's not in Keene Valley this time."

"Or someone wanted to make it look like he ran."

Meyerson's eyes narrowed. "What, are you buying into Payne's conspiracy theory? Next thing you'll be telling me the Cubans, the Mafia, and the CIA killed Kennedy."

"Try coming up with an explanation that fits all the facts of this case—you'll sound like a crackpot, too." Frank fell into step beside Meyerson and told him about the autopsy results as they walked toward the administration building. "What did the arson investigators turn up?" he asked after he'd finished.

"Perfectly straightforward. Gasoline spread around those two rear classrooms and ignited."

"Are there cans of gas stored on campus in the garage or toolshed?"

"Not that we could find. The lawnmowers have all been drained for the winter. Gas cans are all empty. Payne doesn't use snowblowers—he makes the kids shovel. It could've been siphoned out of a few of the teachers' cars, so the loss wouldn't be noticed, but that would take time, and the parking lot's right out in the open."

"So that would seem to eliminate the students as suspects, and brings us back to Payne's idea that he's got an enemy on the inside. Have you spoken to Paul Petrucci?"

"I've been waiting for you."

"Let's do it."

<hr>

PAUL PETRUCCI SAT AT the teacher's desk in an empty classroom, staring out the window at the bare black branches of a huge elm creaking in the breeze. He glanced up as Frank and Meyerson entered the room, but their presence didn't seem to hold his interest.

Frank dropped into a student desk in front of him. "How's it going, Paul?"

Paul turned slowly, his face wan and strained. "My student is a suicide. How should it be going?"

"She didn't commit suicide; she was murdered."

"Murdered! What do you mean? I assumed—"

"Heather LeBron was strangled on the night she disappeared from the isolation room," Meyerson said flatly. "We need to verify a few facts." He riffled through some papers. "Let's see, you were not working that night, correct? You say you were home with your wife and children. Can anyone else confirm that?"

Paul looked back and forth from Meyerson to Frank in astonishment. "No, of course not. Why should I need confirmation?"

Meyerson made a brief notation, shuffled his notes, and continued talking. "You've worked here four years, so you were here when the classrooms at the end of the hall on the second floor of the administration building were remodeled?"

"Yes." Paul looked at Frank. "That's where the fire was, right? Did it have something to do with the remodeling?"

Meyerson asked his next question before Frank could answer. "Do you remember what those rooms looked like before they were remodeled?"

Paul opened his mouth to answer, then closed it. His gaze shifted from Meyerson to Frank and back again. "Not really," he said finally. "I never taught in those rooms. I've always used classrooms on the first floor, or in this building."

Impassively, Meyerson made another note. "Was Heather LeBron one of your favorite students?" he said without looking up.

"Favorite? I don't have favorites." Paul tapped a pencil on the desk. "I was concerned about her. She was quite bright, but very troubled."

"So you made special allowances for her?"

"I don't know what you mean."

"Didn't you make a special effort to get Heather included in the camping trip on which Jake Reiger was killed?" Frank asked.

"I asked Jake if she could go—it was no big deal."

"Why did you want her on that trip?" Meyerson spoke without looking up from his notebook.

"You know about Payne's ridiculous point system." Paul pushed back from the desk and stood up. A bookcase full of paperbacks stood against the wall and he began to rearrange them. "In order for Heather to have a part in the class play I was putting on, she had to have thirty points by the day of the auditions. She needed eleven more. Going on the hike was a way to earn more points. She wanted to be in that play so badly. The poor kid had already volunteered for every disgusting job on campus."

Frank remembered some of the chores Lorrie had mentioned the kids could do to earn points—scrub toilets, shovel manure. He wondered if Heather had ever done any jobs in the kitchen, like scour pots or peel potatoes. He made a note to check with the cook.

"Did Heather like Jake Reiger?" Lew asked.

Paul offered a rueful smile. "Heather didn't really like much of anyone, even me. She didn't like herself, so it's hardly surprising."

Frank crossed the room to lean against the radiator next to the bookcase. "Did you have to plead with Reiger to get him to take Heather on this hike, or was he willing?"

Paul shrugged. "I wouldn't say *plead*—"

"But Reiger had worked with MacArthur Payne before. Presumably he supported his methods. You were trying to circumvent the rules, weren't you?" Meyerson pressed.

Paul, who had seemed preoccupied with his own thoughts at the beginning of the interview, now sharpened his focus. He stopped fiddling with the books and looked hard at Frank, then Meyerson. "Why are you making such a big deal about it? I asked him to do me a favor and he agreed."

"Did you ever ask Jake any other favors? Like maybe to borrow money?"

A muddy red flush spread up from Paul's neck to his face. "No, I never asked him for money."

"But you do need money, don't you?" Frank leaned forward confidingly. "I've heard you're having trouble keeping up with the payments on your house."

"Who told you that? Christ, this town is impossible—you might as well walk around with a sign on your back listing all your personal problems." Paul pivoted and walked toward the window. "We had a few money problems but we straightened them out. Everything's fine now," he said with his back turned to them.

"How did you straighten them out?"

Paul whirled around. "We just did! What's this got to do with Heather?"

Frank was not yet ready to reveal Payne's suspicions about Paul and Glen Costello. It was enough that he'd elicited that defensive response. He'd come back to that line after he knew more about Costello.

"Paul, you must've heard by now that there's some speculation Reiger's death wasn't an accident—that someone intentionally put bacon grease on his sleeping bag."

"Of course I know there was a story in that rag, the *Beat*, but surely you don't believe that?"

Frank's answer was a slight arch of the eyebrows.

"You're not saying you think Heather did it? My God, the poor child's dead, and people are still maligning her! Instead of trying to find out who killed her, you're trying to pin crimes on her. Well, I want no part of it. I have nothing more to say to you." He strode toward the door.

"You're not obliged to cooperate with the investigation, Paul," Frank said. "But if you truly care about finding out who killed Heather, I need help in understanding why she was killed."

Paul paused in his angry march. "What makes you think I know anything about why she was killed?"

"Because you knew her, understood her, maybe better than anyone here." Frank had taken the lead in the interview and Meyerson sat back.

Paul ran his hand through his wavy, dark hair. Frank was sure the teenage girls in his class must find their teacher very attractive—the combination of soulful eyes and a buff body would have to be a winner with the under-eighteen set. He tried to imagine those muscular arms around Heather's neck. Certainly Paul was physically strong enough for the deed, but did he have the stomach for it?

"I don't think I really understood her. I just sensed her pain. I wanted to help her. And I failed—it's too late."

"A lot of people failed her, Paul, including me. Finding her killer seems like the least we can do for Heather now."

Paul's eyes were focused on a scuff marking the linoleum floor, but he nodded.

"Would you say that Heather was very suggestible? Would she have gone along with planting that bacon grease if someone offered to get her out of this school in exchange?"

"But why would anyone—"

"One thing at a time. Give me your opinion. Was she desperate enough to get out of here that she would have agreed to such a plan?"

"She claimed she was anxious to leave, but where would she have gone?" Paul paced up and down as he talked. "She wasn't welcome at either of her parents' homes. She wanted someplace to belong. She might have been able to belong here if I could have gotten her involved in that play. She seemed really enthused about it—it's hard to believe that at the same time she was telling me she wanted to do the play, she was scheming with someone else to pull off this sabotage. But . . ." Paul's gaze met Frank's. "She was a little, uh ..."

"Manipulative."

"I'm afraid so."

"Do you know a man named Glen Costello?"

If Paul was startled by Frank's sudden change of tack, he didn't show it. "No."

He answered without nervousness, but the response came quickly. He hadn't paused to consider the question.

"Did Heather ever mention him?"

"No. Who is he?"

Frank shook his head. "All right, Paul, thanks for your time. We may need to speak to you again."

"Wait—that's it?"

Frank and Meyerson stood. "Yes. For now."

Chapter 23

"Why did you back off when Petrucci wouldn't tell you how he solved his money crunch?" Lew demanded when they were alone. "I would have pressured him to reveal his source."

"Petrucci's a smart guy, and he knows his rights—he won't roll right over. If there's really some truth to this idea of Petrucci and Costello working together, then I want some more evidence of the connection before I confront him. Otherwise, he'll start covering his tracks."

Lew's mouth twisted in disapproval. "Maybe. And what was all that about Heather pouring the bacon grease on Reiger? I thought we agreed there was nothing suspicious there?"

Frank shrugged. "That was before this murder. You know, Heather told me she was afraid someone else was going to die, and she thought it might be her. She knew something was going on at this school, but I wasn't patient enough to get her to tell me everything she knew or suspected."

Meyerson huffed in exasperation. "Frank, you sat there in that meeting with me and the rangers and said yourself that the kids on that campout had no opportunity to get bacon grease and wouldn't know what to do with it even if they had."

"If Petrucci was working with Heather, he could've gotten her the grease."

"If they were allies, why did he kill her?"

"She knew too much, she threatened to talk."

"But you said she was fearful from the time of the campout. If she were in on the murder—"

"All right! All right!" Frank rested his head in his hands. "Look, I know none of it makes sense, but I want to keep my mind open to every possibility. I'm not ruling anything out this time."

"Well then, you're never going to solve this case. Because that's our job—to rule out everything that's impossible and examine what's left for the truth. Jake Reiger's death was an accident. Don't let it distract you from what happened to Heather."

EARL WAS HOVERING AROUND the outer office when Frank strode through the door.

"Frank! Can I talk to you for—" The ringing of the phone interrupted Earl. He answered it, then handed the receiver to Frank. "It's Rollie Fister. Wants to tell you about that problem at the library."

Frank accepted the phone with a sigh. Rollie must've been watching the office from across the green to have called the moment he walked through the door.

"Hi, Rollie. What can I do for you?"

"Someone broke into the library and stole some tools yesterday," Rollie announced.

Frank reached for a pen and prepared to take notes. This was more serious than Earl had led him to believe when he'd called in earlier.

"Except that whoever it was broke in again and returned them today."

Frank dropped the pen. "I wouldn't call that stealing, Rollie. Obviously, one of the guys working over there borrowed them."

"I knew you were going to say that! I just knew it!" Rollie's usually good-natured voice cranked up half an octave. "Then why is there pee in the toilet?"

"Huh?"

"The toilet's been used, and all the guys working over here know that the plumbing's not connected yet, so they go over at Malone's. I asked everyone if they borrowed my rechargeable power screwdriver, and they said no."

Frank knew how fussy Rollie was about his tools, so it was hardly surprising that no one owned up to it. "How did they get in? Have the door or windows been tampered with?"

"No," Rollie admitted. "And they were all locked."

"So whoever *broke* in used the key. How many copies of that key are floating around?

"Well, I have one, and there's one up at Stevenson's . . ." Rollie continued to mutter names under his breath as he counted. "I'd say six."

Frank kneaded his eyes. Why did they even bother to lock the door if everyone and his uncle had a key? "Maybe you oughta consider changing the lock, Rollie, and keeping closer tab on the keys. In the meantime, don't leave any valuable tools over there."

"Good idea, Frank. I'll talk it over with the fellas. 'Course, the electrician's coming this week—we gotta let him in . . ." Frank hung up while Rollie was still mulling over his options.

He slumped in his desk chair with his eyes closed trying to arrange the facts of the academy case coherently. He could hear Earl breathing.

"Go on home, Earl. You've been here all day without a break. There's nothing else we can do tonight."

"I know. But I need to talk to you about something." Frank heaved himself up straight but made no effort to look alert. "What?"

Earl gnawed on his lower lip. "Lorrie's kids are missing."

"What!"

Before Frank could get more worked up, Earl continued his story. "Apparently they weren't in school today, and the school secretary assumed they were sick, even though no one called. But then Peg called the school at the end of the day saying she sent them off to the bus stop this morning and wanting to know why they didn't get off the bus this afternoon."

"What time were they at the bus stop?"

"Around eight, Peg says."

"They've been missing since then and you never bothered to tell me?" Frank slammed a file folder across the desk, sending papers scattering.

"Well, it's not like they're kidnapped—I'm pretty sure they're with Lorrie."

Frank narrowed his eyes. "What do you know?"

"I called the Foleys—their kids wait at the same stop as Lorrie's. Ashley says she saw Lorrie's car pulling away from the bus stop right when she and her brother turned the bend in their driveway. At least, she's pretty sure it was Lorrie's car. So I think the kids are with her."

"And that's why you didn't bother to tell me? Haven't I been searching for Lorrie for three days? Now it looks like as of eight this morning, she was alive and kicking. Didn't you think this might be relevant?"

"I didn't find out 'til after four, when the kids didn't show up on the bus. You were busy with the state police."

"You couldn't have brought it up just now?"

"I tried, but Rollie called. Look, Lorrie can't possibly have anything to do with whatever happened to Heather. Lorrie would never hurt anyone. She must've got scared when she saw that blood . . . thought she'd be in trouble. So she went and got the kids this morning and ran off somewhere."

"But where has she been between the time we discovered the bloody isolation room and this morning, when she got the kids?" Frank jabbed a pen in Earl's direction. "Why did she wait until today to take them?"

Earl scrunched his eyebrows down so far they were actually visible below his straggly bangs. "Uh, I don't know—but I'm sure she must've had a good reason. You're just going to scare her off worse if you set the state police after her. Let me take care of this, Frank. She's my family—I'll find her and make her say what's going on."

"Didn't I warn you about this last week? You can't let family loyalties get in the way of your work."

"They won't get in the way. They'll help—you'll see. If I put out the word that Lorrie's not in any trouble, that we're trying to help her, I bet I'll be able to find out where she is."

"You mean someone in your family knows where she is right now?"

"No, I already made some calls. I don't think so. But if I say the right things to the right people, it might filter through. Sometimes people don't even realize all they know—get what I mean?"

He did get it, and as irritating as it was to admit, Earl was probably right. Wherever Lorrie was with those kids, she wasn't driving on the interstate, using credit cards and a cell phone, and making herself easy for the state police to trace. Earl probably could flush her out, but once he did, could he be trusted to bring her forward?

Frank took a deep breath. "Listen to me, Earl. I'll have Meyerson pull the state police back on the search for Lorrie for a few days. But that's all you've got, understand? And if you find her, you share the information with me *immediately*. No screwing around."

"I will. I mean, I won't. I mean, I'll tell you, Frank. I promise."

FRANK WANTED NOTHING more than to go home and eat a TV dinner in solitude. Unfortunately, his freezer, and every other part of his refrigerator, was bare. Malone's held no possibility of respite, not with that Klotz woman and her laptop camped in the back booth. He considered the Trail's End, but some yowling folksinger was scheduled to perform. Cadging a meal from Edwin and Lucy was his best bet.

He pulled into the Iron Eagle Inn's driveway and parked in back. He peered through the window of the kitchen door and saw a woman sitting alone at the big oak table. Not Lucy, but Penny.

He tapped lightly and opened the door. Penny broke into a wide smile when she saw who was there.

"Frank! I could use some company!"

"Hi, Penny. What are you doing here on a weekday?"

"I've taken a leave of absence from my job. Clyde's health is really failing. It's better if I spend an hour or so with him every day planning the library, rather than try to cram so much work in on the weekends."

"I see." But he didn't, really. Penny hadn't had this job very long; something didn't add up.

"Edwin and Lucy are getting some real guests settled. I'm here so often, I just fend for myself." She gestured to a half-eaten plate of food on the table.

"Well, maybe you can fend for me, too." He opened the refrigerator door. "I came looking for something to eat."

Penny joined him in front of the open fridge. "There's roasted chicken, and mushroom risotto, and these gingered beets were fabulous." He watched her slender fingers tapping the plastic containers as she itemized their contents. Her shiny dark hair fell forward and she pushed it behind her ear as she looked up into his eyes and smiled. "Oh, but you don't like veggies, do you Frank?"

"Beets are fine." When he reached into the refrigerator to pull out one of the containers, their hands brushed together. She nudged him playfully with her hip. "No, that's cat food, silly! These are the beets."

"My wife always said I couldn't even find food in the refrigerator." He laughed, but inwardly cringed. Why in the world had he brought up Estelle?

But Penny didn't seem to notice. "You want wine?" she asked as he fixed himself a plate from the assembled leftovers.

"Sure, I could use a drink."

"Rough day?"

He hadn't wanted to talk about Heather LeBron, but something about the concern in Penny's brown eyes and the way she leaned across the table with her chin in her hand made him want to pour out the clutter of conflicting ideas in his mind. He couldn't discuss the details of an open case, but he could get some insights into a young woman's mind.

"You went to boarding school, didn't you?" he asked without preamble.

"Yes. I hated it."

"Did you ever think of running away?"

He knew she must wonder why he was asking her this, but she simply answered the question. "Almost every day. Once I read a book about a girl who ran away and lived with her dog in the wilderness of Alaska. That was very appealing. But running away from a boarding school in Connecticut, I figured I'd be more likely to end up squatting with street people in Hartford. That kept me from taking off. For all that I fancy myself an iconoclast, I'm a weenie at heart."

Frank suspected that's what Heather LeBron was, too. Despite her bravado, her dreadlocks and tattoos, he didn't see her as bold enough to carry out the sabotage of Reiger's sleeping bag and arrange an escape from the school when she had nowhere to go.

"Is this about Heather LeBron?" Penny asked. "Is it true the poor girl was strangled?"

"Yes, the *Beat* got that much right."

"This case matters to you more than most, doesn't it?"

God, he wished she wouldn't look at him like that, with her eyes sort of squinted and her smile so sad. He jumped up to rinse off his plate.

"I feel like maybe I could have prevented her death if I'd been a little more attentive to what was going on over at the academy," he answered from the neutral zone of the sink. "Anyway," he said briskly before she could offer him condolences he didn't want, "tell me what's going on at the library."

Penny seemed to sense that he wanted the distraction. She chatted on about the computers Clyde was letting her order and the collection of Adirondack folklore she hoped to build. "And I want to start a summer reading club for kids—bring them together for book discussions so they see that reading is fun, not a chore." Penny gestured and Frank watched the silky sleeve of her blouse slide back along her slender arm. "This could be so much more than a little place for ladies to check out romance novels. Just yesterday I showed Elinor how to do some research on pain management, so that when she and Clyde see his doctor they can make an informed choice on his treatment." She thumped the table for emphasis. "Information is power, and that's what I see this library as—empowerment for people who are overwhelmed."

"All this is going to take a lot of your energy, Penny. Doesn't leave you much time for your job in the city." Penny looked up at him from under her bangs as she fiddled with her long silver necklace. "I'm thinking of quitting that job and moving back to Trout Run."

"Really? Why?"

"There are people here who need me."

Chapter 24

Meyerson's background check on Glen Costello had turned up precious little information. No arrests, no restraining orders, no traffic violations. He'd been questioned in the heat prostration death of the student at his and Payne's school in Utah, had cooperated with the investigation, and ultimately the death had been ruled an accident. He now owned a school called Vista del Mar on the west coast of Mexico and lived on-site.

The state police had no luck, as yet, in getting through to Costello directly in Mexico, and Meyerson was trying to coordinate assistance from the Mexican authorities. In the meantime, Frank set Earl to digging for information on the man and his new school on the Internet.

Earl had his nose to the screen when Frank came into the office after lunch.

"Turn anything up?"

"I found the Web site for Costello's school. This Vista del Mar is like a boot camp Club Med. The pictures show these kids laughing and playing volleyball on the beach, but the description of the program sounds like the way Payne talks—points, levels, repercussions, limiting inappropriate distractions. Then there's a Web site for this watchdog group called TeenTurnaround. They rate all the schools for troubled teens."

"Really? That's sounds interesting. What do they say about Payne and Costello?" Frank asked.

"Not much good. Here's the ratings." Earl handed Frank a page he'd printed out.

"Well, it's hardly a ringing endorsement, but it doesn't say anything we don't already know about the place," Frank said after scanning the report. "And 'not recommended' isn't their lowest ranking."

"No, they save that for a few places that are full-time punishment, with no education at all. Wait'll you see what the kids who went to all these schools have to say."

"You mean there's stuff on there from alumni?"

"The TeenTurnaround site is linked to this message board where kids and parents who've gone through the boot-camp school experience can chat. That's what I'm reading now."

Earl tilted the screen so that Frank could see, and they scrolled through pages and pages of messages from teenagers, many of them complaining about the treatment they'd received, but a significant minority claiming that the schools had truly helped them. Sniping between the two camps accounted for half the messages.

Frank skimmed along. The messages from the teenagers all sounded like they could have been written by Heather—full of angst and melodrama. But one titled warning from a mother caught his eye.

"I want to warn any parents on this message board who are considering sending their child to one of these schools to DO YOUR HOMEWORK. Visit the school in person, ask to speak to the students, get recommendations from other parents. If I had done that, my son would not have suffered as he did. I was desperate because of his alcohol and drug use and wild behavior. I sent him to the Langley School in Utah based only on a brochure and a telephone conversation with the owner, Glen Costello. I feel that Mr. Costello misrepresented the techniques the school used and pressured me into a decision. My son was there for six months and he is still recovering from the experience. Thankfully, now, he is under a doctor's care. PARENTS, PLEASE BE CAREFUL."

"If I want to find out more about this woman's story, do I have to post a message on this board for everyone to read?" Frank asked Earl.

"No, you can reply off-list directly to her. Just click here."

Frank quickly sent an e-mail introducing himself and asking the mother, who had signed her self simply Greta K., to contact him. "Now I guess we sit and wait to see what happens."

"WHAT ARE YOU DOING to find my son?"

A man in a very expensive suit and a very starched shirt stood before Frank's desk. According to Doris's terrified introduction, he was Morton Levine, Justin's father.

Frank let Levine bluster a while, and studied the man's tie to pass the time. It was a nice shade of blue, with a dark gold pattern. He couldn't even remember the last time he'd worn a tie. This one probably cost more than all the ties he'd ever owned, combined. He sensed Levine winding down and asked a question. "Why was Justin enrolled at the North Country Academy?"

Levine's tanned face contorted in a scowl. "He was expelled from the Collegiate School, one of the finest private schools in Manhattan. Now none of the others will take him, despite the fact that he had some of the highest scores ever recorded on the admission test. I was so pissed at him, I thought the North Country Academy might knock some sense into his head."

"And why was he expelled from Collegiate?"

"Let's just say he was displaying his entrepreneurial spirit in an inappropriate fashion."

"Dealing drugs, in other words."

Morton Levine smiled, revealing perfectly even, very white teeth. "I like you. You seem a little sharper than that state trooper over in Ray Brook. Look, Justin's no angel, but there's no way he was mixed up in what happened to that girl. He's too smart for that."

"I've never known intelligence to exclude a person from criminal endeavors, Mr. Levine. The fact is, Justin ran away the night Heather LeBron disappeared. I was inclined to believe him when he said that was just a coincidence. Now, he disappears again the night her body was discovered. That's stretching coincidence to the breaking point. I'm worried that he's involved, and that his involvement could put him in some danger."

Levine eyed him in a manner that Frank imagined he'd used to assess adversaries across a boardroom table. Frank felt certain that getting this man on his side might help him solve the case, while having him as an opponent would lead to endless roadblocks.

"Look, Mr. Levine. I'm not trying to pin anything on Justin, but it's possible that he knows something about what's going on at the academy, and that scared him into running. The best thing for all of us would be to find him. Let's work together."

Levine nodded slowly. "But I'm not sure how I can help. Justin and I—" He looked away and cleared his throat. "Let's just say we parted on bad terms. He wouldn't come to me for help; too much pride."

"What about his mother?"

"Not in the picture. She's remarried and living in Italy."

"Who else would he turn to?"

"He has an older cousin living in Boston ..." Levine offered hesitantly. Frank could see by the look on his face that this was a long shot, but he took the name anyway.

"And you live in New York City—has Justin always lived there?"

"All his life."

"He ever gone to summer camp?"

"A week of chess camp at Princeton one year."

So Justin Levine, the smart-aleck drug dealer with a privileged New York upbringing, had made his way through the thick, unmarked forest behind the academy all the way to Keene Valley, and then escaped through the woods again a few days later—something didn't add up. He had to have had help.

"Does Justin make friends easily?" Frank asked.

"Like that." Levine snapped his finger. "I keep telling him, with your head for numbers and your schmoozing ability, you could be anything—an investment banker, a portfolio manager. Don't screw it up." He shook his head. "Kids. Whaddaya gonna do?"

Frank offered what he hoped passed for a sympathetic smile. He had a feeling he knew who Justin Levine had last been schmoozing with.

"RAY! CAN I HAVE A WORD with you?"

The big man lumbering across the lawn of the North Country Academy stopped and turned slowly. When he saw who had spoken his jaw jutted forward, but he waited for Frank to catch up with him.

"I don't have much time," Ray said, glancing at his watch. "I gotta be in building three in ten minutes."

"We can walk while we talk," Frank said.

Ray resumed his trek across the grass. A stiff wind blew his thinning hair back. Despite the cold, he wore only a flannel shirt. He flexed his massive hands, and the motion made his powerful biceps strain against the plaid fabric. Frank found it easy to imagine that arm squeezing the life out of Heather

LeBron. It was harder to imagine why. Just typical Ray bullying, gone out of control?

"Let's go over exactly what you were doing between the time you and Lorrie took Heather to the isolation room and the time you discovered the room empty."

"I already told you that," Ray protested.

"Tell me again. I have a bad memory."

Ray hacked his smoker's cough and spit an impressive distance. "We took the girl there and I helped Lorrie get her in. Then Lorrie went back to the cafeteria, and I went to get ready for Group Encounter in building three."

"Just what is it that happens in Group Encounter?"

"It's part of the procedure. A step they have to go through to get to Level Three."

Frank accepted this nonanswer for the moment. "How are you involved in it? I thought your job was transportation and security."

"Well, sometimes security problems come up in Group." Now Ray's smirk seemed positively gleeful. "They try to leave the room, run away from the group. I'm there to make sure they don't get too far."

"I'm sure you're quite effective. Tell me, Ray, what happens if a kid puts up a fight?"

"I could take on two or three at once, no problem."

"You ever put a kid in a headlock?"

"Sure, if I have to. There ain't a kid here who could win a fight against me. They all know that."

"Did Heather LeBron know it?"

Ray's smirk faded. "I never had any kind of fight with her."

"Not even when you were putting her in the isolation room?"

"She put up a struggle against Lorrie. When I stepped in, she piped down."

"Because you hurt her?"

"I didn't hurt her. She took one look at me, she knew there wasn't no point in fighting."

"So, was there any trouble at the Group Encounter?"

"Nah, just some crying and carrying on. Nothing Steve and Randy couldn't handle."

"The Pathfinders run these groups? How come Lorrie wasn't there?" Frank asked.

"Don't know—you'd have to ask her that," Ray answered with a leer, impressed with his own cleverness.

"How well did you know Lorrie before you started working together?"

"I used to hang with her and Chuck when they were married. After they broke up, it was hard. Lorrie'd complain to me about Chuck, Chuck about Lorrie. I got tired of hearin' it from both of them. But working with Lorrie here—she seemed okay. She was really glad to have the job, worked hard at doing everything right. That's why—" Ray trudged forward with his eyes on his work boots.

"What?"

"I've been thinking about it, and I can't make no sense of what happened in that isolation room."

You and me both, Frank thought.

"I don't see why Lorrie would run off, not when she needed this job so bad. Kinda makes me wonder if something happened to her."

Was that a note of concern, of empathy, coming from Ray? He obviously hadn't heard yet about the disappearance of Lorrie's kids, and Frank chose not to tell him just yet. "Was there anyone here who didn't like Lorrie?" Frank asked.

Ray shook his head. "Lorrie was quiet. She kept to herself."

"Let's get back to the night Heather died. After the Group Encounter meeting, what did you do?"

"Escorted the kids back to their dorms, then started my nightly lockup rounds. That's when I discovered the empty isolation room."

"Between the time you left the dorms and the time you got to the isolation room, who saw you?"

"No one." Ray stopped walking and faced Frank with his hands folded across his chest.

"So we only have your word that when you got to the isolation room it was empty and unlocked."

"Why are you trying to pin this on me?" Ray stabbed his finger at Frank's chest. "You been ridin' my ass ever since you took over as police chief. All I hear from you and Clyde Stevenson and Reid Burlingame is 'Why don't you get a job, Ray? Why don't you clean up your act, Ray?' So now I have a job, a job that pays enough for a man to live on, and you're tryin' to take it away from me.

"I've been doing my work here real good—you can ask Dr. Payne. But when you want a fast way to say you solved this killing, I'm the first one you come after. Why don't you look at that wuss Petrucci? He was always comin' on to Heather. Maybe he killed her to keep her quiet about that—sexual mo-lest-tay-shun. Did you ever think of that?"

They had reached building three, a one-story brick rectangle of newer vintage than the other buildings on campus. Ray pulled a ring of keys from his pocket and unlocked the door.

"Do you have keys for all the doors at the academy, Ray?"

"No, I don't have one for the isolation room. It's got a Yale dead bolt. None of these keys are Yales—check it out." He tossed the heavy key ring at Frank, who barely had time to catch it before it hit him in the face. But Ray was right—there were no Yale keys on this ring. Frank handed it back.

"I got work to do, if that's okay with you," Ray said.

Frank let him go without comment. Their conversation had raised more questions than it answered. Ray had no alibi for the time of Heather's murder, but he had no motive either, other than his general attraction to violence. And Ray had touched a nerve. Was he more suspicious of Ray than of Paul Petrucci simply because he didn't like the man? He had accepted Paul's interest in Heather as well intentioned, but first Payne and now Ray seemed to think there was more to it than that.

And with the concern Ray had shown for Lorrie's safety, it was obvious he didn't know where she and her kids were now, or why they were on the lam. Frank stared at the horizon. The view, beautiful even at this bleak time of year, barely registered. He saw instead the faces of Lorrie and Heather, each unhappy in her own way.

FRANK CHECKED HIS WATCH—2:45, almost the end of the school day at High Peaks High School. He had just enough time to get over there and intercept Brad Fister before he got on the school bus.

He watched the stream of young people pouring from the building, all so carefree. Certainly no one escorted them to meals and their classes, recorded their every indiscretion, locked them up at night. Yet were they all that different from the kids at the North Country Academy?

Frank spotted Brad Fister's tall, lanky figure loping toward the bus with his backpack slung over his shoulder.

"Hey, Brad!"

The boy paused and glanced around. A friend pointed out Frank, and Brad looked at him quizzically. Frank waved him over to the patrol car.

"I need to talk to you for a minute," Frank said. When Brad looked anxiously at the bus, Frank put his hand on the boy's shoulder. "I'll drive you home. Get in."

Looking as if Frank had offered him a ride on the wagon transporting prisoners to the guillotine, Brad got in the car. Frank leaned back in the driver's seat, making no attempt to start the ignition. They sat in tense silence until Brad could bear it no more. "What's this about?"

"I think you know."

Brad began twisting the straps of his backpack. "No, I don't."

The silence dragged on. Frank watched the last bus pull away. A few teachers trickled out of the building and walked toward their cars, peering curiously at the patrol car.

"It's that trespassing thing at the North Country Academy, isn't it? Why are we in trouble for that? We didn't do anything." A frown tugged at Brad's handsome face and Frank could see the shadow of the six- year-old Brad, accused of tracking mud in the house.

"Describe to me exactly what you do out there," Frank said.

Brad took a first pass at answering—they parked, they built a little fire to keep warm, they talked and ate some chips.

Frank sat expectantly, waiting for the story to continue.

"We listen to music on a little boom box."

Still Frank waited. Brad was a zookeeper flipping fish to a hungry seal. How many would it take until he swam away satisfied?

"We smoked some cigarettes."

"We had a few beers ... once."

Frank stretched out his legs and checked his watch.

"I hafta get home—I'm due to work at the hardware store this afternoon," Brad said.

"Well, then, you better tell me what I need to know, and we can get going."

"What? I told you everything!"

Frank smiled and waved to Mrs. Carlstadt, the English teacher, as she walked by, then softly started to whistle "The Old Ship of Zion."

"This isn't fair! I don't know what more you want me to say!"

Ah, fair—life was rarely fair, but Brad was too young to know that. Frank turned his head and smiled. "You do know, Brad, because you're a smart kid. You don't want to rat on a friend, and that's admirable—but all bets are off now, son." Frank sat up straight and leaned in dose to Brad. "Because someone's been killed. Heather LeBron is never going to get her driver's license, never going to wear a cap and gown, never going to kiss a boy again."

Brad's hands gripped his backpack, his knuckles stretching the skin to white. "It has nothing to do with her," he whispered.

"Tell me about it anyway."

Chapter 25

Once the cork had been popped, information flowed out of Brad Fister like cheap champagne. According to Trout Run's favorite son, Justin Levine had mastered getting out of his locked room shortly after he arrived at the academy, but the knowledge didn't do him any good because he couldn't figure out a way to get back to civilization. Then one night he noticed the campfire that Brad and his friends made at the edge of the campus, slipped out of his room, and introduced himself. He filled the kids with stories of how he was being horribly abused, and they hatched a plot to help him run away. The night of Heather's murder, Brad met Justin at the big rock by the stream and drove him to Keene Valley, then gave him a sleeping bag and showed him a place to hide out until the Trailways bus came the next day.

Up to that point, Brad told the story without hesitation. Then, he turned away from Frank and stared out the passenger side window at the now empty school parking lot.

"But Justin got picked up by the police in Keene Valley," Frank prompted gently. "So you tried again?"

Brad nodded. "Justin was totally prepared—we already discussed a back-up plan if the first plan failed. Security was tighter after what happened, so Justin couldn't use his old trick to get out of the dorm. For the new plan to work, he said we needed to create a distraction."

"The fire," Frank said. "But how did Justin set it? I thought all the kids were in their rooms when it broke out."

"They were." Justin's words came so softly, Frank was certain that he'd spoken only because he saw his lips move.

"You set the fire?"

"Yes." Brad's upper lip trembled. "I guess you have to arrest me now, huh?"

Man, this kid had a ways to go before he could run with the academy crowd. "Look, Brad, the most important thing is that we find out who killed Heather and what happened to Justin and Lorrie. If you help me by telling me everything you know—and I mean *everything*—I'm sure we can work out some restitution plan for the fire."

Brad looked like he'd been promised a puppy if would agree to take the trash out every night. "Really? You mean I won't have to go to prison?"

"I doubt it. Just tell me what happened."

The faucet turned on again. "You know, the academy students all wear khaki pants and green T-shirts or sweatshirts with the school logo. Justin gave me his sweatshirt the first time he tried to escape. When we got picked up, no one noticed he was only wearing a T- shirt. So, the afternoon of the second escape, I slipped onto campus wearing the school sweatshirt and a pair of khakis. Some new students had arrived that day, and if anyone on the staff stopped me, I was supposed to say I was one of them. But no one did stop me, and I hid behind the Dumpsters until dark."

Brad told that part of the story eagerly, proud of his cleverness. But when he got to the part where he'd actually committed a crime, he spoke more reluctantly. "Then I slipped up to the back of the administration building, went in and poured the gas around those classrooms and lit it. Pretty soon, the alarm went off and everyone started running around. After they checked Justin's dorm, all the teachers left that building except Oliver Greffe. Then I used my grandfather's tools to dismantle the lock on Justin's window and spring him. We put it back together so no one would be able to figure out how he escaped."

"So that's why the tools were missing from the library," Frank said. "Now, where's Justin?"

Brad's clear blue eyes opened wide. "That's the problem. As I was putting the last screw in, we heard someone coming across the lawn. We each ran in different directions, and I never got to give Justin the stuff that he needed."

"What stuff?"

"A little cash, some food and water, a sleeping bag, warm clothes, and a map. The plan was for him to camp in the woods until one of us could find a way to drive him to Albany to get on the train. Going back to Keene Valley was too risky."

"But without supplies ..."

Justin gnawed on his thumbnail. "I don't see how he could make it. He doesn't know anything about the backwoods. I've gone back to the big rock at night several times, looking for some sign of Justin, but there's never anything there."

———————— ❦ ————————

FRANK SAT IN THE STORE with a cooling cup of coffee, mulling over Brad's information.

"My kids have been kidnapped and you're just sitting here on your fat ass!"

He pushed aside his half-eaten sticky bun and looked with displeasure into the contorted face of Chuck Betz. Frank prided himself on keeping his weight at 170 pounds—there was nothing fat about his ass—but he willed himself to be patient.

"We're doing all we can to find Lorrie and the kids, Chuck. We feel they must be nearby. Without money or credit cards, she can't have gone far. If you would be less antagonistic, she might come back willingly."

"Oh, so now it's my fault that that crazy drug addict has stolen my kids!" Chuck threw some bills at a frowning Rita Sobol behind the cash register and grabbed the pack of Marlboros she offered in return. There was no denying the fact that, on paper, Chuck was the victim here—a custodial parent whose kids had been taken by the noncustodial parent. But the truth encompassed a few more shades of gray. Chuck was a jerk and a bully, Lorrie was a frightened woman who loved her kids, and the biggest danger to everyone lay in not knowing why she was on the run. Was it simply another round in their endlessly troubled custody dispute, or did it have something to do with the murder of Heather LeBron?

"When was the last time you spoke to Lorrie, Chuck?" Frank patted the chair next to him.

"You were there—at her great-grandmother's birthday party."

"And you didn't say anything more to her after that night that might have provoked her into taking the kids?"

Chuck tore open his cigarettes. "There you go again—blaming me."

"I'm sorry," Frank said with exaggerated courtesy. " 'Provoked' was a poor choice of words. I meant, did the two of you have any further arguments that might have given Lorrie the notion to take the kids?"

"Nothing," Chuck said.

"What about your mother? Did Lorrie have an encounter with her in the days between the party and the morning she took the kids?"

"None of us heard from her after she dropped the kids off the night of Grandma Gert's party. So far as we knew, she was planning on picking them up again on Tuesday, her regular visitation day. And then she pulls this stunt at the bus stop."

Frank didn't like the sound of what he was hearing. If Chuck could be trusted—an admittedly big if—Lorrie had no personal reason to run. Which meant her disappearance had to be linked to Heather's death.

When Frank got back to the office, he dropped into the chair in front of earl's desk. "We need to talk about Lorrie."

Earl lifted his head slowly from the paperwork he'd been completing. "What about her?"

"She and the kids are still missing, or had you forgotten?" Frank's vow to be understanding went out the window. If Earl was going to play at being clueless, he was going to come down on him hard.

"I've been doing all I can, but I can't find her. No one's heard from her."

"So you say."

Earl sat up straight and thrust his chin out. "That's not fair! I'm trying hard. I told you I'd share any information I turned up, but there hasn't been anything yet. I can't help that."

"How stupid do you think I am?" Frank's voice rose with Earl's show of defiance. "Lorrie doesn't have any credit cards; her bank account's been frozen; there's an APB out on her car. Now, you tell me how she's surviving unless someone in your family—maybe even you—is supporting her."

Earl jumped out of his seat. "Are you calling me a liar?"

Frank narrowed his eyes. Was Earl out-and-out lying? Maybe not, but he was probably being willfully blind to what his relatives were up to.

"I gave you your chance. I'm putting the state police back on the search for Lorrie."

Earl had crossed the room to the office door. "Well, go ahead and see where that gets you. Nowhere!" He slammed the door behind him.

Frank yanked it back open and yelled after him, "You'll never get into the police academy if you're charged with harboring a fugitive!"

Chapter 26

"I want to talk to you about Petrucci." Meyerson started talking before he was all the way into Frank's office. "I've caught him in major lie."

The papers Frank had been reading slipped from his hand. "Really?"

"On the night of Heather LeBron's murder, he was not home all night with the wife and kiddies. He bought gas at the Stop'N'Buy at ten p.m."

Frank raised his eyebrows. The Stop'N'Buy market and gas station was at least seven miles from Petrucci's home, and directly on the way to the North Country Academy. "What does he say about it?"

"Said he forgot that he ran out to get gas that night."

"But why would he make a special trip to fill up at night when he'd be passing right by there in the morning on the way to work?"

"Exactly. He says he did it because he's always running late in the morning."

"Could be, but with the price of gas these days, he'd be burning up money making that round trip. On the other hand, if he murdered Heather, why stop and buy gas afterward and place himself right in the vicinity of the crime?"

"Murderers are often stupid, you know that. Besides, if he didn't have enough gas to get home, he would have no choice but to stop there. According to the receipt at the gas station, he bought seventeen gallons, and he drives an old Honda Civic. They don't hold much—he must've been riding on empty."

Frank sat staring at his folded hands. He still had a hard time accepting Petrucci as the killer. The guy probably didn't let his kids watch Wile E. Coyote clobber Roadrunner—could he really press the life out of a girl in the crook of his arm? But the evidence was starting to pile up against him. Grudgingly, he shared some more information with Meyerson.

"I caught Petrucci in another lie today, too. Earl happened to mention that two summers ago, he and Paul both worked part-time for the contractor who remodeled those classrooms. Paul helped build those walls—he certainly knew about the crawl space and the little access door."

Frank and Meyerson's eyes met for a long moment. Then Lew spoke.

"I think with the evidence we have of Petrucci's special interest in Heather, and knowing he was near the academy that night and was familiar with the layout of the classroom, we have enough to get a search warrant for his house and his bank account. I want to find out where that cash to make his back mortgage payments came from."

"You asked him again?"

"He and the wife refused to say. Both acted very defensive."

"That doesn't mean much. Katie would act defensive if you asked her where she buys her shoes. Any word from Mexico on Glen Costello?"

"Zilch, and I'm tired of waiting. I want to move forward with this search."

Frank nodded slowly. How could someone so politically correct, so adamantly nonviolent, strangle a young woman?

"Well, see what it turns up," Frank told Meyerson reluctantly.

"If he has nothing to hide, he has nothing to fear."

Frank's mouth twitched in an ironic smile. Ah, the favorite defense of the police state. "If you know what's good for you, Lew, you won't say that to Katie Petrucci when you're tearing apart her house."

———◉———

FRANK STOOD IN FRONT of his closet, contemplating the meager selection of shirts that were neither flannel nor part of his khaki uniform. A white button-down was surely too formal for the dinner party at Edwin and Lucy's. The blue was okay, but when he took it out he realized the cuffs were beginning to fray. A bold stripe caught his eye—the shirt Caroline had given him for his birthday. Why had he never worn it? Oh, it had that silly designer thing embroidered on the chest. She'd paid twenty extra dollars to ruin a perfectly nice shirt. But Edwin's was about the only place in the Adirondacks where he could show his face in that shirt, so he might as well get some wear out of it.

He had his right arm halfway in the sleeve when he hesitated. Would this shirt make it seem like he was trying to impress the ladies? Trying to outdo Bob? Would it make him look like some pathetic Lothario attempting to look young?

Oh, for God's sake—it was a shirt! A perfectly ordinary blue-and-yellow-striped shirt, that happened to have one of those doo-hickeys. He put it on and left the house without looking in the mirror.

On the way over to the inn, he wondered about this friend of Penny's. He didn't recall ever seeing another young librarian at the community college. But since she'd been invited for him, she probably wasn't young. Just a nice middle-aged lady that Penny, in her effusive way, had befriended.

The parking area was full of cars when he arrived. He recognized Bob's and Penny's; he must be the last to arrive. Instinctively, he headed for the back door and entered through the kitchen without knocking, as he always did.

Edwin was engrossed in stirring something and barely looked up. "Hey, Frank—why are you coming in through the servants' entrance? You're an official guest tonight. The others are in the parlor."

"Sorry I'm late," Frank said, making no move to leave the safety of the kitchen.

"You're not late, they all just—" Edwin looked up. "Wow! Nice shirt. Is it new?"

Frank froze. Did the damn thing still have a size label stuck to it? But a quick glance revealed nothing wrong. "No, I've had it for a while."

"Well, you look very handsome. Come on, carry these spinach and cheese puffs for me."

Frank followed Edwin down the hall to the parlor, where he could hear Penny, Bob, and Lucy laughing over the latest snafu in the library renovation.

"Oh, here's Frank," Lucy cried, taking the plate of hors d'oeuvres from him. "Edwin has put him to work. Frank, I'd like you to meet Janice Caldwell. Janice, Frank Bennett."

A thin woman with very short hair rose from the chair next to the fireplace and shook his hand. He smiled and said hello, but her expression barely changed as she sat back down again. She wore navy slacks and a beige sweater. No makeup, no jewelry, no perfume. Janice looked like all she had done to prepare for this evening was scrub her face with a rough washcloth.

Penny played flamingo to her friend's sparrow. A bright coral sweater set off her dark hair and eyes, and an armful of bracelets jangled as she gestured, telling a story.

"Listen to this, Frank." Penny waved him into the chair next to her. "I'm telling them what Clyde said when he found out how much paper towel dispensers for the restrooms were going to set him back."

Frank sat back and watched Penny hold court over the room. Bob sat on an ottoman to her left, leaning forward as if he was afraid he might miss a word. Edwin broke into her story periodically to offer some affectionate teasing. Lucy sat back, beaming at her handiwork in arranging this event, while Janice sat in the corner with her hands folded in her lap.

He felt bad for her—it was hard when everyone else in the group already knew one another and she knew only Penny. Frank moved closer to Janice.

"So, Janice, you're a librarian at the county college?

"No."

"I thought Lucy said you and Penny used to work together."

"I teach there."

"Oh—what subject?"

"Sociology." Janice continued to sit with her hands folded, staring straight ahead.

"I've taken a few sociology courses along the way. I'm a cop, you know."

"Yes."

Geez, this was an uphill slog! He'd interrogated murder suspects who were chattier than Janice. Now he regretted having moved into this corner beside her. He looked longingly at the other four, who were still happily yakking it up. But he could hardly get up and move away from the woman.

Frank tried to get back into the main conversation, but he'd lost the thread. Bob was talking about something going on at the church. ". . . just amazing the progress Matthew Portman is making in his organ lessons with Oliver. I sit in the corner and listen to them sometimes. They don't know I'm there."

"Ah, you go undercover," Penny said. "When I stopped in to listen, I couldn't keep from applauding. Oliver gave me a very disapproving look. I thought it was okay to come in because Matthew's brother Ernie was there."

"Yes, Ernie's the exception. He often comes with Matthew," Bob said. "It's sweet—they're very devoted to each other. Oliver says he used to be the same way when he was young."

"Well, I'll keep my nose to the grindstone in the library and wait for Matthew to make his debut on Thanksgiving Festival Sunday," Penny said. "I'll even make these heathens, Edwin and Lucy, come with me." Frank's ears perked up. Penny was planning on spending Thanksgiving in Trout Run?

Before he could inquire, a faint tinging came from the direction of the kitchen.

"The oven timer." Edwin clapped his hands. "Dinner is served. Frank, show Janice into the dining room. Bob, you'll be next to Lucy; Penny, next to me."

Frank rose and ushered Janice before him. It was going to be a long evening.

FRANK SLIPPED INTO the back of the church on Sunday morning after all the worshippers had left. He knew Augie never locked up until after the fellowship hour, afraid he might miss a slice of Bundt cake or a pecan sandie. Frank hadn't felt up to listening to a sermon from Bob Rush, but he liked being in the sanctuary so soon after the service had ended. The faith of those who'd just occupied the pews seemed to still fill the place. Maybe some of it would rub off on him.

Although no music rang through the church, the sanctuary was not utterly quiet. As Frank stood looking down the main aisle toward the chancel, he heard the unmistakable sound of soft crying. At the far right side of the church, he discovered a hunched figure in the back pew. At the sound of his footsteps, the head rose and Frank found himself looking into the swollen, red eyes of Katie Petrucci.

"I'm sorry to disturb you, Katie."

He expected her to lash out at him, but instead she lowered her head onto the back of the pew in front of her and began crying with no pretense of self-control.

Frank shifted his feet awkwardly. Nothing unnerved him more than a crying woman, especially one whose crying could, even remotely, be attributed to him. Frank was quite sure that Katie must be here in the aftermath of her house being searched, although he wouldn't have pegged her as one to petition the Lord in times of trouble.

Gingerly, he sat down next to her and patted her hand. "Is there anything I can do?"

Her voice was thick and choked with tears, "Try to get my husband out of jail."

Jail? Meyerson had arrested Paul Petrucci? What in God's name had the troopers turned up in the search? It must have been big if they had acted without even consulting with him. "I'm sorry, Katie. I honestly didn't know they arrested Paul, although I did know they planned to get a search warrant."

She lifted her head and clawed away some strands of hair that had slipped from her ponytail. "I don't even know what the police found, but they must have found something. Now they think he killed Heather. That can't be true, but he acted so strange when they took him away. He didn't deny it; he didn't resist. Paul just told me to call this lawyer in New York that I've never heard of. And where are we going to get the money for that?"

The thought of money triggered another spasm of anguish and she cried louder, flinging her head back until she began to choke on her own tears. "The money," she said, mopping her face with her sleeve. "Where did he get that money to pay what we owed on the mortgage? He wouldn't tell me. We should have just let them foreclose. I told him we could start over somewhere else."

Frank felt a pang of guilt. He was sure that in a rational mood, Katie wouldn't be talking like this to a cop. But if she was willing to tell him more about that money, he wouldn't pass up the opportunity.

"How much money was it, Katie?"

"Five thousand dollars. We fell six months behind on the mortgage, and we worked out a payment plan with the bank. But it seemed that every month, something came up to prevent us from paying the extra money we owed. Deirdre got sick, the car broke down, the solar panels malfunctioned, and we needed more firewood and propane. And Paul felt it was all his fault, but it wasn't. We agreed to make the investment."

"What investment?"

"In Nutri-Green. It's a start-up company developing a highly nutritious source of vegetable protein that can be farmed even in the most arid climates.

It has the potential to end world hunger, but of course the agribusiness conglomerates want to suppress it."

Frank brought Katie back to the matter at hand. "So you invested more than you could afford in this company and lost your shirts?"

"No! We thought there would be a payback by now, but with any start-up you can't expect everything to go according to plan. We took a risk and we miscalculated. I still believe in Nutri-Green, but it looks like we won't see a return on our investment for a while yet. Paul wanted to bail out and cut our losses, but I didn't. I said I didn't care if we lost the house, but Paul did. And now I'm afraid he did something crazy to get the money to keep it."

Like kill Heather LeBron for a lousy $5,000 bucks to keep that shack they called home? Frank couldn't believe that of Paul Petrucci. Did his own wife think it was true?

Katie seemed to read his mind. "He couldn't have killed Heather. Paul won't even kill mice. But that money didn't just fall out of the sky; he's keeping something from me." Katie's face crumpled and she let out a howl of anguish that made Frank flinch.

"He's been getting phone calls that he ends when I come into the room. He goes out at night with some flimsy excuse." Katie focused her teary eyes on Frank. "I think he's seeing another woman."

After making some vague assurances that he would look into Paul's arrest, Frank slipped away from Katie and went back to the office. As soon as he reached his desk, he was on the phone to Meyerson. Not finding him at the office, he tracked him down at home.

"What did you find at the Petruccis' house?"

"What makes you think we found something?" Meyerson replied in his most maddening manner.

"Because you arrested Paul Petrucci! You didn't have enough to arrest him before the search. What happened?"

"We found a key to the isolation room in his possession."

"What! He had the missing key ring that was last seen with Lorrie?"

"No. We found a single Yale key on a ring with a tag marked 'room 211.' That's the number of the isolation room. We tried the key and it fits. This proves Petrucci had access to Heather in that room."

Meyerson's news shocked Frank. He had to admit, evidence was starting to pile up against Paul. "What did Petrucci say about it?"

"We found the key in an empty flowerpot on the kitchen windowsill. Petrucci claimed he mislaid it over a year ago. Apparently, the isolation room used to be the darkroom for his photography club during the previous administration."

"That's easy enough to check, and it makes sense."

"It may well be true," Meyerson's voice held an edge of irritation. "It doesn't change the fact that the key gave him access to that room."

Frank refused to debate the issue. "Did you find anything else?"

"We found transactions in his bank account that show he's been receiving one-thousand-dollar cash installments every week to ten days for the past two months."

"Who's it from?"

"We don't know yet. As I said, it's cash. We took his computer to search the e-mail. We're checking his phone records."

"That's it? No direct connection to Heather or Glen Costello?"

"We'll find it. It's there, believe me."

But he didn't believe Meyerson, and he didn't like the man's blithe self-confidence. Most of all, he didn't like that Meyerson had barged in and arrested Petrucci without so much as a "what do you think?" directed to him.

"I don't see the big rush," Frank said. "The man's not a flight risk. I like to have my ducks in a row before I make an arrest."

"The ducks are all there—lining them up won't take long. And I feel better knowing Heather LeBron's killer is somewhere where I can keep an eye on him." Meyerson's voice was taking on that testy edge it got whenever his judgment was challenged.

"I don't see how you can be so sure Petrucci's our man. There are an awful lot of loose ends here. How does this fit in with Jake Reiger's death? What about Justin Levine and Lorrie Betz? I found out some information about them today that leads me to believe—"

"Well, maybe that's your problem," Meyerson snapped. "You're always being led—led by the nose. It's time for you to accept the facts of this case, and stop screwing around with every harebrained theory anyone throws in your path. Reiger's death was an accident. Levine ran away and will turn up when he needs money. Lorrie Betz is on the lam from her husband. Paul Petrucci is the only person with motive, means, and opportunity to commit this crime. He's our man. End of story."

Frank heard a click and stared dumbfounded at the phone. The bastard had hung up on him! He felt a white-hot ball of fury rising inside his chest. But as fast as it flared up, it sputtered out. Maybe Lew was right. Maybe he was so afraid now of overlooking something that he couldn't keep his focus. Was he really letting every unexplained fluke of human behavior distract him from the solid facts of the case? Was he refusing to accept the possibility of any coincidences and trying to connect dots that weren't even part of the puzzle?

Once he had been a cop utterly confident in his gut instincts. Now he was a kid with one quarter waffling in a shop full of candy. What the hell had happened to him? Of course he knew the answer to that—Ricky Balsam. The career-ending case in Kansas City when his gut had led him so far astray that he'd let a killer walk free. Was he so terrified of doing the wrong thing now, that he couldn't do anything at all? That must be what Lew thought. He couldn't bear to stand by and watch Frank foul up another case, so he'd stepped in and taken action.

Frank leaned back in his chair. His mind had been churning so much since he'd walked into the office that he hadn't even noticed the familiar objects that surrounded him. Stuck to the front of his darkened computer screen was a yellow Post-it note covered in Earl's loopy scrawl. "Frank—check your e-mail."

He moved the mouse and the screen leapt to life. Clicking on the e-mail icon, he saw a mailbox full of routine items from various law enforcement agencies, most of which had been languishing for days. But near the top of the list was a message with an unfamiliar return address. The subject line: Call me about Glen Costello.

Within minutes Frank was on the line with Greta Karsten, the mother who had posted the warning on the TeenTurnaround message board.

"What can you tell me about Glen Costello and the Langley Wilderness School, Mrs. Karsten?"

"They nearly destroyed my son there."

Although her words were combative, Greta Karsten sounded not the least bit hysterical. "I've compiled documented evidence of their abuses," she continued, in the tone of a congressional witness on C-SPAN. "They employed techniques of mind control used by tyrants like Jim Jones and Kim Il Jung to break down the kids' personalities and make them totally subservient to Costello and his partner, MacArthur Payne. Anyone who resisted, as my son did, was punished further. The only way to end the abuse was to capitulate to the mind control. Luckily I rescued my son before he died. Others weren't so lucky."

Frank had expected her to talk about the physical hardships imposed by the school, and her words caught him off-guard. "Do you mean the boy who died of heatstroke?"

"No, his death was an accident. Maybe it could've been prevented, maybe not. I'm talking about Tristan Renfew. He committed suicide after being locked in an isolation room for twenty-four hours with the tapes playing."

"Tapes? What tapes?"

"The mind control tapes. They played the same message over and over again. The kids were made to recite the precepts of the Langley School hundreds of times. If they stumbled over a word, they had to start all over again. They had to recite it perfectly the prescribed number of times, or they couldn't get out of the room. Probably you think that doesn't sound so bad—not like getting beaten or physically tortured. But believe me, the damage is far worse. A healthy young person can recover from bodily wounds. But what this did to young minds can't be undone. My son will never be the same. And it killed Tristan Renfew."

"How did he commit suicide?"

"He ran across the room and rammed his head into the concrete wall. Repeatedly. They found him dead of bleeding in the brain the next morning."

"I read about the scandal the other boy's death caused. Why wasn't Tristan's suicide ever mentioned in those articles?"

"It was hushed up. They claimed the child slipped and fell. Even the parents insisted that's what happened. I called them myself and told them that my son knew what really happened, but they refused to believe me."

"How does your son know that Tristan's death was definitely suicide?"

"He was in the isolation room next to Tristan's. He heard the running, the thump of the impact, the scream. He called for help, but no one came."

Frank felt light-headed with the horror of what he was hearing. "But if there was even a remote possibility that this is what happened to their son, why wouldn't Tristan's parents want to verify the truth?"

"I think they felt too guilty. The shock of knowing they sent their son there to meet such a horrible death was too much for them to bear, so they had to deny it. I can understand that. When I realized what I'd done to my son by shipping him off to the Langley School, I felt like committing suicide myself.

"I tried to bring out what happened, but without the parents' cooperation there wasn't much I could do. And my son was in such a fragile emotional state, I couldn't put him through telling that terrible story again and again. I had to do what was best for him. So I try to warn parents off by posting on the different Internet discussion groups. It's not much, but I hope I've saved a few kids."

"I think you did the right thing, Mrs. Karsten. But I'd like to talk to Tristan Renfew's parents myself. Do you know where I can find them?"

"Unfortunately, I do. They both died in a car accident about two years ago. They're buried somewhere in Connecticut."

"Is there any other family?"

"All I know is that Tristan had a brother he called Juice."

"Juice?"

"It was a nickname. That's all I know."

Chapter 27

Frank entered MacArthur Payne's office without introduction or greeting. "Tristan Renfew."

Payne's eyes widened slightly but he showed no other reaction. "What of him?"

"He committed suicide in an isolation room when you and Costello ran the Langley Wilderness School, didn't he?"

"He slipped and fell. The coroner ruled an accidental death."

"That's not what Greta Karsten says."

"Surely you're not listening to that hysterical fool. Her son couldn't succeed in our program, and now she's put herself on a mission to destroy other children's chance for recovery."

Couldn't succeed? Is that what dying in Payne's care constituted—a lack of success? A comeback to such an enormously arrogant remark was beyond Frank.

Payne kept talking. "Even if Tristan's death were a suicide, what has that got to do with Heather? Her injuries most certainly were not self-inflicted—she was murdered by Paul Petrucci. I don't see how dredging up this business about Tristan helps your case against him."

Frank wanted to say that he wasn't looking to build a case against Petrucci, he was looking for the truth. But he didn't feel too firmly seated on this high horse. Maybe this was just another distraction, another blind alley he felt compelled to stumble down. But he wanted to know about this mind-control business. Maybe that's why Heather had been so distraught about the prospect of spending time in the isolation room.

"I'd like to know more about these tapes that Tristan was forced to listen to. Did Heather have to listen to them, too?"

"You've seen our isolation room, Bennett—it's not wired for sound. The tapes at Langley were Glen Costello's preferred technique. I never cared for them. When I established the North Country Academy, I discontinued their use."

"Why, because they drove kids crazy?"

"No, because I didn't think they were the most effective route to lasting, organic change."

Frank looked at the photos of smiling kids and their parents on Payne's wall. Were they smiling because they'd been programmed to smile? As he scanned the montage of photos, one jumped out at him: Steve Vreeland standing between two beaming adults who were obviously his parents. There was a kid whose change had been lasting.

"Steve Vreeland must have been a student at Langley at the same time as Tristan Renfew. Did they know each other?"

"The school was small enough that all the students knew each other. But Steve was well on his way to recovery. He and Tristan were at different levels."

Frank knew what that meant. Steve would have been at the level where he had power over Tristan. "I'd like to talk to Steve. Where can I find him?"

Payne's face hardened. "That won't be possible. The state police have made an arrest in Heather's murder. The case is closed. I can't have my staff disturbed any further—we have to get back to our routine."

ROLLIE FISTER CORNERED Frank in the plumbing department of Venable's Hardware as he searched for an elbow joint. Frank had been tactfully avoiding the older man since his grandson's involvement in the academy fire had been revealed, knowing how ashamed he was that Brad had to go before the county magistrate to face charges of criminal mischief.

"Frank, there's something I need to talk to you about."

"Don't worry, Rollie. I fully intend to come to Brad's hearing and recommend that the boy just receive community service."

Rollie looked muddled. "That's nice of you. I think they oughta lock him in the pokey for a few days, myself. No, what I wanted to tell you is, there's still someone gettin' into the library. Yesterday morning I went in there and found a small sack of groceries."

Frank stopped rooting through the pipe-fittings. "What kind of groceries?"

"Little stuff—some applesauce cups, crackers, a package of American cheese slices."

The kind of snacks a person on the run could use. "You sure it didn't belong to one of the workers?"

"Well, I didn't call them all, but no one had worked the day before, because we're waiting on the electrician and he didn't come."

"Did you ever change the lock over there?"

Rollie hung his head. "After we found out it was Brad who borrowed the tools, we figured there was no need . . ." Rollie turned to look at some browsing customers. "Maybe it's not important."

"I think it might be important," Frank said. "After all, Justin Levine is still missing. He might be crashing there."

"I thought of that. But Brad returned the library key, and his parents have been riding herd on him. I don't think he could sneak out to meet that kid."

The way Rollie said "that kid" he could have substituted "that terrorist." Frank knew that Justin Levine was being portrayed around town as the evil urban delinquent who'd led the innocent Trout Run kids astray. But Brad had displayed plenty of devious ingenuity of his own. Frank nodded toward the key-copying machine near the checkout counter. "Brad could have made a copy of his key and given it to Justin as part of the escape plan."

Rollie looked as if he were about to protest, then caught himself. The boy's recent behavior had obviously undermined his confidence.

"I guess you're right. You want me to ask Brad?"

"No, don't say a word about talking to me or about noticing that someone's been in the building. I'm going to keep an eye on the library for the next few nights and we'll see who turns up."

When Frank returned to the office, Earl was at his desk typing. He continued pounding the keys as Frank passed him. Things had been tense between them since the blowup over Lorrie. Frank refused to apologize; he saw himself as wholly in the right on this one. Still, he found the silence in the office oppressive. He pulled a folded newspaper out from under his arm. "I've got today's *Beat*—I wonder what bullshit Dawn Klotz is printing about us today."

Earl said nothing, but a brief sideways glance told Frank that he'd caught his assistant's attention.

"Let's see," Frank read the front page headlines aloud, " 'Mayor Tells Gov—Come Up with the Dough'; 'Freak Accident Kills Six in Bronx.' Oh, here it is, in a box at the bottom of the page: 'Cover-Up Continues at Tough-Love School (see page 7).' "

Frank braced himself for aggravation and flipped open the paper. There was the headline again with Dawn Klotz's byline. He continued to read to Earl, who had dropped his pretense of typing.

Although state and local police claim to be investigating the horrific murder of 15-year-old Heather LeBron at the North Country Academy, so far their efforts have produced more questions than answers.

"Well, she got that right," Frank commented, then continued to read.

Despite egregious violations of safety and education regulations, the North Country Academy continues to operate under the protection of local authorities eager to preserve the jobs the school provides at any cost...

"Egregious—there's that word again," Earl said. Pleased that he had engaged Earl, Frank lowered the paper. "Was that one of the words in your vocabulary book?"

"No, don't you remember? It was in that article from the Utah paper about MacArthur Payne's other school, the one that closed."

"You're right. Must be a popular word to describe these schools." He found his place in the article to continue reading, then he let the newspaper drop to his desk.

"Where is that article from the Utah *Guardian*—do we still have it?"

Earl shuffled some papers and came up with the article that he'd printed from the Internet. Frank scanned the lead paragraph until he found the sentence, "Battling charges of egregious safety violations, the Langley Wilderness School defended its controversial disciplinary practices." Then his eyes moved up the page to the byline. "By Dawn Trefedi."

He looked at Earl. "Would you say Dawn is a very common woman's name?"

"Not really. I've never known anyone with that name until that reporter showed up."

"So what are the odds that two different reporters named Dawn wrote critical articles about two tough-love schools owned by MacArthur Payne, in which they both used the word *egregious?*"

Earl's brow furrowed. "So you think Payne's right? Someone really is out to close down his schools? Why would this Dawn want to do that?"

"I don't know, but I'm going to find out."

———————— ◉ ————————

FRANK STRODE DOWN THE main aisle at Malone's toward the back booth where Dawn Klotz hunched over her computer. "Well, if it isn't Mrs. Trefedi!"

Her head snapped up. "Why did you call me that?"

"Because it's your name. Or was your name, two years ago when you wrote these articles."

Dawn glanced at the Utah *Guardian* pages that Frank clutched. He saw a flicker of nervousness cross her face, but she regained her composure quickly. "So? I got divorced. What interest is that to you?"

"Your marital woes—none whatsoever. Your journalistic pursuit of MacArthur Payne, on the other hand, interests me quite a bit."

"I happened to work for the Utah *Guardian* when his school there was responsible for a student's death. Now I work for the *Beat,* and Payne has opened a new school in New York where people are dying. I was a natural to cover the story."

"You sure you didn't follow Payne out here for the express purpose of finding a scandal at his school?"

"Don't be ridiculous. I've been at the *Beat* for eighteen months. Check my personnel records."

"So when the news editor of the *Beat* returns the message I left for him, he's going to tell me that he assigned you to this story because of your past experience?"

Dawn slid toward the edge of the blue vinyl booth. "Uh ... yes."

Frank extended one long leg to block her exit. "Only if you're able to get to him before he gets to me, I think. Otherwise, I bet he'll tell me that you came to him with the idea for the story. Reporters can do that, right?"

"You seem to think you know quite a bit about journalism, Chief Bennett. I won't attempt to change your preconceived notions."

"How did you—or your editor—find out about Jake Reiger's death to begin with? The *Beat* doesn't have a High Peaks bureau chief, does it?"

"We have a research assistant whose job it is to scan local papers looking for interesting stories that we can investigate further."

"And a camper being attacked by a bear is the sort of thing this research assistant would flag for follow-up? I don't think so."

"Black bear attacks are very unusual—your ranger friend said so."

"You knew Jake Reiger when you were in Utah, didn't you? You must have interviewed him for your story about the hiker's death at Langley Wilderness School."

"I interviewed him by phone—I never met the man."

"Maybe Jake was providing you with some inside information on MacArthur Payne's latest educational venture," Frank persisted. "Maybe that's why he died."

Dawn shut her laptop with a snap. "It's just a coincidence that a person I once interviewed happened to be the victim in this case. The real issue—which you seem to be blind to—is the terrible abuses that go on in these schools."

"Cops don't believe in coincidence."

"You should." Dawn clambered over Frank's leg and exited the booth. "There was a big article about it in the Sunday *New York Times Magazine* a while back. People assign mystical or sinister meaning to coincidences because they don't understand the mathematical principles of probability." With a toss of her hair, she marched toward the door of the diner.

"I don't think your showing up in Trout Run has anything to do with advanced mathematics, Ms. Klotz," Frank called after her.

———— ◉ ————

IT HAD TAKEN FRANK quite a while to unearth the tiny clip-on book light Caroline had given him for Father's Day years ago so that he could read in bed without disturbing Estelle. Now that he slept alone every night, he didn't need it. He could stay awake with the lights on as late as he wished—small consolation for his loneliness. But the book light was coming in handy on this late-night vigil at the library.

Rather than watch the building from outside, which would have been impossible to do unseen, he had very casually walked in the front door of the Store and bought something, then exited through the back door and slipped around the backs of the other buildings on the green until he came to the back door of the library. He used Rollie's key to let himself in, and sat on the risers where Penny planned to have her children's story hour, reading by the tiny glow of the battery-operated light as he waited for Justin Levine to appear.

He had finished *Jane Eyre* during one of the restless nights he'd lain awake worrying about Heather. Tonight he was starting a biography of Alexander Hamilton, and more than once his chin had hit his chest and the book had slipped from his hands.

He had read the same paragraph on Hamilton's monetary theory three times when a soft click registered deep in his cop's subconscious and jolted him into instant alertness. The doorknob rattled and the back door opened with a creak. Frank clicked off the book light and let his eyes adjust to the dim illumination provided by the moonlight slanting through the front window. The back hallway, where the intruder would enter, was utterly black.

Frank heard footsteps and a rustling sound, then a slight clunk as the intruder set something down. He had his hand on his flashlight, ready to shine its powerful beam into the hallway.

Then he smelled something, and knew exactly what to expect.

Chapter 28

The shriek that cut through the night when Frank flicked on his flashlight must have been heard in Albany.

"Penny! What the hell are you doing here at this hour?" The familiar floral scent had tipped Frank off to whom he would find in the hall when he turned on the light, but he was still shocked to see Penny standing there with two plastic bags from the Stop'N'Buy at her feet.

Penny's right hand clutched her chest and her left reached out to the doorframe to steady herself. She hadn't recovered the power of speech after her initial scream, when the sound of another key scraping in the lock made them both look toward the door. Penny's eyes widened in panic as she looked from the door to Frank and back again. Frank moved to pull her into the room where he stood, to protect her from whomever was about to come through that door.

But she shoved him away with surprising strength. "Don't come in!" she shouted. "Run! Run!"

Frank staggered backward, nearly losing his balance. It took him a moment to comprehend that Penny had been calling out a warning to whomever was outside. Now he headed purposefully to the door, while Penny clung to his arm to hold him back.

He tried to shake her off, but she was tall enough to put up a good struggle.

"For God's sake, Penny, what's gotten into you? Who's out there?"

Frank finally reached the door and jerked it open. He shone his flashlight into the clutter of construction debris behind the library. The snow had been trampled by the passing of many work boots into a lumpy gray mess of ice and slush that made it impossible to discern fresh footprints. The intruder might have run behind the buildings toward the Store, or might have gone in the other direction, toward the road. But Justin Levine didn't have a car, and he could hardly set off marching down the road in plain sight, so Frank chose to follow the path behind the buildings. He swung his flashlight from side to side, illuminating garbage cans and propane tanks and flattened cardboard boxes. A movement made him pivot to the right, only to meet the glowing eyes of a hefty raccoon eating the remains of a sub sandwich.

He rotated the light again, and heard a slight whimper from behind a tower of plastic milk crates at Malone's kitchen entrance. Another animal? He stepped closer and this time heard an unmistakably human voice.

"Mommy!"

Frank knocked the milk crates aside with a clatter. Lorrie Betz huddled on the ground, clutching her two children in her arms.

FRANK SAT THE KIDS down in the library and let them have at the snacks in Penny's bags. The emergence of juice boxes and Cheese Nips quickly quieted their sobs. The two women were not as easily consoled.

Lorrie leaned against the wall glumly staring into space, while Penny paced, periodically raking her fingers through her hair, which somehow did not disturb its sleek lines.

"Will someone please tell me what the hell is going on here?" Frank asked.

Apparently, Lorrie didn't feel this question was directed at her and continued to contemplate the unpainted walls in sullen resignation. Penny leaped into the breach.

"Frank, you can't tell anyone that you've seen Lorrie and the children."

She had chosen exactly the wrong approach. "Don't tell me what I can and can't do, Penny. Lorrie is wanted for questioning as a witness in a murder investigation, and she's taken these kids in violation of her custody agreement."

Penny recoiled as if she'd been slapped. He hadn't meant to sound so harsh, but what the hell was she doing in the middle of Lorrie's mess? He wouldn't have thought the two women even knew each other, and here she was acting like Lorrie's bodyguard.

Penny went over and put her arm around Lorrie and the two kids scampered into the group hug, shooting filthy looks at him as they went. They formed the kind of heartrending tableau of innocent victims newsmagazines put on their covers to boost circulation. He was losing this battle before the first shot had been fired.

He started the process of regaining the upper hand. "Lorrie, where have you been since the night of November twelfth?"

"I've been at the old Luhan place."

Frank knew she was lying. The house, set back in the woods at the end of Beaver Dam Road and deserted since elderly Mrs. Luhan had been carted off to a nursing home, had been one of the first places the state police searched when they realized Lorrie was missing.

"The state police checked there, Lorrie. You weren't there on November twelfth or thirteenth."

"No, I mean I've been there since the fourteenth. It was a good place to stay with the kids, since the furniture was still in there. And it was close enough that I could walk down here and pick up the food Penny left for me. It was too risky for her to drive out there to bring it to me. Everyone knows her little sports car." Frank tried to picture the end of Beaver Dam Road. When he drove down these twisting country lanes, he was often surprised at where he popped out at the other end. There must be a path that led from the back of the Luhan property down into the valley where the village sat. But it would be a steep walk back up, especially with two tired kids.

"How long did you plan on keeping this up?"

Penny and Lorrie exchanged a glance. Lorrie shrugged but remained silent.

Clearly Penny was the brains of this operation and had been hatching some plan to relocate Lorrie. He'd pry that out of her later. The right thing to do now would be to take Lorrie directly to state police headquarters for questioning in the murder investigation. But Lew was so determined that the case was solved that he probably wouldn't bother to interrogate her properly. And if Lorrie told them something that didn't support their case against Petrucci, would Meyerson even bother to record it as evidence? No, there was no big rush to get Lorrie to the Ray Brook Barracks.

"Tell me what happened the night of Heather LeBron's death."

"Wait!" Penny laid her hand on Lorrie's arm. "She should have a lawyer. Weren't you going to tell her that?"

"She's not under arrest. She's not even a suspect." Frank glared at Penny. "I simply need to know what she knows about that night."

"He's right. I knew this would never work out." Lorrie looked mournfully at Penny. "You may as well take the kids over to their grandparents' house." Her Charlie Brown-like fatalism would have been almost funny if the stakes weren't so high.

Penny shook Lorrie's slumped shoulders. "No! You can't just give in."

Frank felt truly exasperated with Penny now. Here was Lorrie trying to do the right thing, and Penny wanted to talk her out of it. "Listen," he began, winding up to a lecture.

But Lorrie spared him the effort. "Give me your cell phone," she said flatly.

When Penny complied, Lorrie handed it to Frank. "Call Chuck's folks and tell them the kids are on their way."

"I still don't think you should talk to the police without a lawyer," Penny said as Frank ended his call to the Betzes.

"She has nothing to fear," Frank said. "Haven't you heard? Paul Petrucci's been arrested for the murder."

"Paul? Paul didn't kill her!" For the first time that night, Lorrie's mask of exhausted defeat slipped and her eyes lit with animation.

"You know who did?" Frank asked.

"No, of course not. But it sure wasn't Paul."

———————●———————

BACK AT THE OFFICE, Frank had brewed a pot of coffee and sat sharing it with Lorrie. The buzzing fluorescent tube over their heads emitted the only light in downtown Trout Run.

"Start from the moment Heather knocked over her milk at dinner and tell me everything that happened that night," Frank said.

Lorrie swirled her coffee around and around with a plastic stirrer. "I didn't actually see her spill the milk, but all the other kids said it wasn't an accident. I didn't want to send her to isolation—I just wanted a nice quiet night. But the other kids kept insisting it was done on purpose, and that was the kind of shit Heather liked to pull. I had no choice but to send her to isolation. It would've looked funny if I hadn't." Lorrie stopped and bit her lip. "Oh, God—I shouldn't speak ill of the dead. I can't believe she's dead! And maybe she wouldn't be if I hadn't—"

Frank knew all about remorse and second-guessing when it came to Heather LeBron. He patted Lorrie's hand. "It wasn't your fault. Tell me what happened next."

"She freaked when I told her I was sending her to isolation. Started screaming and kicking, so I had to get Ray to help me take her."

"Did Ray hurt her?"

"Nah—he picked her up under one arm and started carrying her across the dining room. Kids started laughing, so Heather settled down and he let her walk the rest of the way."

Poor Heather, hauled off like a squealing piglet. Another humiliation to add to her list of injustices. "What's so terrible about the isolation room, Lorrie? Do you know why she hated going there so much?"

"Beats me." Lorrie chewed her swizzle stick flat. "I wouldn't mind a few hours of total peace and quiet. I could sleep, even on that cold, hard floor."

"Was there anything she was forced to listen to in there? Tapes playing with a motivational message?"

Lorrie cocked her head. "Tapes? No, what made you ask that?"

Frank moved on. "So you got her there—then what?"

"I took her shoes and her belt. Searched her pockets. She didn't have anything in them."

"You're sure?"

"Absolutely. I reached in and pulled them inside out myself. She put up a fight again when we tried to shut the door. Ray had to push her inside, then slam the door fast."

"Who locked it?"

"I did. I turned the key until I heard the lock click, then I tried the door-knob just to be sure." Lorrie paused and twined the swizzle stick between her fingers. Frank watched as she wove it up and under each finger, then pulled it out and started over. The silence stretched to a full minute.

"And then?"

Lorrie looked at him, her eyes full of hopeless despair. "You don't know what it's like. He's always watching me, just waiting for me to fuck up."

"Payne?"

Lorrie snorted. "Dr. Payne likes me. I'm talkin' about Chuck."

"What's Chuck got to do with what went down at the academy?"

Lorrie took a gulp of her coffee. "I was supposed to work until midnight. Except I met this guy a few weeks ago. He's really nice and he wanted to take me out someplace special for my birthday. On my days off, Chuck's always watching me, or he gets his buddies to do it. He always knows if I have a date, and he starts calling me a whore and threatening to tell the judge that I sleep around and create an unsafe home life for the kids.

"So I figured if there was a way I could meet this guy on a night when Chuck thought I was working, then I could see him and maybe—" She blushed a furious red.

Frank wasn't interested in the details of Lorrie's sex life. "So did you arrange to leave work early to meet this fellow? Did Payne know that?"

"No, Dr. Payne doesn't approve of last-minute schedule changes. I already had to ask for time off when Tiffany got sick—I didn't want to do it again. So I got, uh, a friend to cover for me."

"What friend?"

Lorrie's face hardened. "I'm not telling you that. He was only trying to help me—I'm not going to screw up his job for him. I won't do it." She folded her arms across her chest.

Frank decided to let this pass and return to it later; he didn't want to antagonize Lorrie this early in the interview.

"All right, so you left the academy at what time to meet your date?"

After a moment's surprise, Lorrie leaned back in her chair and crossed her legs. "I left at nine. I had parked my car out on the road behind some trees so the guard wouldn't see me leave. I drove to Willsboro and Gary and I had dinner there."

"Very clever. And you spent the night at his place, which is why you weren't at home when the state police checked after the isolation room was discovered empty and full of blood."

Lorrie nodded sheepishly. "In the morning I drove on up to Plattsburgh to do some shopping. It was my day off and I had planned to do that. It wasn't until I was driving home that I heard the news on the radio that the police were looking for Heather and me, and that they suspected foul play. I panicked!

"I went back to Gary's house and talked it over with him. He thought I should call the police and tell them exactly what happened." Lorrie's eyes welled with tears. "He just didn't understand. It would mean I'd lose my job, and if I lost my job, I'd lose the kids. We argued about it. I could see he thought I was crazy. I spent that night there, still thinking about what I should do. The next morning I went and got the kids from the bus stop and took them to the Luhan place. We've been there ever since."

Frank looked at Lorrie's forlorn but defiant face. Her life had been one long string of bad decisions and this was just one more. This Gary might actually be a man with his head screwed on straight, but Lorrie had probably blown her chances with him. Certainly the job was lost, and her actions had doomed her chances of regaining custody of the kids. Great-grandma Gert was right—Lorrie did go through life with a dark cloud over her head.

"How did Penny get involved?" Frank asked. It wasn't pertinent to the case, but he sure wanted to know.

"Me and the kids ran into her in the green one day. She started talking to them about the new library and everything she wanted to do for kids there. She had some books in her bag and pulled them out and started reading to Tiffany and Charley right there on a park bench. She was so nice." Lorrie said it in such a wondering tone of voice that it was obvious she wasn't used to Penny's brand of spontaneous kindness.

"She gave me her cell phone number because she said she wanted to test out some ideas for her children's programs on real kids. So when I needed someone to get me food, I called her. I knew if I called anyone in my family, somehow the word would get out. They'd want me to turn myself in. Penny understood what it's like to have a husband who scares you."

Frank got up to pour himself another cup of coffee; his throat felt awfully dry. Of course it made sense that Penny would feel solidarity with Lorrie. Lorrie's scheme was crazy, but she'd already crossed the Rubicon of taking the kids by the time she'd called Penny. He could see how Penny would feel she had no choice but to abet Lorrie in her quest to keep the kids.

"Did Chuck ever hit you?"

Lorrie scowled. "About a million times when we lived together, but not anymore. I was too stupid to take pictures of how I looked after he beat me so I'd have evidence. At the time I was so ashamed—I thought it was all my fault. Now it's my word against his."

"But you say he follows you and watches you—that's considered stalking. You should file for a restraining order. Fight fire with fire."

Lorrie looked at him with new interest. "You really think I could fight him, even now?"

A part of Frank regretted having spoken. He'd be the one called upon to enforce that restraining order, and it wasn't easy to keep menacing men away from the women in their lives. But Lorrie needed some shred of hope. How could he not give it to her? "I think you need some good legal advice. You should talk to Reid Burlingame."

"I can't afford a lawyer," Lorrie said, disconsolate again.

"Reid offers flexible terms. Norm Feeney paid him for straightening out his mother's will with two hundred gallons of maple syrup."

For the first time ever, Frank saw Lorrie's lips touched by a smile. She really wasn't a bad-looking woman. While he had her in this mellower mood, he quickly moved forward.

"What made you say Paul Petrucci couldn't possibly be the killer?"

"Paul was so nice to Heather, and all the kids, really. I would sit in on his classes as the Pathfinder in charge of discipline, and I'd get so interested in what he was teaching that I'd forget about watching the kids. I wish I could've had a teacher like him when I was in high school. I might not have dropped out."

"Was Paul the friend who covered for you the night of Heather's murder?"

Instantly suspicion returned to her face. "He wasn't even working that night."

"He didn't drop by the school for any reason on Thursday?"

"Of course not. He—" Lorrie clamped her lips together, and Frank could see it had dawned on her that she was narrowing the field of prospects. Again, he backed away from that line of questioning.

"Lorrie, how well did you know Jake Reiger?"

The same blotchy flush that had appeared when she talked about her tryst with Gary spread up her neck and across her cheeks. Apparently Jake had been quite the ladies' man.

"Lorrie, you know there's been some suspicion that Jake's sleeping bag was sabotaged with bacon grease, that the bear attack wasn't accidental. At first I didn't believe that, but I'm starting to feel that it might be true. And if I knew who was behind the attack on Jake, I'd know who killed Heather."

Lorrie scrutinized him for a long, silent moment. He couldn't blame her for not trusting him—her track record with men didn't inspire confidence. Finally, she began to speak.

"Jake said he wasn't sure he believed in Dr. Payne's methods anymore. He thought this school would be better than the one out in Utah because Dr. Payne's partner wasn't involved. But once he got here and started working, he had doubts. I know he was looking around for another job when he died."

"Did Payne know that Jake was unhappy?"

Lorrie shook her head. "I don't think so. Dr. Payne doesn't like suggestions from the staff. You're either with him or against him. Jake knew to keep his mouth shut until he found another job."

"What about other people on the staff—Randy, Paul, Steve—did they know?"

Lorrie shook her head. "I don't think so. He made me promise to keep it secret. I think the only reason he told me was—" Her voice trailed off and she twisted a strand of hair, which was much blonder at the end than at the top. "He, he was trying to be honest. To let me know that it couldn't last, that he wouldn't be around that long."

"Do you know more about why Jake was dissatisfied at the academy?"

Lorrie shrugged. "Just that it was too much like the other place."

"Did he ever mention a boy named Tristan Renfew, who died at the school in Utah?"

"No."

Lorrie didn't seem to be holding back. Frank supposed she and Jake hadn't spent their time together having long philosophical discussions. "Jake knew Steve Vreeland from his days at the Langley Wilderness School, right? How did they get along?"

Lorrie rolled her eyes. "That Steve creeps me out. Jake made fun of him behind his back, talking in that robot kind of voice."

This time Lorrie didn't realize that she'd once again narrowed the field of friends who could've helped her on the night of Heather's death. It wasn't Paul or Steve. Ray had been a friend of Chuck's when Lorrie had been married, so Frank couldn't imagine Lorrie would call on him for help in setting up her romantic getaway. Of the men on duty that night, that left only Randy Ohlandt and Oliver Greffe. And Frank was pretty sure which of them a woman in need would turn to.

Frank rose abruptly. "It's almost morning. I'd better take you home so you can get some rest. The state police will want to talk to you today. And I suggest you call Reid and let him help you out with this custody thing."

Lorrie looked amazed. "My friend's not in trouble?"

Frank smiled. "Don't worry about it."

Chapter 29

Sleep was impossible after all the coffee he'd drunk with Lorrie. The information he'd gleaned from her and Dawn Klotz filled him with the urge to get working, but he had to at least wait for the sun to rise. He went home to shower and make a plan, but was back in the office as the first rosy glimmer touched the eastern sky. Before the sun had cleared the top of the Verona Range, Earl walked in.

"You're at work early," Frank said.

"I heard you found Lorrie last night. I heard it was Penny who was helping her."

Ah, he'd forgotten that this meant he owed Earl an apology after all.

"Earl, I—"

Earl held up his hand. "It's okay, Frank. No one could've known that it was Penny."

Frank stared at his desk. Nothing was more unnerving than Earl's generosity of spirit. "You gave me your word that you weren't helping her. I should have trusted you."

Earl shrugged. "To tell you the truth, I suspected some of my own family. I thought one of them was lying to me. Anyway, she's found now. What's going to happen to her and the kids?"

"I guess that's up to Chuck—he could persuade the DA not to press charges."

"Ha! That'll never happen."

"I told Lorrie to talk to Reid. Maybe he can broker a deal."

Earl shoved his hands in his pockets, making his pants droop even more than they normally did on his skinny hips. "So, what are *you* doing here so early?"

Frank brought him up to speed on all he had learned from Lorrie and Dawn. Reviewing it for Earl helped him see the case more clearly in his own mind. "Here's my goal," he concluded. "To know these three things by the end of the day." He ticked them off on his fingers. "If Oliver Greffe let Heather out of the isolation room. Why Dawn Klotz is covering this story. And what the hell happened to Justin Levine."

Earl glanced at his watch. "Are you going out to the academy now?"

"No. I've had it with MacArthur Payne. Every time I talk to that man, he skews the facts to fit some new theory. And Meyerson's got his mind made up already, no matter what new information comes in. I'm doing everything from here."

Earl looked dubious.

"I can talk to Oliver when he comes to town later today to give Matthew his organ lesson. And now that I know a little more about Justin Levine, I have a hunch who might be helping him hide out."

"Who?"

Frank shook his head. "It's just a guess. I'll let you know if it pans out. In the meantime, I have a project for you."

Earl seemed eager to have something to distract him from his concern for his cousin. "What can I do?"

"I want you to find out everything you can on the public record on Dawn Klotz: where she was born, went to school, when she got married, when she divorced, her work record." Frank nodded toward the computer. "You can start that now. I'm going to wait until it gets a little later and call Reiger's sister again. I want to see if she knows the names of the women Reiger was involved with."

"Why?"

"Think, Earl. Reiger was a good-looking guy who couldn't stay away from the ladies. He left Utah because of trouble with a woman. Dawn Klotz is a beautiful woman who divorced her husband when she lived in Utah. She reported on a story at the school where Reiger worked. What are the chances that they knew each other?"

Earl grinned. "In the biblical sense?"

"That's what I'm thinking."

Frank left Earl poring over vital statistics Web sites and drove out of town toward High Peaks High School. A quick stop at the school office told him the girl he needed to speak to would be leaving homeroom for biology in a few minutes.

Frank stood in the hall and waited until the ringing of the bell unleashed a torrent of teenagers. Rachel Portman, with her cascade of dark wavy hair, was easy to spot.

"Good morning, Rachel. Can I speak with you for a minute?"

Alarm clouded her pretty, dark eyes. "What is it? Did something happen to Ernie? Was my dad in an accident?"

Frank laid a reassuring hand on her shoulder. "Nothing to worry about, your family are all fine." He steered her gently toward an empty classroom. "I wanted to talk to you a bit about Justin Levine."

He felt her shoulder stiffen. Rachel slipped away from him and stood with her back to the frame of the classroom door, unwilling to step across the threshold.

"I believe you were with the group who met Justin a few times on the big rock by the creek at the academy?"

"So? We haven't been there since ... since what happened with Brad and the fire."

"No, I know the group hasn't been there. But you've been there, haven't you?"

Rachel moved her right foot backward, but there was no place further for her to edge away from Frank. "How would I get there? I'm only sixteen—I don't have my license yet."

"No, you don't get that piece of paper until you turn seventeen, but you know how to drive, don't you?" Rachel bowed her head over the stack of books she clutched in her arms.

"It's been a bother for your dad, being the only one in the family who can drive, hasn't it? He can probably hardly wait until you pass your test. He only agreed to let Matthew take organ lessons because he could walk up to church for them on his own, right? But when the weather's cold, I bet you help your brother out, don't you, and give him a lift to the end of your road. I bet your father even says it's okay, as long as you don't drive on the main road."

Rachel looked up from under the screen of her long hair. "How do you know that?" she whispered.

Frank conjured up an inscrutable smile that he hoped conveyed he possessed all sorts of mysterious knowledge.

Somewhere in Doris's endless prattle she had imparted the fact that Matthew got a ride as far as Route 12, but that his father couldn't be bothered to drive him all the way to the church for his lessons. "So it didn't take that much more nerve to borrow your dad's truck at night and use it to get out to the North Country Academy. After all, it wasn't just for a joyride, it was to help a friend."

She lifted her head and met his eyes now, and there was a flash of fierce defiance there. "Brad chickened out. When that teacher at the academy saw them the night of the fire, Brad was afraid to go back. So I took the camping gear to the big rock."

He had Rachel pegged, all right. She was the nurturer, the caregiver. With Mrs. Portman dead, she had to take care of her brothers and sister, but he suspected she'd taken on that role even before the crash that killed her mother. Rachel had never known a time when she hadn't had to take care of Ernie. From her first awareness, he had always been there demanding attention, protection, help. Giving those things was second nature to this girl. No wonder Justin Levine, with his dark good looks and insinuating charm, had been able to persuade her to come to his rescue.

"Justin was in danger at the North Country Academy and no one would help him—not his dad, not the state police . . ." Rachel squared her shoulders, gathering some courage now. "Not you."

Well, he deserved that, didn't he? Rachel's bold response said it all—he was the man who'd let Heather LeBron die; he could hardly be trusted to protect Justin Levine or anyone else at the school, for that matter.

"Look, Rachel—I need to figure out what's going on at the North Country Academy. But whether the school stays open or not, I think everyone will agree it's not the right place for Justin. His dad is worried about him; he wants him home safe."

"Really?"

He could see how much she wanted to believe this. It wouldn't take much more to persuade her.

"I think his dad regrets ever sending him to the academy. He was just mad at Justin about the trouble he got into at his other school."

"What trouble?"

"Justin was expelled for selling drugs. He never mentioned that?" Rachel was kind and generous, but she wasn't a fool. Frank waited and watched as the information he delivered perked through her mind. He could see doubt beginning to creep into her eyes.

"It's getting colder every day, Rachel. You know Justin can't camp out all winter. He wants you to drive him to Albany so he can hop a train, doesn't he?"

She flinched as his question struck home. The class change over, the halls of the school were silent now. "I'd have to drive on the Northway," she whispered.

"Where your mom had the accident. I think we both know that's not a good idea." Frank took Rachel's elbow and guided her to a chair in the empty classroom. "Take me to the spot where you meet Justin tonight, Rachel. I'm going to need you to help me persuade him to come in."

Rachel searched his eyes, looking for some assurance that she could trust him. "You promise you're not going to arrest him or send him back to the academy?"

"I promise. It will all work out for the best."

Frank returned to the office and found Earl waiting with an eager-beaver expression that must mean he'd accomplished all that had been asked of him.

"Whaddaya have?"

"Dawn Klotz, born 1975 in Westerville, Ohio," Earl read from his notes. Graduated high school in 1993; graduated New York University with a BS in communications in 1997. Worked for one year on the Sanborn, Ohio, *Sentinel,* then moved to Utah where she worked on the Utah *Guardian* from January '99 to February 2004. Got married to Anthony Trefedi in 2000; got divorced in December 2003. Went to work for the New York *Beat* in March 2004 and has been there ever since."

"Great work, Earl." Frank held out his hand. "Let me see your notes."

Frank studied the time line. "The timing of her divorce would be about right for her getting involved with Jake Reiger. The story about the Langley School was breaking early in the last year of her marriage."

Earl cleared his throat. "I, uh, went ahead and called Reiger's sister in Utah. I remembered last time you talked to her it was before she left for work. You were gone so long, I thought you would miss her."

Frank glanced at his watch. "You're right, I would have. What did she say?"

"She said she didn't remember Jake dating a woman named Dawn, Trefedi or Klotz, but she says he had so many girlfriends she couldn't keep them all straight. She seemed to recall that there was one who was some kind of writer, but she thought she was a poet, not a reporter."

Frank frowned and continued to scan Earl's notes, willing something pertinent to jump out at him. "What is this word?" he asked, pointing to a scrawl that looked like "Uzbekistan."

"University." Earl pointed to the line above. "She graduated New York University in 1997."

"New York University—NYU. Isn't that where Katie and Paul Petrucci went to school?"

"Yep. Katie got a full scholarship, and that's where she met Paul."

"How old are they, exactly?"

Earl immediately began the elaborate process that allowed him to calculate the age of anyone in town. "Let's see... Katie started out in the same grade as my cousin Donald's older sister, but she skipped a grade, so that would make her..." Earl ticked off the years on his fingers. "Thirty, or maybe thirty-one."

"And Paul must be about the same age if they met in school," Frank said. "Dawn Klotz was born in '75. That makes her thirty. Could she and Paul have known each other in college?"

Earl shrugged. "Isn't NYU, like, a really big place?"

"It is. But Dawn was just telling me that I ought to believe more in coincidence. Maybe she's right."

<hr />

FRANK PULLED KATIE Petrucci out of the class she was teaching at the nursery school she ran in the Presbyterian Church. Drained of the passion she brought to every task, Katie looked drawn and haggard.

"Did Paul get his undergrad degree at NYU as well as his master's?"

Too exhausted to inquire why he wanted to know, Katie simply nodded. "Yes, in communications."

Dawn Klotz's major. Now he was getting somewhere. "What year did Paul graduate?"

"Ninety-seven. Why?"

"Dawn Klotz graduated NYU with a degree in communications in ninety-seven. They must have known each other. Do you remember her from those days?"

Katie frowned. "I seem to recall there was girl named Dawn in his study group." Her eyes got a faraway look as she tried to conjure up the memory. "They used to meet in Bobst Library. There was Paul, and Ted, Carlos, Jillian, and—yes, it is her! She had brown hair then and she was about thirty pounds heavier, but it's the same woman. Dawn Klotz was the fifth person in the group." Katie's eyes opened wide and she took a step back from Frank. "What does this—? She's, she's the woman he's been sneaking out to see, isn't she? Oh my God, I can't believe that's what he wants—"

Frank touched her arm lightly. "I suspect it's not quite what you think."

Chapter 30

F rank heard the music from out on the flagstone walk, even though the church doors were closed against the freezing air. He slipped inside the narthex and sat in an usher's chair, listening. There was no need to interrupt Matthew's lesson.

"That was fantastic," Oliver said. "You've obviously been practicing."

"You think T.J. would like it?"

"I think T.J. would love it."

"What about that spot at measure 157?"

Frank waited impatiently while they discussed some technicality involving key changes. Now that the music had ended, he was eager to start talking to Oliver. Finally Matthew emerged from the sanctuary with his backpack over his shoulder. The narthex was so dimly lit, he didn't even notice Frank in the shadows and went out the door.

Frank popped his head around the corner and saw Oliver with his head bowed over some sheet music. He spoke softly to himself. The notes on the page were obviously as riveting to him as the words of a best-selling novel. Estelle had read music in just that way.

Frank knew he would startle Oliver, but there was some advantage in that. "Working on something for your own repertoire?"

The sheet music flew out of his hands. "Geez, you scared me! How long have you been standing there?"

"I caught the end of your lesson with Matthew. I didn't want to interrupt."

Oliver bent to retrieve the music. "Then you heard how good he's getting. It's a pleasure to teach him."

"Takes your mind off what's going on at the academy, huh?"

Oliver's head emerged from under the organ bench. "What *is* going on, Frank? Yesterday evening they announced that Paul Petrucci had been arrested for Heather's murder. That can't be right, can it?"

"You tell me."

"What's that supposed to mean?"

"What happened when you went to let Heather out of the isolation room that Thursday?"

Oliver seemed to stop breathing for a moment. His eyes flicked back and forth, glancing at the door, the pulpit, everywhere but Frank's face. "Lorrie's back?" he whispered.

"Yes. So why don't you tell me everything from the point when you agreed to help Lorrie meet her boyfriend."

Oliver turned his back on Frank and began picking out a tune with one hand on the organ keyboard. "I felt so bad for Lorrie. She worked hard and never had a chance to enjoy herself. When she was on duty in the rec room in the boys' dorm, we would talk a little. She used to sing in the church choir here when she was a kid. She has a nice alto voice."

Frank almost smiled. Typical that Oliver would be won over by a woman's ability to carry a tune. Some men let their dicks lead them astray; Oliver let his ear do it.

Oliver continued the story of how he'd agreed to cover for Lorrie while she slipped away early that night. His version matched hers in every detail.

"Heather being in the isolation room kind of complicated things, but Lorrie gave me the key and I figured I could let her out at ten without anyone noticing." Oliver's long slender fingers endlessly picked out the same ten or fifteen notes as he spoke. "If Heather said anything about it, we figured no one would believe her since she had such a reputation for lying.

"But when I got there, the door was ajar. I opened it up, saw the blood, saw the room was empty." Oliver shuddered but his fingers kept playing. "I didn't know what had happened."

That tune was driving Frank crazy. He reached out and removed Oliver's hand from the keyboard. "You didn't call for help?"

Finally Oliver looked at him. "I know it sounds crazy. I still can't believe I didn't. But I panicked. I was worried about Lorrie and about myself, too. I knew we'd both be in trouble. Neither one of us could afford to lose our jobs, but especially not Lorrie. I thought I'd wait to do anything until I could talk it over with her. But then she never came back. I didn't know what to think."

Oliver leaned forward, his face so close that Frank could see a loose eyelash on his pale cheek. He almost brushed it away as he would have done for Caroline when she was a child.

"I understand your reaction at the moment, but you must have realized that your evidence would be important once the state police and I started to investigate."

Oliver squirmed and hung his head, looking no older than Matthew. "As I went back to my room that night, I saw Ray going into the main building doing the final security round of the night. I knew he would find the room and call in the alarm. So really, what could I add? Ray saw exactly what I saw, just a few minutes later."

"What about the keys Lorrie gave you? Did you have them in your pocket all evening?"

"W-e-e-ll, not exactly."

"Where exactly were they?"

"Lorrie gave me her entire key ring, and it was big and lumpy. It jabbed into my leg when I was sitting in the boys' rec room trying to read. So I took the keys out and laid them on the end table. Then the boys started a card game and wanted me to play, so I moved over to the card table, and the keys were left on the end table by the sofa. But they were still right where I left them at ten when I went to let Heather out, so I don't think anyone touched them."

"Did you have your back to the end table while you were playing cards?"

"Yes."

"How long did the game go on?"

"An hour and a half."

Frank stared into the young man's eyes. "This is important, Oliver—who entered and left that room while you were playing?"

He didn't answer immediately, and Frank saw his hand stray back to the keyboard. Then Oliver pulled it back, as if restraining himself from a security blanket. "As I remember it, there was a lot of activity that night. Steve Vreeland passed through twice looking for Mac. And Ray Stulke came in, because we'd been having trouble with a window that wouldn't close all the way." Oliver grinned. "Ray got it shut, no problem. Oh, and earlier, Justin Levine came in and asked to join in the card game, but the other boys wouldn't let him."

"Why not?"

"They said he cheated. We were playing blackjack and Justin could count cards."

That figured, another skill to add to Justin's dubious resume. "Did Justin stay in the rec room after you turned him away from the game?"

"No, he made some wisecrack about our playing, then he went back to his room."

"Was that the last you saw of him that night?"

"Hmm. Now that you mention it, he did come back in right before lights-out to see who had won."

"What about Steve Vreeland? You said he came in twice—how much time passed between visits?"

"I'm not sure—maybe an hour." Oliver paused for a moment. "You mean you think Justin or Steve could've borrowed the keys, gone to the isolation room, and brought the keys back again?" Before Frank could answer, Oliver continued, "Oh, wait! That was the night Justin ran away, the first time."

"Exactly. And when we brought him back and questioned him, we let him go because he convinced us that his running away had nothing to do with what happened in the isolation room. But we didn't realize he had had access to the keys. The keys were missing—we thought they were still with Lorrie. And now Justin is gone again." Frank stood up and glared down at Oliver. "Your information changes everything."

He got back to the office as Doris was ending a phone call. "He just stepped out for a minute. I'll send him over as soon as he gets back."

"Send me over where?"

"To the Rock Slide. There's some problem with a customer who's giving the girls a hard time and won't leave."

"Threatening them?"

The uncertainty etched on Doris's face indicated that she had once again failed to obtain complete information from a caller.

Frank pivoted and headed out the door with a sigh. He was eager to act on this new information, but it would only take a few minutes to check on the situation at the Rock Slide. Better safe than sorry.

The ride to the sports equipment store was quick— in less than ten minutes, he could see the bright yellow coils of climbing rope that festooned the porch outside the log cabin-style building. There were only two cars in the parking lot. One was the old Volvo station wagon driven by the two sisters who worked there; the other must belong to the irate customer. At least he wouldn't have to settle this in front of a crowd.

He walked in and immediately saw a young man with a stony expression sitting in an Adirondack chair. Standing behind the counter looking equally grim were the two sisters, whose names he could never keep straight. Frank glanced from the man to the others and had a "what's wrong with this picture" moment. For the man in the chair was none other than Pathfinder Steve Vreeland.

"Hello, Steve, ladies. What seems to be the problem here?"

"I've been cheated," Steve said in a flat voice.

The girls immediately began jabbering in response, interrupting each other in their eagerness to tell Frank their side of the story.

"He's trying to make a return without a receipt."

"He mighta bought it on sale—"

"He wants his money back, but we can only give store credit."

"Without the receipt we can't—"

As the girls' voices grew shriller and louder, Frank saw Steve's lips move but no sound came out. He thought he might be counting to himself.

Finally they paused for breath and Steve spoke again in that uninflected tone. "The merchandise still has the tag. It has never been used. I paid full price. The receipt must have fallen out of the bag." He kept his eyes focused on a display of ice crampons as he talked.

Frank could see why this debate had reached a standstill. By asking a few questions of both parties, Frank determined that Steve had paid by credit card, got the girls to look up the transaction, and had them credit Steve's account. It seemed to him that reasonable people could have figured that out without the help of the police, but he'd seen more trivial matters escalate into violence. And in truth, the sisters at the Rock Slide had done him a favor. He wanted to talk to Steve Vreeland, especially in light of what he'd learned from Oliver and Greta Karsten, and Payne wouldn't willingly give him the opportunity to see the young man on campus.

Frank held the door of the store open and ushered Steve out to the parking lot.

"Thank you for your assistance." Steve gave a curt nod and headed toward his car.

"Say, do you have a minute?"

Steve paused and turned slowly.

"Do you remember a kid named Tristan Renfew from your days at the Langley Wilderness School?"

Frank thought he detected a slight break in Steve's wooden demeanor. The kid's Adam's apple bobbed up and down before he answered. "I knew him. He's dead now."

"Committed suicide, I believe?"

Steve stared at the Rock Slide's hanging sign, which creaked in the stiff breeze. "It was an accident."

"He died in an isolation room, just like Heather, didn't he?"

"Paul Petrucci killed Heather. Nothing like that happened to Tristan."

"What *did* happen to him?"

"He refused to accept the program. He resisted it, and his resistance brought him down."

Frank felt a chill that had nothing to do with the cold, gray weather. How could Steve be so utterly unsympathetic to another young man whose troubles must have been so similar to his own? He had completely bought into the notion that Tristan's horrible death was his own fault.

"Did you spend much time with Tristan in the weeks before his death?"

"I participated in all the encounter sessions to help Tristan admit his transgressions and accept accountability for his actions."

Did you ever notice that you were pushing the poor kid right over the edge? But Steve wasn't the one to blame; he hadn't been calling the shots.

"What about Jake Reiger—was he involved in Tristan's, uh, treatment?"

"He was Tristan's interventionist."

"His what?"

"He led an intensive one-on-one intervention to try to bring Tristan in line with the program's goals."

"Obviously he failed."

Steve's hands clenched and he rubbed his right thumb and forefinger together over and over. "Why are you asking all these questions about Tristan and Jake? Paul Petrucci killed Heather, and he must've set up that bear attack, too. None of this has anything to do with Tristan Renfew. He had an accident."

"The night that Heather was taken to the isolation room, did you visit the boys' rec room?" Frank asked.

Steve appeared relieved to have left the subject of Tristan Renfew. "Yes. I was looking for Mac. He wasn't there; he was in the girls' dorm."

"But you went back to the boys' rec room again."

Steve continued to stare straight ahead, his eyes not quite focused on Frank. "Yes. It's not entirely appropriate that Oliver participates in the boys' recreation activities. I wanted to be sure he implemented the proper lights-out procedure."

"Did you happen to notice a set of keys lying on the end table by the sofa?"

"Keys? What keys?"

"The keys to the isolation room. They were lying there that night. Several people had access to them. Someone used them to go and kill Heather."

"Paul—"

"I doubt it." Of course, Paul had his own key to the isolation room, but Frank was interested to see Steve's reaction without that piece of information.

For the first time in their conversation, Steve's eyes met Frank's. "What's going on? How could what happened to Tristan and Jake and Heather be connected?" There was a rising note of hysteria in Steve's voice. "Paul's the one who killed Heather. He did it because he hates Dr. Payne and he wants to make the school look bad. He knows Dr. Payne is going to fire him as soon as he can find a replacement. So Paul wants to see us fail."

Frank could believe Paul hated Payne and wouldn't mind discrediting the school, but he couldn't imagine him sacrificing an innocent child to ruin the academy. But what if Paul had hatched some plan with Heather and Justin that went horribly wrong? Could one of them have killed her accidentally? But it still didn't make sense.

"I'd be more likely to buy this idea that Paul killed Heather if the body hadn't been hidden," Frank continued. "Why not leave it there to be found right away if the point was to create a scandal?"

Steve just stood there, glowering.

"Moving Heather's body was very risky. Paul didn't have a reason to take that risk. And now I know that you and Justin Levine had access to those isolation room keys."

Frank's words wrought a bizarre change in Steve Vreeland. His eyes bulged, his fists clenched, and his breathing came in short, raspy puffs. He looked to be holding in enough steam to blast himself clear to Lake Champlain.

Finally, he blew. "I hid Heather's body!"

Chapter 31

"**I** was scheduled to help Randy with Group Encounter after dinner," Steve said. "I realized I didn't have the notebook in which I record transgressions. I had been showing it to Mac earlier in the day, and I forgot to get it back from him." He looked down at his clasped hands. "It was very careless of me.

"First I looked for Mac in the boys' dorm, but he wasn't there. I went to check his office. He wasn't there either, but I saw a light shining into the hall upstairs. There would be no reason for a light to be lit on the second floor of the admin building at that time, so I went up to check."

Steve shut his eyes. A muscle twitched at the corner of his mouth. He took a deep breath before continuing. "The light was coming from the open isolation room. Heather was in there. The room was covered with blood. I ran to her. She was warm. I couldn't see where the blood was coming from. I checked her pulse. I couldn't feel anything."

Frank watched him. Most people showed signs of stress when they recounted finding a body; some even became physically ill. Steve spoke like a soldier reciting name, rank, and serial number.

"I started CPR, but in a few minutes I could tell that it was useless. She was dead." Steve clenched his teeth; the tendons in his neck grew taut. "I couldn't believe that stupid bitch had killed herself."

Frank drew back. He'd been in interrogation rooms with gang executioners and cop killers, but this guy scared him as much as any hardened con. "You made the decision that she couldn't be saved yourself? You didn't call for help?"

Steve's face regained some of its former impassivity. "I'm very well trained in first aid. I could see there was nothing more to be done. The important thing became how to protect the academy. Mac couldn't afford another scandal. I moved Heather's body to the crawl space behind classroom 210. My intention was to leave it there temporarily until I could bury it in the forest. I planned to go back to the isolation room and clean up the blood, so it would look like Heather had simply run away." Steve frowned. "Of course, an escape wasn't good either, but it was better than a suicide. Heather's parents would believe she'd run away, with her history."

"How did you know how to access that space behind the classroom?" Frank asked.

"Ray Stulke showed it to me when he first started working security. He noticed the little removable panel that had been put in. He said it must be in case there was ever trouble with the pipes or wiring, but that a kid could hide in there. He wanted us Pathfinders to be aware." Steve bobbed his head in approval. "Ray is very attentive."

"What about the blood? You didn't get a chance to clean it up?"

Steve fidgeted with the zipper of his jacket. "It was hard to fit her through that little opening."

Yes, it would've been easier if she had crawled in, but she was dead, remember?

"Then I had to get the panel back in place, and I had trouble with that." Steve exhaled a little grunt of self-disgust. "By the time I was done, I needed to get to Group Encounter. Missing it would have raised too many questions—I had to let the blood go. I figured you all would think Heather had injured herself trying to escape."

"You didn't know that Lorrie and Justin would also go missing."

"No, it muddied things. Made everyone more suspicious." Steve's eyes narrowed. "Especially that bitch reporter."

"What about MacArthur Payne? Did you tell him what you did to help him out?"

"No!" Steve twisted around to face Frank. His cold eyes were alive with passion now. "No, Mac knew nothing about this. It was my idea. I did it to help him and the school, but it didn't turn out the way it should have. That's why I'm telling you now."

He reached out and grabbed Frank's wrist. "You have to help him. You have to get this cleared up so everyone knows it wasn't Mac's fault. None of it is Mac's fault."

Fifteen minutes with his wife in the visiting room of the county jail brought about the confession that a team of state troopers had been unable to elicit from Paul Petrucci. Now he sat talking to Frank and Meyerson, his handsome face at once dejected, relieved, and defiant.

"All right, let's go over this from the top," Frank said. "You say Dawn approached you about being her paid inside informant. And since you disapproved of Payne's educational methods and needed the cash, the opportunity was too good to pass up."

"Yes. She called me out of the blue in September. I hadn't heard from her since we graduated from college."

Frank and Lew exchanged glances. "So she was on the trail of this story before anything suspicious happened at the academy?"

"She said she wanted to do an investigative report on abuses at tough-love schools, and she needed inside information. She said she'd be getting information from other schools like this, as well."

"And paying for it?"

Paul shrugged uneasily. "I know it's unorthodox. Dawn says the *Beat* is trying to upgrade its journalistic image by doing more serious pieces. That's why she came to work for them. She knew this could be a hot story, but she hasn't established all the sources she needs, so ..." Paul's voice trailed off. He knew his justification for taking the money was feeble at best.

"You got the money as cash payments. Are you sure it was coming from the *Beat?*" Frank asked.

Paul looked puzzled. "Well, yeah—where else could it be coming from?"

"Payne claims his ex-partner Glen Costello is out to ruin him. Couldn't the money for your information be coming from him?"

Paul grew very still. Frank watched as a tiny muscle near his right eye jumped. It was the reaction of a highly intelligent man who realizes he's been hoodwinked.

"The lawyers—" Paul's voice emerged as a croak. He cleared his throat and tried again. "The lawyers said they were the legal team from the *Beat* and they could get me off if I just kept my mouth shut about the payments."

"I've talked to Dawn's editor," Frank said. "He's never heard of the lawyers who were representing you. He also hasn't heard from Dawn in two days. He says that surprised him because she's been so hot on this story, she's even been covering some of her own expenses. Apparently she sees it as the story that's going to make her journalistic career."

Paul pulled himself together for one last offensive. "Of course he would say that—he's not going to admit he's been paying for a story."

"Maybe, maybe not. We'll keep pursuing that line. Right now I need to know one more thing from you. Dawn Klotz wrote her first story about the possibility that Jake Reiger's death was not accidental at a time when no one knew about the bacon grease on the sleeping bag except the state police, me, the DEC, and Payne. How did she get that information?"

"I told her," Paul admitted.

"And how did you know?"

Paul paused to think. "We were all sitting around talking about it in the staff lounge the day after the attack. Steve, Oliver, Randy, Lorrie, Ray—I think that's all." Frank leaned forward. "Who brought it up? Who mentioned the bacon grease first?"

Paul shrugged. "I can't remember—what difference does it make?"

"Because that person could only know if he—or she—was the person who planted it."

Lew Meyerson sat in his office with Frank, looking none too pleased. "Well, you've certainly been busy, haven't you?"

"I'm sorry if the truth undermines the basis of your case against Petrucci."

The two men glared at each other. Lew was first to look away.

"All right, let's review what we have." Lew tapped the corners of an already straight stack of papers on his immaculate desk. "Petrucci was being paid to provide inside information about the academy for Dawn Klotz's so-called expose. And you think Costello is actually providing the money?"

Frank leaned back in his chair and steepled his fingers. "He might be behind what's going on at the academy. Paul said Dawn approached him about doing a story on the academy as soon as she learned that Payne had opened a school in New York, and that someone she knew was teaching there. She set up Paul as her inside source as if she knew something would soon be happening. And sure enough, a couple weeks later, Reiger was attacked."

Lew regarded him with expressionless eyes. "So, we're back to this notion that the bear attack was sabotage."

Frank sprang out of his chair. "How can it not be? Why are you fighting me on this? Justin Levine and Steve Vreeland were both present when Reiger died. Steve Vreeland was present when Paul learned about the bacon grease.

Steve, Jason, and Oliver all had access to the keys to the isolation room when Heather was murdered. Someone at the academy—maybe more than one person—is responsible for both deaths. I want to bring in Levine tonight, then I want to interrogate everyone until I get some answers that make sense."

Lew nodded. "What about Dawn Klotz?"

"Get your boys to track her down. It shouldn't be hard—she strikes me as a woman who can't survive long without her credit card and cell phone."

"What's the plan for apprehending Levine?"

It wasn't lost on Frank that Lew said "the" plan, not "your" plan. They were back to collaborating, but Lew would never cede control of the investigation.

"Rachel Portman has described where she meets Levine. He's been camping in a lean-to near Owl Pond, but he keeps out of sight during the day and walks down to meet her at a spot between the lean-to and the trailhead. I thought we'd send in a few officers dressed as hikers to conceal themselves along the trail. Then I'll ride with Rachel in her father's pickup so Levine isn't suspicious."

"I don't like involving a civilian in this." Lew's jaw clamped in a hard line.

"We don't have a choice," Frank said. "Levine's not armed. It will work out."

Frank sat slumped down in the passenger seat of the Portman family's pickup. He had driven most of the way to the Owl Pond trail and nervously turned the wheel over to Rachel a half mile from the trailhead. But his fears were groundless—Rachel proved to be a perfectly competent driver, despite her lack of a license.

The trail was accessed from a dirt road off Route 12. They passed a few vacation cottages nestled in the woods, then the forest closed around them. The truck's headlights sliced into the night ahead of them, making the blackness to their sides more intense. If Frank had been driving he would have missed the trailhead, but Rachel expertly pulled the truck off the road into a small clearing. Frank could just about discern a wooden sign with "Owl Pond" and an arrow painted crudely in yellow.

"This is it," Rachel said. "I beep the horn three times to let him know I'm here. Then I head up the trail. He usually meets me in less than five minutes."

The plan was for Rachel to head up the trail with a flashlight, with Frank following behind without a light, keeping her beam in view. But when he stepped out of the truck and realized how absolute the darkness was, he began to doubt he could pull it off.

"Don't look at the light. Give your eyes some time to adjust," Rachel advised. "You'd be surprised how much you can see." Then, without waiting for his okay, she reached through the window of the truck and gave the horn three long blasts. The sound reverberated through the forest, sending unseen creatures skittering through the underbrush. No choice but to proceed.

Rachel set off briskly up the trail. Now that she had agreed to help bring in Justin Levine, she seemed determined to get it over with as soon as possible. Frank struggled to keep her flashlight beam in sight, turning his ankle on indiscernible rocks on the trail, and scratching away branches that lashed at his face.

Only a few minutes passed before Frank heard a low, indecipherable male voice. The meeting was coming sooner than expected, which meant the state troopers were posted too far up the trail.

"How are you holding up?" Rachel asked.

"Terrible. I'm so damned cold. Rachel, I can't last out here much longer. You gotta take me to Albany. C'mon—you promised you'd help me."

"I am going to help you, but I—"

Frank stepped into the circle of light created by Rachel's flashlight.

"You bitch!" Justin screamed. "You tricked me!"

Justin lunged at Rachel. Frank stepped forward to stop him, but his eyes, which had dilated fully to accommodate his hike in pitch darkness, were now blinded by the flashlight that Rachel swung from side to side.

In a flurry of confusion, the flashlight fell, Frank stumbled into a tree, and Justin grabbed Rachel. When Frank regained his balance, Justin stood before him with his arm crooked around Rachel's neck. Her hands clung to his sleeve, trying to pull the vise open; her feet kicked ineffectively at his shins. Was this how Heather had spent her last moments of life?

"Justin, let her go." Frank rested his hand lightly on his service revolver, but did not draw the weapon. He noticed Justin's gaze following his movement. "There are three state troopers heading down the trail right now."

"You're ly—" But the sound of running and a cascade of small rocks choked off his words. His eyes darted wildly. "Don't send me back there! I'm not going back to that school!"

"No, Justin." Frank spoke in a low, soothing voice. "You're not going back to North Country Academy. I've been in touch with your dad. He wants to bring you home. But first I need you to tell me everything you know about Heather LeBron's murder."

"You won't believe me." Justin pulled Rachel more tightly into his grasp. "No one will take my word."

Chapter 32

Twelve hours had passed since the arrival of three burly state troopers on the Owl Pond trail had put an end to Justin Levine's hopeless siege. They had their man, and now Frank and Lew sat at the Ray Brook Barracks trying to decide what to do with him.

"You know what we're up against with his old man," Lew said. "If we interrogate him without a guardian present, Morton Levine and his lawyers will have anything the kid says ruled inadmissible in court."

And Morton Levine was nowhere to be found. They'd called his home and cell phone numbers and left messages. When they called his office number, Levine's recorded message informed them he would be out of the office for the next week. They left one of Meyerson's staff trying to rouse a human being at Levine's office who could track him down.

"I can't stand this." Frank paced around the office like a tiger in a cruelly small cage. "We can't wait days for Levine senior to show up. Any minute now, the Portman kids will start talking about what happened last night and the news that we've got Justin in custody will be out. However that kid's involved in the deaths at the academy, I'm sure he's not in it alone. We've got to act fast to reel in everyone who's responsible."

Lew looked unmoved. "The proper procedure would be—"

With his rigid expression and pontificating tone, Lew bore an unpleasant resemblance to Steve Vreeland in that moment. Frank had heard quite enough about procedure. Unyielding adherence to some arcane rules was precisely what had gotten poor Heather killed. He wasn't going to stand by and let her killer do more damage or escape, just so procedure could be followed. His gut told him he needed to act now.

Frank headed for the door. "I'm going to talk to Justin off the record."

"Risky. You could blow—"

The office door opened as Frank reached it and a trooper stuck his head in. "Chief Bennett, Justin Levine is requesting to see you."

Lew's lips barely moved when he spoke. "Go. Go see what he has to say."

When Frank entered the interview room, Justin Levine had his head cradled in his folded arms on the table. He raised it slowly and Frank could see that the cockiness of their previous meetings had disappeared, replaced by exhaustion and maybe fear. Someone had given him an extra-extra-large state police sweatshirt, which made him look scrawny and very young.

"How's it going?" Frank asked. "Did they give you something to eat?"

"Eggs. They were good." Justin pulled himself up straight and locked eyes with Frank. "I am truly fucked this time, aren't I?"

No pleasantries; Justin wanted to cut to the chase. That was fine with Frank.

"You're in trouble, Justin, I won't deny that. But you've got two things going for you: you're smart and you're rich. The vast majority of people on this planet don't hold those two aces. You don't have to bluff and cheat to win—you could win playing the hand you've been dealt."

"That's not too exciting."

"Excitement is overrated."

"You got a point." Justin sighed. "All right, I'm gonna tell you what I know. Some of it doesn't make sense, even to me, so you're probably not going to believe it. But I don't care—I just want this thing over with."

"So do I. Tell me about Heather."

Justin pushed the sleeves of the huge sweatshirt up, revealing sinewy arms and long, nimble fingers. "Heather was one of the first people I met at North Country Academy. I could tell right away she was the kind of girl who could be useful to me."

"Useful?"

"Heather was the kind of chick who needs a lot of attention. If you gave it to her, you could get her to do anything for you." Justin studied Frank's stem face. "Hey, that's the way of the world, man."

Frank thought it was sad to understand the way of the world so well at only sixteen, but merely nodded encouragement.

"Anyway, Heather told me right away she had an ally who was going to get her out of the school. She said she'd take me with her. I knew it was bullshit, but I played along. Because I had a plan of my own—"

"And you thought she might come in handy."

"Exactly. But after the bear attack, Heather started acting sort of scared. She said things hadn't worked out like she expected, as if she had something to do with what happened on the campout. I couldn't tell if she knew something, or she was just acting like she did to get attention. Then she said it didn't matter because Jake Reiger got what he deserved."

Frank sat forward. "What did she mean by that?"

"I'm not sure. With Heather, it was always yak, yak, yak." Justin mimicked a talking mouth with his hand. "I tuned out most of what she said. But I remember she said Reiger had something to do with the death of a kid named Tristan."

"Tristan Renfew. He died at MacArthur Payne's school in Utah. How did she know that?"

Justin shrugged. "If I asked too many questions, she'd go all mysterious and secretive. Honestly, I wasn't that interested."

But Frank was. Steve Vreeland and Payne himself were the only ones at the North Country Academy who knew about Tristan Renfew's death. But no, Paul Petrucci knew as well, because Dawn had told him about Payne's past. He resisted the urge to question Justin at this point and just let him talk.

"Then on the morning of the day she died, Heather told me this was it—she was getting out tonight and she'd make sure her friend got me out, too. I was like— 'yeah, right.' I had my own plan for that night, but I didn't tell her that."

Justin flexed his long fingers and twined them together. "She was all hyped up—she kept talking and talking even though we're supposed to be silent when we walk between classes. I was trying to ignore her so I wouldn't get in trouble. Then the Pathfinder in charge gave Heather a warning, but she still muttered one more thing. Something like, 'This whole school's coming down to make up for what happened to Juice's brother.' "

"Tristan Renfew had a brother nicknamed Juice," Frank said.

"That makes sense. At the time I didn't know what she was talking about, and I didn't care." Justin rose and pulled off the baggy sweatshirt. The atmosphere in the tiny interview room was getting stuffy.

"Rachel probably told you what happened next: I got out of my room, met up with Brad, he took me down to Keene Valley, and you guys brought me back the next day. I didn't find out about Heather and the isolation room until you told me about it when I got back. So I kept my mouth shut, because I figured it must be part of Heather's plan, and I wasn't going to screw it up for her."

Frank said nothing, but anger radiated from his taut face.

"All right, all right, so I should have said something. I've had plenty of time to think about it since I've been alone in the woods all those days. Do you want to hear the rest, or what?"

"Continue."

"Two nights later, I made my second escape from my room after Brad set the fire and picked the lock on my window. We were supposed to run into the woods together, but we ran in different directions when we heard someone coming."

"Yes, Brad told me that."

"Did he tell you who it was who saw us?"

"No. He didn't know."

"It was Oliver Greffe. We looked right at each other. But he didn't try to stop me; he didn't call for help. He let me get away."

Frank stared at Justin and tried to absorb what he'd just said.

"See, I knew you wouldn't believe me." The boy's expression turned sulky. "Because it doesn't make sense. Why would Oliver—"

Frank held up his hand for silence. Little bits of information were floating into his consciousness, and he had to grab them before they got away. He pictured the form Oliver had filled out before Al towed away his car. He had printed "Oliver J. Greffe." O. J. Greffe.

Juice.

Oliver had told him he was an only child, but now Frank remembered something Penny had said at that dinner party, about overhearing Oliver say that Ernie behaved as Oliver had done. The significance hadn't struck him at the time, but she'd meant that Oliver had been an admiring brother, just as Ernie was.

He remembered that time he had walked in on Matthew's organ lesson in the church. Matthew had asked, "Do you think T.J. would like it?" T.J. must be Tristan J. Renfrew. The brothers shared a middle initial although they didn't share a last name.

Oliver had sought out the job at the North Country Academy, not for money but for revenge. No wonder he had tried to cover up by saying Payne had recruited him.

"Did Heather really have someone helping her escape?" Justin asked. "Was it Oliver? Then who murdered her?"

Frank's only reply was a weary shake of the head.

Chapter 33

Weak winter sun shone through the dusty leaded-glass windows of Trout Run Presbyterian, dressing the sanctuary in long shadows. When Frank had gone to the North Country Academy to talk to Oliver, the gatekeeper told him he'd gone to the church to practice. But the church was silent.

A slight rustle made him look up. Oliver was visible to Frank only as a darker darkness behind the ranks of organ pipes in the loft.

"Oliver, couldn't you come down from there? We need to talk."

"About what?"

"Your brother, T.J."

In answer, a shot rang out, its report obscenely loud in the solemn stillness of the church.

"Oliver! Don't be—" Frank had been about to say "crazy" and Oliver knew it.

"Get out of here, Frank. I don't want to hurt you. I'm waiting for MacArthur Payne. I'm going to make him explain why he did what he did to my brother. Then I'm going to kill him."

Crisis negotiation required infinite patience and delicacy, qualities Frank knew he didn't possess. One ill-considered response could trigger disaster. He reached for his radio. The call might provoke Oliver, and it could be half an hour before any backup arrived, but what choice did he have? "Trout Run One, requesting assist—"

Another shot whizzed overhead, embedding in the column behind him.

"Don't say another thing into that radio, or my next shot will be through the window. Maybe I won't hit anyone outside; maybe I will."

Frank decided to simply leave the radio switched on so that everything that transpired in the church would be broadcast. With a little luck, Earl would catch on to what was needed, and intercept Payne before he barged into the church. But if only Doris heard him .... There was no point in worrying about what he couldn't control. He would keep Oliver talking, and hope for the best. Maybe he could calm him down, reason with him.

He wasn't feeling all that compassionate toward Payne, but he didn't want him gunned down in the center aisle of the church. More even than protecting Payne, he wanted to protect Oliver, to keep him from doing this last terrible thing that would seal his fate forever.

"Tell me about Tristan. Was he a musician, too?"

"He sang like an angel, the purest tenor you ever heard. And he used to play the flute until our stepfather discouraged him so much he gave it up."

Just keep him talking. "Why did he discourage him— the money?"

"No, money was never an issue. Our stepfather wanted to erase everything in us that he felt came from our real father—our music, our names ... our insanity."

"Your father had, er, problems?"

"You might say that. Maybe you've heard of him. James Renfew—he made his Carnegie Hall debut playing Paganini's Violin Concerto at seventeen. He went on to earn a PhD in mathematics at Princeton. He froze to death on a subway grating in New York City when he was thirty-two. Paranoid schizophrenic. Psychotic. Auditory delusions. My mother left him when Tristan was two and I was an infant. She remarried a year later. Phil Greffe was the only father Tristan and I ever knew." Oliver shifted position slightly, maybe to be able to see Frank's reaction to his story. "He did everything for us that a father is supposed to do for his sons—coached Little League, led our Boy Scout troop, took us to football games. Except we never really were his sons. He couldn't stand those arty names our father gave us: Tristan James and Oliver James. He made us T.J. and O.J. He hated that we were both musical, not athletic although he tolerated my organ playing because it impressed the pastor of our church." Oliver gave a bitter laugh.

"How did Tristan end up at the Langley Wilderness School?"

"When T.J. was fifteen, he started to act out. He insisted on being called Tristan, he spent all of his time in his room, listening to music and singing. His grades went to hell."

"Typical teenage rebellion," Frank said.

"That's what my parents thought. But then he got weirder. I could hear him in his room at night, talking to himself. It seemed like he never slept.

He told me he had enemies; that people were watching him. It scared me—I knew something was wrong with him."

"But your parents ... ?"

"They refused to acknowledge it. My mother watched my father fall apart. She had to know what was happening to Tristan, but I guess she couldn't bear for history to repeat itself. And my stepfather—he just wouldn't allow Tristan to be schizophrenic. For him, it was all pure willpower. He decided all T.J. needed was a change of scenery, in a place no one would indulge him like our mother did. So they sent him to the Langley Wilderness School. To straighten him out."

Silence descended on the church. Frank didn't need to hear more to know how this story ended. The program at Langley Wilderness School obviously had exacerbated Tristan Renfew's budding schizophrenia. Frank shuddered to think of the effect Costello's mind-control tapes, played over and over, must have on a person who was suffering from auditory hallucinations to begin with. Payne, with his scorn for traditional psychiatry, had completely overlooked Tristan Renfew's serious mental illness, and as a result, the boy had killed himself.

He could understand why Oliver hated Payne, but why had he killed Jake Reiger and poor Heather? Surely she had been a victim of Payne's treatment as much as Tristan had been. He didn't want Oliver to get more agitated, but he had to keep him talking and try to steer the conversation in a direction that would send a signal to Earl over the radio that Payne should be intercepted.

"What about Jake Reiger, Oliver? Was he involved in your brother's treatment in Utah?"

"Reiger was the person who drove my brother over the edge. I got a long, rambling letter from T.J. a month before he died, saying Reiger was after him. Later, I learned more from the mother of the boy who heard T.J. kill himself."

"Greta Karsten? You spoke to her?"

"No. I listened on the extension when she told my mother that Reiger played into T.J.'s paranoia. Told him he was always watching him and could see everything T.J. did, even when he was alone. Could read T.J.'s thoughts. Instead of helping my brother, he made his delusions seem even more real. I hated him for what he did to T.J."

"So you sabotaged his sleeping bag with bacon grease?"

Oliver laughed, an unpleasant sound that trickled down from the organ loft like felling plaster.

"I didn't know that the bear would kill him; I wasn't even positive there would be a bear around the area. But I wanted Jake to be terrified, just like my poor brother was. I knew even if he woke up in the morning safe and found that bacon grease, he'd know someone was after him.

"I got the grease from the kitchen the day before. I was always hanging around there, looking for a snack. I noticed Mrs. Pershing saved up the grease in a coffee can in the freezer. I took it and hid it in my car."

That information hit Frank with the force of a punch in the gut. He'd meant to talk to Helen Pershing again, but never had. If he had followed up, got her talking, he might have learned about the coffee can... found out that Oliver frequently visited the kitchen... and prevented Heather's death.

"The night they camped out," Oliver continued, "I hiked in to their site using a different trail and poured the grease on Jake's bag. No one suspected me, because I always made a big deal about not doing anything outdoors that could injure my hands. But hey, I was a Boy Scout. I know all about backpacking."

"And Heather? Why did she have to die?"

Oliver hung his head. "Heather was a mistake. I feel very bad about that."

A mistake? Backing your car into a pole was a mistake to feel bad about. Murdering someone was in an entirely different league. He was beginning to see how truly unstable Oliver was. But he was careful not to let his voice betray that.

"How did it happen with Heather?" Frank asked. Oliver let out an impatient huff. "Heather was so unpredictable. One minute she'd be willing to do anything for you; the next minute she'd turn on you."

He didn't seem to sense the irony in his statement. Frank jollied him along. "What did she agree to help you with?"

"The isolation room. I wanted to call attention to how they tortured kids in there—you know, for Dawn's story—and Heather agreed to help. But after she made the mess with the blood, it all went wrong."

Oliver turned his back and his voice drifted into an unintelligible murmur.

"What did you say? I couldn't hear you."

Oliver whirled around. "She started screaming. She screamed and screamed and wouldn't shut up. She screamed because I was late letting her out of the room, and being alone with the blood freaked her out." His voice rose. "I had to make her stop! I put my arm around her neck. Then finally she was quiet."

Oliver began to pace in front of the organ pipes. Every time he turned in the narrow space, his gun clanked against a pipe. What had he meant about Dawn's story? But now was not the time to press for answers. Clearly Oliver was getting more agitated.

Had Earl heard all this? Had he understood what was going on? At least he hadn't come charging across the green on his own, but had he called the state police for assistance? Everyone was up in Ray Brook, waiting for Morton Levine. Was there a patrol car out on the road somewhere closer to Trout Run?

"Why is MacArthur Payne meeting you here at the church, Oliver? Does he know Tristan was your brother?"

"No, the fool still hasn't figured it out. He's so sure that his ex-partner Costello is behind all the problems he's been having here, he doesn't even suspect me. I invited him to come here for a private recital—Bach played just for him. He doesn't know the only piece on the program is a requiem."

Unless *requiem* had been one of Earl's vocabulary words, Frank didn't think the significance of that remark would hit home. He needed to make sure Earl knew Oliver was armed and dangerous.

"Why don't you put down the gun, Oliver? You and I can talk to Payne together when he gets here."

"I have one thing left to do before I go." Oliver spoke in the voice of a person making a to-do list before vacation. "I have to kill to MacArthur Payne. Where is he? Why hasn't he come yet? Did you tell him not to come?"

Without warning, Oliver spun and fired off another shot. Frank, who had let his head peek above the pew as he talked, felt the slug whistle by his left ear. He dove for the floor.

"Steady, now, Oliver. Why don't you put that gun down?" He couldn't afford for Oliver to start shooting wildly; the side walls of the church were fifty percent glass. Hadn't anyone heard this gunfire? But if they had, they probably just thought it was hunters.

"You warned him not to come!" Oliver shrieked, and the gun discharged again. The shot went high this time, embedding in the oak beam that supported the arched ceiling. A few inches in either direction and it would have gone through the window.

"I didn't warn him, Oliver." Frank needed his full concentration to keep his voice low and soothing. "You've been right here with me all along. I never called anyone."

But he prayed that Earl was watching for Payne, because if the headmaster came walking through that door, Oliver would see him first. He could shoot before Frank had a chance to bring Oliver down. Yet he couldn't bring himself to shoot the boy now, even as a precaution; it would be like killing in cold blood.

"Oliver, I want you to do something for me, okay?"

"What?"

"While we're waiting for MacArthur Payne, let's sing."

"Sing?"

"Yeah, it would make the time go a little faster. Besides, we're both a little jumpy, no? Let's sing—" He cast about for something they both would know the words to. "Let's sing 'Amazing Grace.' "

Frank started out, "Amazing Grace, how sweet the sound."

Soon he heard Oliver's sweet, clear tenor drifting down to him. They continued in unison, "that saved a wretch like me. I once was lost, but now am found..." Frank heard a door creak. Was it Payne, or had his backup finally arrived? Either way, he needed to keep Oliver singing. "Was blind but now I see," he thundered, then started the second verse with barely a pause. "Through many dangers, toils, and snares, I have already come."

A tall, broad-shouldered figure moved through the shadows in the narthex. Too big to be Earl. Was it Payne, or Meyerson? The figure moved forward without hesitation. Surely Meyerson would be more cautious.

Frank's gaze shot back to Oliver. He was singing with his eyes half shut, the gun dangling loosely in his right hand. If Frank called out a warning, would the person in the back of the church have time to take cover before Oliver snapped back to attention and started firing? If it was Meyerson, probably; he would be anticipating trouble. But Payne had no idea he was walking into danger. Besides, that man never followed commands without question.

Frank kept singing as he skimmed though his options, the words to the old hymn so ingrained in his memory that they came reflexively. " "It was grace that taught my heart to fear, and grace my fear relieved." He would wait until the man just came into view under the organ loft, then wave him back, as long as Oliver appeared still lost in song.

"Hey!" a loud voice rang out from the shadows. "You're singing my favorite song!" The man stepped into the dim light of the sanctuary, and Frank's C natural ended in a croak.

It was Ernie Portman.

Chapter 34

E rnie's brash greeting changed everything.

Frank sprang up, but twenty rows of pews divided him from Ernie. "Ernie, get down!" he shouted.

Ernie turned his broad, vacant face toward Frank and squinted. "Huh? Who's there? Where's Oliver?"

"I'm here, Payne."

Frank looked up and saw Oliver, his face contorted with determination, his right arm fully extended, and the gun aimed straight down at the top of Ernie's head.

"I killed your school and now I'm going to kill you."

Ernie raised his sweet face up toward the organ loft and lifted his hand in a wave, as if to greet what was coming his way.

Frank took aim and fired.

Oliver's slender body buckled, crumpled over the organ loft railing, and fell in a graceful somersault to the stone floor just a few feet from Ernie.

"Oh, no! Oliver fell. I think he's hurt."

Frank made his way through the pews and put his trembling arm around Ernie. "It's okay, Ernie. I'll take care of him."

Frank emerged from the church to find two state police squad cars zooming into town, lights flashing but sirens off. So, Earl had called for backup. Then why in God's name had he let Ernie Portman wander into that church?

Meyerson trotted across the green to meet him. "Frank, what's going on? Where's Oliver Greffe?"

Frank waved a weary arm in the direction of the church. "He's in there. He's dead—I had to shoot him to save Ernie. Where the hell were you?"

"We got the call from Earl fifteen minutes ago. I was in Ray Brook; Pauline was in Keene Valley. We came as fast as we could."

Frank glanced around. Where was Earl? He never passed up a chance to be in the middle of a big operation.

Meyerson continued explaining. "Earl was clear over by Beech Pond. Someone called in a report of a bear wandering around. Since it was near Corkscrew, he thought it might be Reiger's killer. He notified Rusty and went out there to keep an eye on it. It wasn't until he got back in the patrol car after the DEC showed up that he heard your transmission and called us."

"Did you head off Payne? Is that why he never showed up?"

"Yes, I caught up with him as he was pulling out of the school driveway. I had the dispatcher call the church to warn them to keep people away, but no one answered in the church office."

Frank felt an irrational rage welling within him. He wanted to blame someone, anyone, for this senseless death.

Why had Ernie walked into the church at just that moment? Why had that damn bear, who had eluded them for so long, chosen this morning to reveal himself? Why the hell couldn't Earl have been watching out the office window? He spent seventy-five percent of every other workday doing just that—why not today? Why couldn't Augie Enright have been sitting in the church office chatting with Myrna when the state police had called, so he could run out like the busybody he was and direct everyone away from the church?

The questions chased through his mind, a continuous round of recrimination: Why had he been forced to kill Oliver?

Chapter 35

The week that followed the shooting in the church was filled with steady activity.

The state police and district attorney conducted a pro forma investigation and commended Frank for his handling of the crisis. The bear suspected of killing Jake Reiger was captured and relocated to a remote section of the Adirondack Park, far from the possibility of human interaction. Steve Vreeland was charged with being an accessory after the fact and obstructing justice. Paul Petrucci was released without being charged with any crime and he insisted on returning the money he'd received.

The final piece of the puzzle had fallen into place when Dawn Klotz had been located back in Ohio. She revealed that it was Oliver, not Costello, who had financed her "research" into the North Country Academy. Using insurance money he'd received after his parents' death, Oliver had paid Dawn to pursue the expose of tough-love schools, hoping to create enough scandal that the entire industry would be shut down. She had hoped to launch her own career as an investigative reporter with the story, but the plan had backfired on both of them.

From the moment he awoke every morning, Frank was busy meeting or on the phone with the state police, the DA, the DEC, the county social worker, the press, and parents of academy students. All the action allowed him to fall into bed at night, exhausted, and sleep until the ringing phone woke him again in the morning.

But by the end of the week, the workload lessened. He had time to walk across the green for a donut at the Store, to eat lunch at Malone's, to drive the afternoon patrol.

Time to think.

He replayed that awful moment over and over: Ernie calling out a greeting, Oliver raising the gun, his threat to shoot, Ernie's utter incomprehension of danger.

Then Frank saw his own right hand raised, his view along the barrel of the gun as he took aim, the tremendous pressure required to squeeze the trigger, the moment of impact, the falling body.

He had never killed a man before. He'd wounded a man once—a bad guy who'd shot at him first—and that had been bad enough. The fact that he had been cleared of wrongdoing—commended, in fact—was absolutely no consolation.

Every morning right before he opened his eyes, a voice in his head would murmur, "Something's wrong with this day," and in that moment he would remember: *I killed Oliver Greffe. I killed a troubled, talented, very young man. I took his life and nothing will ever change that.*

The knowledge sat on him, a huge rock that crushed the joy out of every day. No joke was funny, no meal had flavor, no music was tuneful.

"What're you looking at? Don't you have something to do?" he snapped when he felt Earl's watchful gaze on him.

Earl's reaction was neither hurt nor anger, but something much worse. "It's okay, Frank." He touched Frank's shoulder lightly. "I understand."

But Earl didn't understand because he'd never killed a man. And neither did the state police psychologist, whom Frank dutifully visited. The man said all the appropriate things, to which Frank made the appropriate responses. The doctor was satisfied; Frank left feeling worse than when he'd arrived.

He ran into Edwin later that day. "You look like shit," his friend said, eyeing him up and down. "You should talk to someone about this."

"I just talked to the state police shrink. He pronounced me cured."

Edwin scowled. "What kind of shrink goes to work for the police department? He probably graduated at the bottom of his class. Go see a real doctor."

"Like who? You can't find a doctor to set a broken bone around here, let alone straighten out a cracked brain."

Edwin thought a moment. "You should talk to Bob. I think he could help."

"Bob who?" Then Frank took a step backward as understanding struck. "Bob Rush! That's a laugh. The two of us are like oil and water."

"You underestimate Bob." Edwin gave Frank a long look and his usual irony was missing when he spoke again. "And you're wrong about his regard for you. Give him a chance. He could help you if you let him."

FRANK SAT IN THE MIDDLE of the darkened church. It was freezing in there. Now that Oliver was no longer giving organ lessons, Augie left the heat turned back to fifty until Saturday morning, when he set it on its slow climb to sixty-eight.

He let his head fall back against the pew and gazed up at the thick beams supporting the vaulted ceiling. He could still see the spot where Oliver's bullet had lodged in one. One tiny hole in the oak beam—the only outward sign of the desecration that had occurred here.

And the silence.

According to the scuttlebutt at the Store, Matthew hadn't laid a finger on the organ keyboard since Oliver's death. Another thing the town could thank him for— ruining their prospects for a new organist.

A rustle of cloth and the creak of a floorboard roused him. Bob Rush stood in the chancel, surveying the decorations for Thanksgiving Festival Sunday. He adjusted the cornucopia the ladies had filled with fall produce, knocking loose the acorn squash keystone of the arrangement. Butternuts and mini-pumpkins and gourds bounced off the communion table and rolled down the aisle.

"Shit!"

Despite his morose mood, Frank laughed.

Bob spun around, glaring. Then he, too, began to laugh.

"Oh, man, I'm in trouble now."

Frank slid out of the pew and chased down an errant squash. "I'll help you put it back together. Ardyth and Bernice will never know."

"Don't bet on that. Ardyth has the location of each vegetable imprinted in her memory. If I don't confess, she'll think Bernice sneaked in here and changed it."

"In that case, you definitely shouldn't confess. Sit back and enjoy the fireworks."

Recreating the cornucopia was like building a house of cards. After a few collapses, they finally hit on a successful arrangement.

"What do you think?" Bob surveyed their work from a few steps down the main aisle.

"Don't preach too loud on Sunday. Sound waves could trigger another avalanche." The instant he mentioned sound, Frank's high spirits drained out of him. They wouldn't have to worry about vibrations from the organ, would they?

The transformation of his mood must have passed across his face. Bob's tone grew gentler in response.

"Matthew *is* going to play on Sunday. Did you know that?"

Frank shook his head. "How did you change his mind?"

"I didn't change it. We've been talking a lot. He came to the decision himself." Bob perched on the edge of the first-row pew, while Frank remained standing. "He doesn't blame you for what happened, Frank. He's been blaming himself."

"Matthew? Why? He did nothing wrong."

"He stayed silent. Matthew was closer to Oliver than anyone here. He suspected for a while that there was something wrong with his teacher. He knew about Oliver's father; knew that his brother had killed himself although not all the details. Matthew told me that when he came into the church for his lessons, he often would find Oliver talking to himself. Sometimes Oliver would have flashes of irrational suspicion. But Matthew overlooked it all because he liked Oliver so much. He didn't want there to be anything wrong with him. Now he thinks if he had come to me or you for help, maybe things would have turned out differently."

Bob paused and took a deep breath. "Maybe they would have, maybe not. I think you and I were seduced by Oliver's charm and talent, too. I'm not sure we would have believed Matthew."

Frank had been listening with his eyes focused on the cornucopia. The colors and shapes swirled before his eyes, an abstraction of his seething doubt. "Nothing changes the fact that I'm the one who shot him. I should have been able to talk him down. I should have been able to get the gun away from him."

"He would have shot you, Frank, if you had tried. And then he would have shot Ernie when he came in. How would that outcome be any better?"

Frank jammed his hands in his pockets and looked up at the organ loft. "That's just it. I'm sure he wouldn't have shot Ernie. If I'd waited a second longer, Oliver would have realized the person below him wasn't Payne. I shot too soon."

"Oh, I think Oliver was quite aware that Ernie wasn't Payne, and he would've fired the shot anyway. Maybe he would've missed, maybe not. And then you would've fired."

For the first time in their conversation, Frank's gaze locked on Bob. "What do you mean?"

"Frank, has it ever occurred to you that Oliver *wanted* you or the state police to kill him? He put himself in an unwinnable situation because he didn't want to walk out of this church alive. He wasn't quite brave enough to turn the gun on himself. He let you do the job."

Frank could hear his own breath going in and out through his mouth. "There's a name for it. Suicide by cop."

"Yes. You were simply the weapon he chose."

Frank turned away. "Not quite. A gun doesn't have a say in how it's used. I didn't have to let him co-opt me."

"Frank, there was no possibility for a happy ending here. Even if you had managed to talk Oliver down, he would have been convicted of Heather's and Reiger's murders. He would have spent the rest of his life in prison or a mental institution. The Oliver we had come to love was already dead."

No possibility of a happy ending. Bob had hit it, there. That was what ate at him all day and night. "Why? Why did this have to happen?"

"God—"

Frank held up his hand. "Don't say 'God works in mysterious ways.' Please just don't say that."

Bob looked miffed. "I was going to say that with God, the worst thing is never the last thing. After the Crucifixion came the Resurrection. Some good will come of this, Frank."

"You really believe that?"

"I couldn't go on doing what I do if I didn't. Some good will come."

"Like what?"

Bob rose and embraced Frank without awkwardness or embarrassment. And for a longer moment than he would have admitted, Frank allowed himself to be held. He pulled away, and Bob looked him in the eye.

"Be patient. Watch, and you'll see it."

Chapter 36

There was no miraculous rolling away of the guilt stone. But in the days following his talk with Bob, incremental erosion made the weight bearable.

On Friday, Earl greeted him with a cheery, "Have you heard the news?"

"Augie Enright came through his hemorrhoid operation—Doris beat you to it."

"No, not that. Big news—the North Country Academy is under new ownership. MacArthur Payne wants out of the therapeutic school business for good. He's retiring to Montana."

Frank's head snapped up. "Some other crackpot has taken it over? Forgive me if I'm not blocking the streets for a parade."

"Not a crackpot," Earl protested. Then he hesitated. "Well, I guess they are kind of crackpots, but okay ones. And now the school won't close, and Lorrie gets her job back. And with Chuck's parents moving south for the winter, Chuck's given up on trying to keep full custody of the kids. Everything's working out great. Except for Ray—I don't think they'll be needing him anymore."

"What the hell are you talking about? Who's taking over the academy?"

"Paul and Katie Petrucci."

Frank gave Earl the look he had perfected for those occasions when his assistant dragged in some half-baked rumor and laid it at his feet like a cat presenting a dead mouse.

"I'm serious, Frank. It's for real. Katie and Paul are buying the school from Payne."

"Buying it? They can't even make their house payments."

"That's the other part of the news. You know that company they invested in—Nutri-Green? Well, it went public. They made half a million bucks just like that." Earl snapped his fingers. "They're selling some of the stock and using the money to make a down payment on the academy. Then Paul's going to find some other investors—maybe some of the parents, since a lot of them are rich. And he and Katie are going to run it. It's still going to be for screwed-up kids, but Paul's going to treat them better. Use some different methods, or whatever."

Would Paul and Katie have the skill to pull this off? Payne's authoritarian approach had certainly led to disaster, but he suspected academy kids would run roughshod over Katie and Paul. This was not a group who responded to time-outs.

"How do you know so much about it?" Frank asked.

"Paul's over at Malone's right now, telling everyone. You should go over."

"I think I will."

By the time Frank reached Malone's, Paul's crowd of eager listeners had dissipated. He sat in the back booth, poring over a stack of papers and writing notes.

"Hi, Paul. I hear you have big news."

Paul looked up, a radiant smile transforming his severe features. Frank realized he'd never seen the man happy before.

"I guess Earl told you the basics. Katie and I take over the academy next month." He nodded at the papers before him. "I'm working on a revised curriculum and a new prospectus."

"That's terrific. Congratulations."

Paul began to chatter happily about his plans—the expansion of the creative arts programs, the counseling professionals he would hire, the camaraderie he hoped to foster among the students.

"And then we're going to—" Paul cocked his head. "You don't think we can pull this off, do you?"

Had the expression on his face been that transparent? Frank stammered in embarrassment, but then found his voice. Paul had given him an opening and he was going to take it. There was too much at stake to offer nothing but mindless assurances.

"Look, I don't pretend to know anything about educational theory, but can I offer you a little advice based on life experience?"

"Go right ahead." Paul's encouraging words didn't jibe with the purse of his lips.

"I'm glad you're taking over the academy, I really am. I think the changes you're planning will be great." Leading off with positive reinforcement didn't come naturally to Frank, but he gave it his best shot. "Just think about this: Sometimes, when you don't like someone, you can't imagine that anything they've ever said or done could be right. I lost my job in Kansas City because I couldn't bring myself to listen to another cop who I happened to think was an ass."

Frank paused. "You and MacArthur Payne were at odds, but some of what he did at the academy had value. Those kids *do* need discipline, and structure, and close supervision to turn their lives around. They're not equipped to handle complete freedom."

Paul listened to all of this while staring at his folded hands on the table. When Frank stopped talking, Paul never raised his eyes.

So much for the dispensing of free advice. Paul obviously had his own vision for the academy, and the opinions of an old fart like Frank didn't play into it. He stood and walked toward the door.

"Frank."

With his hand on the door, he looked back.

"I hear you."

Leaving Malone's, Frank had a strong impulse to hear what Bob had to say about this new development. The pastor had the phone held to his ear as Frank approached the door, but he wasn't speaking. He waved Frank in. "Just listening to messages. I'll be done in a second."

Bob made a note on his calendar, pressed a button to move to the next message, and began to laugh. "Listen to this—you probably have the same message on your phone. Lucy's planning another one of her matchmaking dinner parties. I wonder who she has in store for us this time?"

"Why's she calling you? I thought she already found success in that department," Frank answered, feeling much less amused than Bob.

"With Janice the sociologist? No thanks. I don't know why everyone thinks pastors should be attracted to drab, earnest women."

Frank wasn't sure what shocked him more—Bob's brutally honest assessment of the charmless Janice or the implication that he and Penny were not an item. "Wait a minute, Lucy didn't invite Janice for you, she invited her for me."

Bob tossed a crumpled message slip across the desk toward his wastebasket and sank the shot handily. "Don't be ridiculous. Everyone can see that Penny only has eyes for you."

Frank was so flabbergasted he couldn't respond.

"I could never date Penny," Bob continued. "She's still a member of this congregation—she never transferred to a new church after her divorce."

Frank coughed in an effort to regain his composure. "Well, surely there's a way around that..."

"I don't want to get around it. I like Penny, and she likes me, but there's no chemistry between us."

This had to rank as the weirdest conversation he'd ever had—discussing sexual chemistry with a Presbyterian pastor. He felt himself gaping like a fool.

Bob continued with a twinkle in his eye. "Come on, Frank—I'm just a man like anyone else. I want a woman I feel a spark with, but finding someone is not easy when you're in my line of work, especially in a small town. Try going to happy hour in Lake Placid and striking up a conversation with a girl. As soon as you tell her what you do for a living, she's heading for the ladies' room. I tell you, I could empty out an entire bar in a couple of minutes."

Frank laughed out loud. He'd never seen this side of Bob before—or maybe he'd chosen not to notice it—and suddenly he understood why everyone else liked the minister so much. "You're right, it's not easy being a bachelor in the Adirondacks. I guess we have no choice but to keep accepting Lucy's invitations."

"Actually, I have a date this Friday night. If it goes well, maybe I can afford to turn Lucy down."

"Who's the lucky girl?"

Bob looked sheepish. "I haven't exactly met her yet. We've only exchanged e-mails. She's a schoolteacher in Burlington. We got in touch through this Internet dating service for clergy—men-of-the-cloth-dot-com."

Frank roared with laughter. "Maybe I should see if they have one for cops—men-with-badges-dot-com."

"Don't bother." Bob glanced out his window at the town green. "You don't have to look any further than our new library."

THANKSGIVING FESTIVAL Sunday dawned crisp and cold. Four inches of snow had fallen during the night, just enough to make the world fresh and new. The ultra-efficient county road crew had already cleared it, so there was no excuse for missing church.

Frank put on a tie and sports coat, unnecessary formalities for services at Trout Run Presbyterian, but he deplored the current trend toward attending worship looking like you'd just left off chopping wood. Besides, he sang better when dressed up.

He arrived early to get a good seat—one in the rear. The pews filled up quickly around him. Frank read the bulletin, stared at the cornucopia, studied the pew Bible—anything to keep himself from looking up at the organ loft or the beam with the bullet hole. He noticed Penny come in—she marched down the aisle and took a seat front and center in the second row. Despite the pastor's disclaimer, Frank was sure she wanted Bob to be aware of her presence.

Soon the choir filed in, the crowd silenced, and everyone rose for the processional hymn. Penny kept glancing over her shoulder anxiously. In a moment he realized why. Her reluctant converts—Edwin, Lucy, and Olivia—slipped in and squeezed into a rear pew. But even after she acknowledged them, Penny continued to look for someone. Finally her gaze found Frank in the crowd, and she smiled that dazzling Penny smile. After that, she turned and opened her hymnal.

From the organ pipes above and behind him, the first notes of "Come, Ye Thankful People, Come" rang out. The choir, all ten of them, sang along, sounding better than he'd ever heard them. The congregation chimed in, getting stronger with every verse as they realized Matthew would not lead them astray with some sudden tempo change or key shift.

To his left, he heard a strong baritone that faded out on the second and third verses but came back strongly on the refrain. He glanced over and saw Ernie Portman singing lustily, a discarded hymnal on the pew behind him. A beam of sunlight slanted through the high window, a celestial spotlight illuminating his joyous face.

The hymn ended with a rumbling flourish of the Bombard pipes. An appreciative murmur ran through the crowd as heads turned toward the organ.

Frank turned and looked, too. The final crescendo still hung in the air. Matthew sat with his fingers on the keyboard, his eyes cast down, maybe listening, maybe praying. For a moment the crowd disappeared—it was just Frank and the musician and the sound.

Then Matthew looked up and spotted his brother in the crowd. He lifted his fingers in a tiny salute.

Ernie smiled.

It was enough.

THE END

Scroll the page to read the first chapter of Frank Bennett's next adventures, the three short stories in *Dead Drift*.

Chainsaw Nativity

The Thanksgiving turkey had not yet been served, but as soon as the first snow fell, signs of Christmas began popping up around Trout Run, New York. The ladies crafts circle hung an elaborate wreath on the door of the Presbyterian Church, while the bartender at the Mountainside strung tinsel over the beer kegs and mounted an erratically lighted sign that proclaimed Merr Ch istmas, a slurred Teleprompter for the patrons perched on his wobbly barstools. North Country Country 93.3 played Dwight Yoakum's "Here Comes Santa Claus" at least once an hour; every night a few more houses glowed with fairy lights. And, on the town green, Bucky Rheinholz's chainsaw Nativity was unveiled.

Frank Bennett dodged through the Nativity-viewing crowd, already dense at ten in the morning. He would have liked to pause and look at the statues again himself, but was already late for his meeting with Pastor Bob Rush. Charging into the church office out of breath, Frank saw he needn't have hurried. No Myrna at the front desk, no Bob in the pastor's study. Then, from the kitchen he heard voices.

"Yesterday the milk disappeared, today it's the sugar. I tell you, I can't put anything in this kitchen without it being carried off."

"You know they need it, Myrna. Just go buy some more."

Frank came around the corner in time to see Bob pull ten bucks from his pocket.

"If they need help, all they have to do is ask. This is stealing, plain and simple."

"Problem?" Frank asked.

Myrna and Bob froze. "Nothing we need police help with, thank you anyway, Frank. Myrna's being called to do God's work."

Myrna took the cash and stalked out the door.

"Seems to be a little static interfering with His signal."

Bob smiled. "If everyone could hear the message loud and clear, I'd be out of a job. Now, tell me what you want to do about this traffic problem I've created."

They walked to the front door of the church as a tour bus from Albany pulled up to the green, disgorging fifty camera-toting senior citizens.

Frank had watched in amazement the week before as Bucky Reinholz and three burly men wrangled the well-wrapped pieces of the Nativity off a flatbed truck borrowed from the lumberyard. Each statue was as big as the men who carried it, and by the time they had them all unloaded the crew was red-faced and sweating even in the brisk November air.

Frank had helped cut away the paper and padding protecting the figures and as each cover fell away, he grew more amazed. Chainsaw art cropped up all over the Adirondacks, in little souvenir shops, craft fairs, or set up on front lawns with hand-painted "for sale" signs. Mostly totem poles or bears sitting on their haunches—if you'd seen one, you'd seen them all.

Frank fell squarely into the "I don't know much, but I know what I like" school of art criticism, but even to his unschooled eye, Bucky Reinholz's chainsaw Nativity qualified as a masterpiece. The kneeling Mary radiated a tender joy; the shepherd looked curious and a little fearful; one of the three kings glanced skyward as if he wasn't sure that star could be trusted. The infant Jesus in his manger had been carved from an enormous stump, the baby emerging as if the tree itself had given birth.

Frank had wandered from statue to statue, entranced. Up close, the rough cuts of the chainsaw seemed to obliterate the figures' features, but when you took a few steps back you saw that the grooves themselves were what created their astonishingly lifelike expressions. The effect was magical, and Frank couldn't stop examining them.

"You did all this with a *chainsaw*?"

"A five horsepower Husqvarna, mostly," Bucky said.

"How long did it take?"

"Umm, close on to three years, I guess. Had a little trouble with the first baby Jesus. Wood wasn't fully dried, and after I had it all carved, I came out to the shop one morning and found it cracked right down the middle." Bucky grinned, revealing the large strong incisors that had given him his nickname.

Frank thought he seemed awfully good-natured about his setback. "Didn't it bother you to lose something you'd worked so hard on?" He'd built a pretty mahogany end table once, and a wild little friend of his daughter's had knocked it over and taken a big chunk out of it. He still bore that kid a grudge, twenty years later.

"Oh, no use to complain. Besides, the second one turned out even better."

"Are you going to move all this back to your shop after Christmas?"

Bucky slapped his thigh. "Hell, no. This is my gift to Trout Run. Pastor Bob and Ardyth Munger have some crazy notion it'll be a tourist attraction to raise money for the church."

And the crazy notion had proved true. Which brought them to today's problem. The chainsaw Nativity was attracting so many sightseers that traffic in the one-stoplight town was totally balled up. "Earl spends his whole day out here directing traffic," Frank complained to Pastor Bob. "The kid hasn't had a day off since the Nativity went on display."

"You're not suggesting we take it down, I hope?" Bob asked. "All the businesses in town are benefiting."

"No, no—I really like it, too. But could you organize some guys from the church to help with traffic control?"

"No problem. I'll pitch in myself if you think Earl will let me wear that orange reflective vest."

They strolled onto the green, wandering among the statues. This time, Frank took particular notice of the Joseph. Bucky had carved him sitting, gazing at his wife and the child. He looked stunned, as if he couldn't absorb what had happened to him. Frank remembered feeling that way himself in the delivery room, staring at Estelle and the wrinkled little bundle that was their daughter, Caroline.

"I think of all the statues, Joseph is my favorite."

"Yes, I like him too," Bob agreed. "Joseph is so underrated. Just think—his fiancée comes to him with this extraordinary story that she's pregnant, but still a virgin, and the child she's carrying is the son of God. And instead of casting her out to be stoned to death for adultery, he agrees to protect her and marry her and raise the child as his own." Bob touched the puzzled but trusting wooden brow of Joseph. "He believes Mary."

Frank continued to stare at the statue. Trust. Maybe that was what made the Joseph so unusual. Trust wasn't an expression you saw much on the face of a grown man. And Bucky had somehow captured that with his chainsaw. Go figure.

Crime in Trout Run peaked each week between 4PM on Friday afternoon when the men at Stevenson's Lumberyard received their paychecks, and 2AM on Saturday when they had drunk them half away at the Mountainside Tavern. Frank made a point of stopping by the Mountainside late every Friday night.

Tonight's crowd wasn't rowdy, but a certain edginess hung in the air. A group of men in hunters' camo sat at the bar complaining.

"Greg Haney's had my rifle for close on two weeks and he still don't have it fixed. What am I supposed to do, with buck season starting in three more days?"

"I don't care if he is a cripple—that just ain't right."

"I heard he kept Herb's shotgun for nearly a month."

"And what's more, when you call up to ask about it, he won't talk to you. Make's his girl say he can't come to the phone. Hides out behind his kids 'cause he knows I won't swear at them."

"I have half a mind to go out there and collect my gun. I don't care if it's in a million little pieces."

"Greg's a helluva gunsmith, but it seems like he can't keep up with the work since the accident."

The grousing continued, but since everyone agreed about Greg Haney's poor service, and the object of their complaint wasn't present, Frank left them to it. He checked out the action in the game room, where Ray Stulke was trying to hustle a pool game from two young men clearly marked as tourists by the lift tickets stuck to the zippers of their expensive ski jackets. They might as well have worn signs reading Fleece Me. Frank sat down, estimating ten minutes for Ray to lure them into a double-or-nothing bet, three for him to sink every ball on the table, and thirty seconds for the fight to break out.

But the tourists were both better gamblers and better pool players than Frank gave them credit for, and Ray had to work hard to win. The game ended in laughter and backslapping and offers to buy the next round. Frank rose to leave as the jukebox began to play "God Rest Ye Merry, Gentlemen." He'd judged the atmosphere at the Mountainside all wrong. Maybe, just for the Christmas season, he should take a page from Joseph's book and be a little more trusting. The sound of the crowd joining in on the refrain followed him into the parking lot, and hung in the still, cold air:

"Oh tidings of comfort and joy, comfort and joy."

As Frank drove past the green on his way home, the floodlights illuminating the Nativity snapped off. In the split second before the brilliance evaporated, Frank thought he noticed something off-kilter. He drove around slowly, waiting for his eyes to adjust to the soft reflection of moonlight on snow. The wooden shepherd offered genuine concern for his shivering lambs. The three kings still marched toward their goal. The donkey's big eyes studied the store and the diner.

When Frank reached the third side of the square, he realized what was wrong.

Joseph was gone.

To keep reading, download *Dead Drift*[1].

THANK YOU FOR READING *Blood Knot*. To help other readers discover this book, please post a brief review on Amazon[2] or Goodreads[3]. I appreciate your support!

Receive a FREE short story when you join my mailing list[4]. You'll get an email whenever I release a new book. No spam, I promise!

---

1.   *https://www.amazon.com/Dead-Drift-mysteries-Adirondack-Mountain-ebook/dp/B00HE34YX0/ ref=tmm_kin_swatch_0?_encoding=UTF8&qid=1486847849&sr=8-3*

2. https://www.amazon.com/Blood-Knot-mystery-Adirondack-Mysteries-ebook/dp/B00Y3DE6NM/ ref=tmm_kin_swatch_0?_encoding=UTF8&qid=1486768944&sr=8-3

3. https://www.goodreads.com/book/show/25587836-blood-knot

4.   http://swhubbard.net/contact/

Like my Facebook[5] page for funny updates on my writing, my travels, and my dog. Follow me on BookBub[6] for news of sales. Meet me on Twitter[7] and Goodreads[8], too.

---

5. https://www.facebook.com/swhubbardauthor/

6. https://www.bookbub.com/authors/s-w-hubbard

7. https://twitter.com/SWHubbardauthor

8. https://www.goodreads.com/author/show/746045.S_W_Hubbard

Have you read all the books by S.W. Hubbard?

Frank Bennett Adirondack Mountain Mystery Series

The Lure[1]
Blood Knot[2]
Dead Drift[3]
False Cast[4]

1. https://www.amazon.com/Lure-outdoor-adventure-Adirondack-Mountain-ebook/dp/B07BXG95Z4/ref=sr_1_18?s=digital-text&ie=UTF8&qid=1523039445&sr=1-18&keywords=the+lure

2. https://www.amazon.com/Blood-Knot-mystery-Adirondack-Mysteries-ebook/dp/B00Y3DE6NM/ref=sr_1_fkmr0_1?ie=UTF8&qid=1485977644&sr=8-1-fkmr0&keywords=Blood+Knot+s+w+hubbard

3. https://www.amazon.com/Dead-Drift-Bennett-Adirondack-Mysteries-ebook/dp/B00HE34YX0/ref=sr_1_1?s=digital-text&ie=UTF8&qid=1474222841&sr=1-1&keywords=dead+drift#nav-subnav

4. https://www.amazon.com/False-Cast-mystery-Adirondack-Mountain-ebook/dp/B01N2U1IBW/ref=sr_1_1?s=digital-text&ie=UTF8&qid=1486848250&sr=1-1&keywords=false+cast

Palmyrton Estate Sale Mystery Series

Another Man's Treasure[1]
Treasure of Darkness[2]
This Bitter Treasure[3]
Treasure in Exile[4]

---

1. https://www.amazon.com/Another-Treasure-romantic-thriller-Palmyrton-ebook/dp/B009ZFP3DA/ref=sr_1_1?s=digital-text&ie=UTF8&qid=1474222895&sr=1-1&keywords=another+man%27s+treasure#nav-subnav

2. https://www.amazon.com/Treasure-Darkness-romantic-thriller-Palmyrton-ebook/dp/B00QXWYUF0/ref=sr_1_1?s=digital-text&ie=UTF8&qid=1474222949&sr=1-1&keywords=treasure+of+darkness#nav-subnav

3. https://www.amazon.com/This-Bitter-Treasure-romantic-Palmyrton-ebook/dp/B01CKEZ4BS/ref=sr_1_1?s=digital-text&ie=UTF8&qid=1474223009&sr=1-1&keywords=this+bitter+treasure#nav-subnav

4. https://www.amazon.com/Treasure-Exile-read-all-night-mystery-Palmyrton-ebook/dp/B079CQYVQY/ref=sr_1_1?s=digital-text&ie=UTF8&qid=1523039739&sr=1-1&keywords=treasure+in+Exile

Acknowledgements

Very special thanks to Anne Tomlin for suggesting the title for this book. I would like to offer my sincere thanks to fellow writer Lieutenant Kenneth Didion, NYS DEC DLE, for generously sharing his knowledge of black bears in the Adirondacks and DEC procedure (any errors are my own), and for allowing me to draw inspiration from his tales of bear behavior and misbehavior.

I continue to be grateful for the guidance and support of Pam Ahearn, Pamela Hegarty, Ann Hubbard, and Kevin Hubbard. Finally, I'd like to thank Dr. James Hicks, organist of the Presbyterian Church in Morristown, and Carol Hubbard, my mother- in-law, for instilling in me a love of the king of instruments, the pipe organ, played well and played loud!

About the Author

S.W. Hubbard is the author of the Palmyrton Estate Sale Mysteries, *Another Man's Treasure, Treasure of Darkness,* and *This Bitter Treasure.* She is also is the author of three Police Chief Frank Bennett mystery novels set in the Adirondack Mountains: *Take the Bait, The Lure* (originally published as *Swallow the Hook), Blood Knot,* and *False Cast,* as well as a short story collection featuring Frank Bennett, *Dead Drift.* Her short stories have appeared in *Alfred Hitchcock's Mystery Magazine* and the anthologies *Crimes by Moonlight, The Mystery Box,* and *Adirondack Mysteries.* She lives in Morristown, NJ, where she teaches creative writing to enthusiastic teens and adults, and expository writing to reluctant college freshmen. To contact her, invite her to your book club, or read the first chapter of any of her books, visit: http://www.swhubbard.net.

———————◆———————

THANK YOU.

Made in the USA
Las Vegas, NV
05 April 2023

70199972R00144